AUTUMN AT WHITEWALLS

Christine Richard

To Stephen with
warmest wishes from

Christine

Published by New Generation Publishing in 2016

Copyright © Christine Richard 2016

First Edition

www.newgeneration-publishing.com

 New Generation Publishing

Acknowledgements

Thank you so much to everyone who has encouraged me to continue writing fiction. Especially my appreciation to Fiona Richard for producing a lovely cover for this book – as she did for its predecessor, 'Whitewalls'.

Also I am grateful for the professional proof-reading provided by a good friend.   New Generation Publishing have been, once more, so helpful and particularly David Walshaw.

Finally, this book is dedicated to my late husband John, to Fiona and Andrew and to all my extended family and my friends.

Chapter One

The Church - Stitcholme

As Lady Elizabeth walked steadily into the tiny church at Stitcholme in the Scottish Borders to marry her long-time friend and now husband-to-be, Colonel John Prendergast, the small congregation turned to look with appreciation, fondness and delight. They applauded spontaneously. This reaction went well with her chosen music, 'The Arrival of the Queen of Sheba, played on a recording as the church organ had long been defunct. In charge of the CD player was her great-grandson, John who took his job very seriously. He was nearly nine years old. His twin sister Minty was the only bridesmaid. She had chosen her rose-pink taffeta dress herself and she walked solemnly behind Lady Elizabeth, a little slowly as her right leg, was still very stiff after being badly broken when she was knocked down by a car outside her school earlier in the year. Minty looked very pretty and was entirely composed.

The bride's usual vibrant colours had gone in favour of a gentle almond pink coat and dress in slub silk. Her soft, but normally wild, white curly hair had been tamed and Betty wore a very fetching pill-box hat to match the rest of her outfit. It had a small cream rose on the side.

Jamie, her son-in-law, gently supported her on his arm as they processed down the short aisle to the simple altar, decorated with pink and cream late roses. John turned his head and gave her a look of such tenderness and love there were few, if any, who did not have a lump in their throats.

The Reverend Michael Martin smiled warmly at the couple who looked so serene and happy. He began the service,

'Dearly beloved, we are gathered together in the sight of God and in the face of this congregation to join this man and this woman in Holy Matrimony.' The marriage

1

ceremony was underway.

Betty's daughter Rosie and her husband Jamie had collected almost the whole of their extended family to come to the wedding. Betty's only son Hugh was there with his wife Virginia who had wanted to come from the Cotswolds despite being very heavily pregnant. With them were their two grown-up children Roberta who preferred to be called Bobby, and her brother Alexander. Polly and Richard, John and Minty's parents, whose own marriage was going through a very bad patch, felt tense and distant but were determined not to spoil the day. The family party was completed by Charles, Rosie and Jamie's soldier son and his beautiful girlfriend Maggie, a rising star in the world of stage and screen.

The congregation sang 'The Lord is My Shepherd' to the tune of Crimond and rounded off the service with simple prayers and 'Praise my Soul the King of Heaven'. They sang their hearts out. Jamie had a moment of sadness thinking of his father Roddy who had died only months ago in the spring and wishing so much he could have been with them all. Then he gave himself a mental shake and smiled.

Michael Martin did not preach a long sermon. He had decided that, for a couple in their eighties, blessings and good wishes were more appropriate. Michael had never married, though behind a shy and gentle exterior there was still a romantic soul and, after all, he was only in his fifties.

After the Register had been signed and witnessed at the front of the church, in full view of everyone John and Betty walked - arm in arm down the aisle to a Bach cantata which young John managed to start just in time on the CD player. He felt proud of his contribution.

As the couple reached the middle of the church a shaft of bright sunlight lit up the one stained glass window and bathed them in bright light which seemed a symbol of optimism and happiness.

A collection of family cars, plus one driven by John's

chauffeur Percy who was himself ex-army, took the congregation, including the Minister, back to Whitewalls for the reception.

Whitewalls

Rosie and Jamie had decided a marquee on the south lawn would be ideal for the afternoon tea reception. It was draped inside with pale pink and cream hangings. The family was joined by a good number of friends of all ages from the surrounding villages. For once, Polly had not been involved in the catering although her business had expanded into providing for weddings such as this. However, she had insisted on baking the wedding cake. Polly was very pleased with it. She had decided on a feather-light sponge with cream icing and pale pink roses. The traditional bride and groom figures were placed on the top layer.

Polly was determined to be as relaxed as possible, considering the current state of her marriage, and share in the pleasure everyone else seemed genuinely to be feeling Also she was really fond of her grandmother and had come to value John's calming and loving presence in their lives.

Molly, the Douglas' housekeeper and family friend, had stayed behind to make sure, as she put it: 'All they people messing about in my kitchen aren't doing any damage.'

There had been some debate about speeches. Neither Betty nor John had wanted a very official occasion so they decided to ask Jamie if he would 'say a few words'. The guests were milling about enjoying the food and champagne as well as the party atmosphere, so Jamie had to tap on a glass more than once to get their attention. John and Betty, who couldn't stop smiling, stood next to him.

'Betty, my dear mother-in-law as you all know, who has always been so uncritical of me as the husband of her darling daughter, asked me if I would say a few words on this occasion. And she did mean a few.

'I guess it is usual for the best man, or whoever is given the task, to wish the young couple long life and happiness and lots of children. Well, I don't think either Betty or John will mind too much my sharing with you that they have both reached and celebrated their 80th birthdays, so possibly the 'lots of children' will not apply. In fact, they have enough of us already.'

Betty interjected: 'Oh do get on with it, darling. And anyway we might decide to adopt!' John looked so horrified everyone laughed. Yes, this was the feisty woman they knew and loved.

Jamie ploughed on manfully. 'As I was saying, what I believe we all wish for them is great happiness in the years they will spend together as Colonel John and Betty, Lady Prendergast. Would you all please raise your glasses for the toast. I give you the bride and groom!

Everyone raised their glasses, including the twins, John and Minty, who were drinking orange juice with the tiniest drop of champagne. They both felt very grown up. The cry 'The bride and groom' echoed round the marquee and people kissed each other, whether or not they were any more than acquaintances.

Jamie concluded: 'Now I will ask the bride and groom to cut the cake.'

Betty and John moved to the top table where Polly's beautifully decorated cake was placed ready for the ceremony which would also signal the reception was coming to an end. More applause came from the guests, as with John's freckled hand over Betty's tiny one, they cut the cake.

'That's quite enough' said Betty. And it was.

Then, just as the bridal couple had left the marquee to spend the evening and night at Stobo Castle, Virginia let out a horrific scream and slid dramatically to the floor. Hugh, her husband, lumbered across to her side,

'Darling, what's wrong? Are you in pain? Is it the baby?'

'Yes, no, I don't know. Get me some help, she cried,'

and at that moment her waters broke and painful contractions began.

Michael Martin, who was always good in a crisis and who thankfully had first aid training ran across to the small crowd gathering around Virginia.

'Could you all move back, please' he said with his quiet, authoritative voice. Give her some air, and Hugh, make yourself useful and call an ambulance'

Jamie, seeing what was going on, suggested as it was a lovely late afternoon the guests might like to take their recharged glasses out into the garden. They took little or no persuading and were moving outside as the ambulance, which had been in the neighbourhood, screeched to a halt on the driveway in front of the house. The two paramedics, Jane and Nigel, jumped out and ran into the marquee where Virginia had calmed down somewhat with Hugh holding her hand and Michael mopping her sweating forehead with a damp napkin.

Nigel took Virginia's pulse whilst Jane timed the contractions. They looked at each other.

'Yes, better take her to the General Hospital said Nigel.

'When is her due date?' asked Jane.

'To be honest, we're not quite sure as it was all a bit of a surprise,' answered Hugh, 'but we thought there was another month to go which is why we came up for my grandmother's wedding.'

Michael intervened: 'Let's not hang about then and get her to hospital'. Deftly, Virginia was transferred to a wheelchair and taken into the ambulance insisting not only Hughie as she called him but also the Reverend Michael went too. This didn't suit Rosie one little bit as she liked to be in control of events, but she conceded it would not be possible for her to leave the guests. 'Telephone my mobile the minute there's any news,' she instructed Hugh as he clambered into the ambulance after his wife and the Minister.

So, without any more discussion, Nigel drove the ambulance down the drive as gently as he could whilst

Jane attended to Virginia whose natural control was returning. However, it didn't last long and soon she was screaming again as Hughie held her hand and Michael mopped her brow.

The General Hospital

Not a moment too soon they arrived at the General Hospital and Virginia was swiftly wheeled inside, gently placed on a stretcher and taken to the maternity ward.

Mistakenly believing Michael to be the father, the receptionist asked him for details of the patient.

'I'm really sorry, I can't help you,' he said. 'I'm the local minister and I've just conducted a wedding service.'

The girl couldn't help herself. 'Left it a bit late, haven't they?' she exclaimed.

'No, no, not these two. His grandmother,' explained Michael, accurately and seriously, at which the girl whose badge said 'Jessica' on it, couldn't help laughing. Michael laughed too.

'I know it must sound odd,' he said, 'but it's absolutely true, Virginia is Lady Betty Prendergast's granddaughter, and Hugh, who's gone in with her, is Virginia's husband and the baby's father'.

At this point in the proceedings, Hugh came back to reception.

'Thanks so much for coming with us, Reverend.' The Minister interrupted him.

'Please call me Michael. Reverend sounds so ancient.'

'Sorry, Michael then. They're waiting to see if it's a false alarm but don't think so. I think it's on its way.

Will you come with me, please, Michael? You can wait outside the delivery room if you like, but I am really, really nervous'.

'I'll get us some coffee. Milk and sugar?' asked Michael as they sat on the practical pink and blue plastic chairs, found outside every ward in every hospital in the country.

Michael had just come back with some dubious-looking

fluid in plastic cups which, might be coffee though it was hard to tell. They had just started a conversation about gardening, one of Michael's interests, shared by Hughie, when a nurse appeared in front of them.

'Mr Bruce, your wife is asking for you,' she said, looking at Michael.

'No, it's not me,' he replied' quietly amused, and, turning to Hugh said: 'I think you are wanted in a bit of a hurry, Hugh.' So Hugh left with the nurse and shortly afterwards Jamie appeared.

'It's really good of you, Michael, to hold the fort. Do you want to get away now? How are things going?' Michael thought of the empty small manse waiting for him and said he was willing to stay.

'In that case, once we've got an update, come back with me for a family dinner at Whitewalls. We'd love to have you.' Michael smiled. He liked Jamie and Rosie and was delighted to be included.

'I'd love to come. Thanks, Jamie.'

The nurse came out into the corridor again. 'We think she's going to be a while yet though it's not a false alarm and she has gone in to labour. She wants her husband to stay so why don't you both go back to your guests? We'll look after your sister-in-law and her husband as well and ring you when there's any news.'

'Come on, Michael. Let's leave them to it and get back to Whitewalls. I'll just ring Rosie and put her in the picture, then we can call at your place and you can get out of your dog collar, that is if you want to do. It's only family this evening and no dressing up needed. In fact, I'll be glad to get out of these tails.'

After telephoning Rosie who was becoming anxious, the two men made their way to Jamie's Land Rover which had been the nearest vehicle he could get out of the Whitewalls grounds, and they left the General Hospital both amused and bemused at the turn of events.

With her usual organising skills, Rosie had despatched Polly to Edinburgh to buy some essential baby clothes and other necessary supplies from the Gyle shopping centre on the outskirts of the city, with a firm instruction to be back in time for the family supper. Polly, who by now was finding the whole "family occasion" not only overwhelming but also reminding her, yet again, of the fragile state of her own marriage, was glad to escape for a couple of hours.

Edinburgh

Polly had a swift drive to the shopping centre. As soon as she had parked her car she took out her mobile phone, switched it on and sent a text. David McLean, with whom she had enjoyed a passionate affair for the past few months until they were found in bed by her husband Richard, was still very much in her life. He had tried, though not succeeded, to get her to leave Richard and take the children with her. Richard was unaware the affair had resumed and Polly was playing a very dangerous game.

David replied straight away and drove from his flat in Moray Place in the elegant Edinburgh New Town to meet her for a quick coffee and brief encounter in the anonymity, or so they thought, of the shopping mall.

'It's so lovely to see you, darling,' was David's greeting after kissing her passionately on the lips. 'You'll be with me once all this family stuff is sorted out. I miss you so much. Come to the flat tomorrow afternoon!'

She thought quickly, and was very tempted.

'I will if I can,' she answered, with a little caution. 'I'll text you.' This had become their preferred way of communicating when they couldn't be together. Polly felt it was safer and, though it was tempting to save David's loving and passionate texts, she made herself delete them once she had read them, just in case she left her mobile phone where Richard or anyone else could pick it up and read her messages.

Infant clothes and other baby shopping swiftly completed, Polly drove as fast as possible back to the

Borders to deliver the goods and find out the progress Virginia was making. It was hard in a way to think of her aunt, who had always seemed so aloof and totally in control, giving birth when her other offspring had grown up and left home.

Back in the labour ward at the General Hospital things were starting more quickly. With the benefit of pain relief and the almost surprising, to Virginia, comfort of Hughie holding her hand and encouraging her, it was clear the birth was well underway. The midwife, Deborah, was gentle and the consultant Andy looked in from time to time and reassured both Virginia and Hughie things were progressing well. He was a reassuring young man with a kind and courteous manner which calmed everyone.

After that it all happened very fast and, with one final push, Fleur Bruce was born. Deborah checked the baby was all right and breathing, indeed crying lustily, then she wrapped her in a blanket and handed her to Virginia who at once was engulfed with overwhelming feelings of love and wonder.

'Just look at her, Hughie. Isn't she beautiful?' His face was alight with pride and love as Virginia handed him Fleur to hold for the first time. It was a magic moment for both of them.

'Who'd have thought it, old girl, at our age we could make something so beautiful and perfect?' Fleetingly, Virginia thought of Anthony. Surely he couldn't be Fleur's father, could he? At once, she dismissed the idea from her mind.

Whitewalls

Back at Whitewalls, Rosie answered the telephone, then, with a beaming smile, beckoned Jamie from the drawing room where the family was gathered. 'Wonderful news. Right, let's get the champagne out.'

Tattinger champagne was being poured by Jamie with a double family toast. He tapped the rim of a glass and the chatter stopped.

'Everyone, firstly this is a most happy occasion and also a momentous one. Not only can we drink a toast to John and Betty but also, wait for it, to little Fleur Bruce who was born safely at the General Hospital just over an hour ago. She is premature but perfect, and Virginia and she are just fine. Hughie, on the other hand, is rather overcome so Percy, John's driver, has gone to bring him back here. Then later, when the bride and groom have left for their secret destination, Rosie, Hughie and I will go back to see Virginia and the baby. So please raise your glasses, and that includes you, Molly, to John and Betty and Virginia, Hughie and Fleur.'

No-one needed to be asked twice.

Before long, John and Betty, driven by Percy, had left for their 'secret' destination. It wasn't really such a secret as most of the family knew they were going to Stobo Castle, the famous and luxurious health spa a few miles away.

'Ma, I know you'll be happy with John. You deserve someone looking after you and taking care of you.' Rosie's voice choked for a moment. Betty smiled tenderly at her daughter.

'Oh, darling, I'll be fine and so will John. Thank you so much for all your care and help over all these years. I'm sure things will work out and Polly and Richard will heal their differences.'

Hugs, kisses and a final glass of champagne later, the Daimler made its stately exit down the long drive, with Betty and John going happily towards their future as if they were in their twenties. Jamie reflected that happiness was not dictated by age and came in many forms, often unexpected ones like this.

With what seemed to Michael almost immediate order out of chaos, it was not too long before everyone was organised. Hughie had made another visit to the hospital accompanied by Polly with the baby clothes. Percy had driven Michael to the manse so he could collect a few essentials for spending the night at Whitewalls and Rosie was singing in the kitchen, producing appetising food apparently from nowhere!

Michael realised he was happy. It had nothing, or almost nothing, to do with the champagne or food though both were excellent but more the feeling of belonging and being part of a family. He had not realised how much he missed that closeness and though he knew families and indeed individuals were all imperfect in many ways at times like this, he tended to feel momentarily bereft.

Rosie glanced across at Michael, thinking what a sweet, kind face he had and felt an affection, or at least she thought it was just that, towards him. Events later were to cast some doubt on this.

The drive to Stobo Castle health spa did not take long. Percy would return there the following morning with the couple's main luggage which had already been packed, ready for the honeymoon in Tuscany.

John put his arm round Betty's shoulders. She took off her hat and threw it on to the seat and said: 'Well, what an eventful day, and trust Virginia to spring a surprise, but the best is being married to you and having a future together!'

Stobo Castle Health Spa

As Percy drove in a stately fashion up the drive to the imposing front door of Stobo Castle Health Spa, the owner - tall, elegant Stephen Winyard was waiting for them.

With a porter directly behind him to carry the bags, Stephen opened the car door as helped Elizabeth out of the back whilst John made his way round to the front of the steps. 'Welcome to Stobo, Colonel, and to you Lady Betty' he said, shaking them warmly by the hand. 'We've reserved the Cashmere suite for you. I expect you would like to go there first.'

Betty smiled radiantly. Yes, thank you so much Stephen, as always a lovely welcome. Let me get rid of my hat and this bridal stuff, then we might go for a swim.' For a moment both men thought she meant it! She didn't.

As they entered the Cashmere suite John's eyebrows rose and Betty grinned. Everything from the wall coverings to curtains, to luxury throws on the bottom of the cashmere-enfolded double twin beds was the epitome of luxury. There were even plasma screens discreetly mounted in the walnut panelling at the foot of each bed. Stephen showed the couple how the screen worked with remote controls, but neither John nor Betty took much notice. 'Just phone reception for anything at all. Also if you would like to have dinner here in your sitting room, that can be arranged, or you can join the other guests in the dining room.'

'What shall we do, Betty?' asked John,' It's just after half six.'

'Why don't we try out these lovely bathrobes and go and relax in the spa then we can have dinner in our room? Best of both worlds, set us up for the night,' she replied with a decided twinkle in her eye. So it was agreed and, quite unselfconsciously they changed, put on slippers and went upstairs to sample the delights of the spa.

Later they enjoyed a simple dinner of smoked salmon, followed by tournedos rossini finishing with lemon sorbet. Somehow they managed a little more champagne.

John took Betty gently in his arms. 'How do you feel?'

'Very happy and very married,' she replied. 'Let's go to bed'.

So they did and shared one of the beds in a gentle and natural coming together. It all felt just right.

The next morning Percy arrived to take them to the airport. Stephen Winyard was there to see them off and told them the bill had already been settled. Waving to them as the car disappeared round one of the many corners of the long winding drive he reflected he had not seen a couple of any age so at ease with themselves for a long time. Percy, looking discreetly in the rear mirror shared the same thought. It was never too late and you were never too old to be happy.

The journey to the airport took an hour during which time Betty and John talked quietly and, it has to be said, rested their eyes from time to time.

Whitewalls

Rosie organised everything and everyone. Richard, Polly and the children were dispatched to the Lodge.

'Off you go. I think we're all exhausted. We'll catch up with everything tomorrow.' she asserted, and off they went to the Lodge, which was little changed from when Roddy, Jamie's late widowed father, had lived his bachelor life there. But at least Richard and Polly had bought new beds and the bathroom was heated. Also, the old cream Aga had been coaxed into action again and, as the evening cooled, it provided some welcome heat too.

Whitewalls was still very busy with overnight guests, including Hugh as well as Roberta and Alexander who were both due to return south the next day and Michael, who had been warmly invited by both Rosie and Jamie to stay over too.

Micheal sat back nursing yet another drink, whisky this time, observing the family at close quarters and feeling somewhere deep in his heart how much he would have enjoyed being part of a real family. The family of God was food for the soul, but not the body or the senses he thought.

Then just when everything seemed to be settling down Jamie came over to Michael who was sitting comfortably by the fire and said; 'Fancy coming out for ten minutes to take the dogs for a walk? They need it, I wouldn't mind clearing my head and it would give you a break from happy families before we all turn in for the night.'

Michael got to his feet with alacrity. 'Thanks Jamie, sounds like a good idea.' So it was in the gathering twilight the two men accompanied by two very bouncy black Labradors, Tweed and Heather, strolled out of the house and down to the river bank. Thus began a warm friendship which would stand the test of time and the various adventures still to come.

Not surprisingly, John and Minty were completely exhausted and both fell soundly asleep as soon as they got into bed. As at Whitewalls, they shared a room, but one thing on which Richard and Polly agreed was the children needed their own rooms at the Lodge. Richard, if not Polly, envisaged their spending much more time there as a family.

Roddy had left the Lodge and stables to Richard in his will, much to the surprise of everyone but he loved racehorses and was knowledgeable about them. Truly he preferred country life to that in the city even though his career as a lawyer had recently taken off and he had been made a partner in his firm. Finally, Richard and Polly went to bed. They were using Roddy's old room as it was the largest in the cramped quarters. A little later Richard turned to Polly and kissed her deeply. She pushed him away, not very gently

'Richard I am absolutely exhausted and you must be as well. I'm really not up to love-making right now.' 'Maybe in the morning?' he asked hopefully. 'We'll see' was her reply and with that she turned her back on him. Things were no better in the morning and, with the arrival of the twins and their Norfolk terriers, Pixie and Pod, into the bedroom demanding to know when they could get up and go outside, the possibility was in any case again lost.

Things did not improve when after breakfast Polly said 'Richard I need to get straight back to Edinburgh to make some calls and I haven't got my computer or even address book here. Will you come later this afternoon with the twins?'

His predictable response was 'For heaven's sake Polly, can't you give it a rest for a few more hours?' She realised Richard might become very suspicious again if she rushed back to Edinburgh. He didn't know her affair with David was still going on and she was torn between wanting to see

David and keeping it a secret.

Her mobile phone rang and she grabbed it quickly. It was her mother.

'Darling can you come over later and help me get sorted. Hugh is going to stay here until Virginia and Fleur are allowed out of hospital and then all of them for a little while until the baby can travel!' 'Yes, Mum, I'll be over soon.' It was decided for her. She would walk to the house and phone David on the way.

David was not pleased. 'Can't you ever get away from that blasted family of yours?, I want you, I need you and soon.'

'When we get back to Edinburgh and the children to school we'll have an afternoon together, I promise.' His response was silky but determined: 'Better not leave it too long. I still love you, as well as wanting you.' There was almost a note of menace in his voice which she ignored.

Chapter Two

Edinburgh

Polly and David were making love with the ferocity of a couple who had not had the opportunity for some time. For once, though they were in his Moray Place apartment, they had not gone to bed. The large, comfortable cream sofa served just as well.

The doorbell rang, 'Ignore it, David' 'Better not. My car's outside, so whoever it is will know I am at home'. She was cross and sat up, pulling her silk slip down.

Completely naked, David dashed into the cloakroom, grabbed a towel and opened the door a fraction.

'I hope it's not a bad time.' It was Frank Hitchman, David's neighbour whom he hardly knew, though they did, as was the habit in the New Town pass, courteous greetings to each other when they met on the landing or in the lift or lobby.

'Sorry, Frank, just changing. May I give you a call or come round later?'

Frank was a gentleman of the 'old school' and embarrassed. 'Of course' he replied hastily. 'I want to talk to you about a recital I want to put on with me playing the piano and William Berger singing, but it's not urgent and can wait!'

David breathed a sigh of relief as Frank retreated to his own apartment.

'What on earth was all that about?' By this time Polly was sitting upright on the sofa though she had not dressed.

'Oh it's Frank, one of my neighbours, something about a recital he's holding. I'll talk to him later about it. I suppose you're going to dash off and leave me in this state!' She laughed. 'Not yet, come here.' And he did!

Polly arrived home in Murrayfield just in time for first John and then Minty arriving home from school. 'Mummy, your blouse is all done up wrong.' This was Minty who noticed such things. In her haste to dress, Polly hadn't noticed and she hoped Minty would not go on about it when Richard arrived home from the office.

When Richard did arrive, the children had already done their homework and had one of their favourite meals, macaroni cheese, and were about to go and have their baths as it was a school night.

After Polly had served dinner, a good steak eaten almost in silence but with a couple of glasses of Merlot, Richard cleared his throat and said, 'Polly I think we need to have a good talk about the future - the Lodge, renovations, my job, your business, children and where we are going.

'Does it have to be this evening Richard? I'm tired and I've stuff to get ready for tomorrow. Also, she did feel a twinge of guilt at spending much of the afternoon in very vigorous and exciting love-making with David. How much longer could she get away with it?

Richard was, for once, unbending, 'Yes, it does have to be this evening'. The consequences would be far-reaching.

The Haute Savoie

Sir Alistair Douglas, as Betty's divorced former husband, had naturally not been invited to the wedding. Although, much to Rosie's surprise, Betty had thought about doing just that. Common sense prevailed, however, and Alistair had returned to France from Scotland to decide what his next plan would be.

Generously, Betty had offered to let the Pele Tower, where she had lived for many years, to Alistair partly furnished on a recurring lease. In the absence of any better offer he had accepted, relieved at the modest rent she was asking.

Alistair really could not envisage his new wife Madeleine would want to live in the Scottish Borders in a rented property formerly occupied by Lady Betty.

When his taxi from the station at Chambery turned into

the driveway in the taxi he was genuinely surprised to find signs of life at the Chateau. Madeleine was not caught unawares as Rosie had sent her an e-mail telling her Alistair was on his way back.

Alistair was even more surprised to find Madeleine on the steps of the chateau waiting for him. 'You look lovely. It's so good to see you. How did you know when I was coming back?'

'Rosie sent me an email when I was in London with the Marchmonts,' Madeleine replied. 'There was a great drama apparently when Virginia had her baby suddenly in the local hospital. I think they were having some sort of party at the time.' Of course, hearing this he wasn't going to tell his present wife that his first wife had remarried - not on the steps anyway.

That evening Madeleine produced an excellent dinner. She did steak and frites. A salad was the only accompaniment needed and good French cheese rounded off the meal. Alistair had opened a bottle of Burgundy which was a perfect complement to the food.

After dinner, when they were each enjoying a large glass of brandy, he brought out his explanation when he finally told Madeleine of Betty's marriage and her moving from the Pele tower.

'So you see, my dear, we will move into the Pele tower as our base until I get possession of Whitewalls again.' Madeleine smiled but whilst she did not believe Alistair, she went along with the pretence over Whitewalls.

'Of course', her reply was, in itself a little startling. 'And we can see your friends in Perthshire and Edinburgh as well as the Borders. We could even take a pied de terre in Edinburgh.' Alistair smiled, soothingly 'Anything is possible.'

Over the next week both Alistair and Madeleine were busy. He spoke to the Leseures who told him they had decided to sell the chateau and vineyard.

Maurice Leseure was complimentary.

'You have looked after our property and the vineyard so

well we have decided to repay you one year's rental and a bonus of 2,000 euros.

Hallelujah, Alistair thought. What he said was; 'You are very kind. It is totally unnecessary but very much appreciated, so I accept with thanks.'

'We can discuss the time-scale a little later, perhaps next week but I already have someone interested in buying. Another reason for the bonus.' Both men chuckled insincerely and the call ended.

Madeleine, who had a good business mind when she chose to use it was in negotiations of her own. The shop in Chambery, already stocking a limited range of tartan-wear was interested in the proposition of buying through Madeleine. Sophia, her shop manager, had been confided in, and sworn to secrecy, about the impending return to Scotland. Madeleine assured her she could easily ship tartans and cashmere at an excellent price.

Then there was Henri, Madeleine's lover. Both realised no future for them together would be possible but sexually they were more than equals. In bed, on a late summer afternoon, after a particularly satisfactory two hours of making love, he said:

'Cherie, you will always have a special place in my heart.' 'And elsewhere,' she laughed, fondling him provocatively again. 'Come here' he said She did, once more. Madeleine smiled with the satisfaction of a well-fed cat. Yes things would work out to her advantage, bien sur.

Chapter 3

High Wynch Park

Late motherhood suited Virginia. After the early birth Fleur was still a small, though pretty and healthy baby. With his increasingly good financial stability from the house and grounds, which were which were in demand from television producers and film-makers plus with the arrival of his lovely little daughter, Hugh was a happy man.

'Why don't we get a nanny for Fleur?' Hugh asked. The 'new' Virginia looked up from the low armchair where she was contentedly breast-feeding Fleur. Her dramatic arrival into the world which started at the reception following Lady Betty and John Prendergast's wedding at Whitewalls did not seem to have adversely affected her in any way. Virginia was even happy that Fleur had been born in Scotland and close to Whitewalls. In the past she had at times been jealous of all the attention Rosie and Jamie seemed to get from the family but not any longer.

'I don't think so, darling. Really, I am enjoying this but some extra help in the house would be good. Sally's daughter is looking for part-time work and she'll be good for baby-sitting too.'

With that agreed, he went off whistling to talk to the contract gardeners who were tidying the area to be used for the next TV documentary. This was to be a programme about making old properties earn their living and so was very appropriate.

The following weekend would be a busy one. Piers Romayne was due to come and finalise arrangements for the next big contract for a new film. It wasn't clear whether or not Anthony Goodman, who was just possibly Fleur's real father, would be coming with him. Virginia had consigned her one fling with him to the very back of her mind, but maybe seeing him again would bring the excitement back. Yes, he had treated her badly, but could she forgive him? After all, he was in a big way part of Hughie's new- found business and solvency.

There was also the chance that Roberta and Alexander, Virginia and Hughie's grown up children, would come from London for the weekend. The pair had been absolutely horrified when they knew their mother was pregnant with Fleur and even more so when she had decided to go ahead and have the baby. Slowly, though, they were coming round to the idea. So this new phase in the life of Rosie's brother and sister-in-law began. It was going to have far-reaching consequences for them all.

Manor House Farm Yorkshire

Charles Douglas, Jamie and Rosie's son, loved his life in the army. He also loved his beautiful actress girlfriend, Maggie. She had shiny red hair, which if left to itself turned into bouncy curls. Charles loved this, though Maggie was always trying to straighten her wayward hair. He wanted them to be engaged and Charles realised how lucky he would be if she agreed when she was at such a critical point in the development of her career, both on stage and on screen. The fact that he might soon be posted to Afghanistan again had certainly helped Maggie to think seriously about Charles' proposal though she would not admit this, even to herself.

As far as Charles was concerned, he saw such an assignment as simply being in the line of duty and part of his chosen life as a soldier. In fact, he was now a captain with his own platoon of men and considerable responsibilities. Somehow these did not weigh heavily upon him.

Maggie had enjoyed the family wedding at Whitewalls and the drama of the arrival of Fleur, and helping Rosie with everything afterwards had made her feel very much part of the family. Her own parents had been killed in a car crash and, although Florette, her grandmother, who had bought her the mews house in London, and Nigel, her step-grandfather, were her close family, the lack of any extended family had really affected her sense of identity. Then she met the Douglas and Bruce clans and somehow felt a sense of belonging.

Charles and Maggie made the journey from London to Yorkshire to spend the weekend with Nigel and Florette at Manor House Farm, from where Florette ran her successful cashmere business and Nigel happily farmed. By now they were all very relaxed with each other and the tradition had become established whereby Nigel always took Charles and the dogs to the local pub for a pint or two and a man-to-man talk.

'So, Charles I am wondering if you have decided what you want to do when you come out of the army?'

'I hadn't really thought about it. I suppose I am looking on the army as a career as much as anything else. Why do you ask?' replied Charles. 'Well, I won't go on farming here forever and unless you are going to follow your father at Whitewalls and farm there, you might be interested in taking on this place after you and Maggie are married and you've left the army.'

H'mm, time to think about it, Nigel?' 'Of course, let's have another pint then we'll go and see what the women are doing.' So it was left. Life at Manor House Farm was in some ways similar to that of Whitewalls though, apart from the dogs, quieter. Florette's business was flourishing and she was now expanding into selling her unique soft cashmere range on-line. She was very excited about this and Maggie so admired her enterprising grandmother who in her seventies was still embracing new ways of doing things.

After a very convivial supper with just enough impeccably cooked food and wine, a fish terrine with crusty bread followed by perfectly done steaks and salad ending with crème brulee, the four went to the library where a fire had been lit as a mark of impending autumn to keep off the slight chill.

'Anyone fancy a brandy?' As ever Nigel was a good host. So the evening ended with the four sitting round the fire, sipping brandy and going over the adventures of Betty and John's wedding. Even Nigel, who was very conservative in his views had found the whole episode both fascinating and fun.

Much later, after some exhilarating love-making, preceded by a shared bath Charles and Maggie were wound round each other in a most gentle 'after-glow' when she became serious. Taking Charles's face in her hands and looking steadily into his eyes said: 'Darling do you know how much I love you? It gets more and more, all the time. I never want to let you go.'

The room was very dimly lit by a bedside light and the moon shining softly through the open curtains. Charles thought his fiancée's face was even more beautiful than ever. He hugged her tightly, 'And I never want to let you go.' Then a cloud passed over the moon. They slept.

Before Charles and Maggie left the following day, whilst walking the dogs Nigel spoke again to Charles about the possibility of his joining him at Manor House Farm after the army. 'I don't want you to decide right away, Charles. Talk it over with Maggie, but I think you would fit in really well and I know the locals would take to you!'

'Thanks, Nigel. I do appreciate the idea though Maggie and I haven't had time to talk about it yet.' Nigel replied with what was almost a knowing smile, 'Of course you haven't. Better things to do! Just promise me you'll discuss it'. Charles had already become very fond of Nigel and found it easy to agree. 'Yes, we will, as soon as we get back to London. I promise. There it was left, for the time being.

Burnmouth

Despite Polly's protests, David had insisted they steal a

23

day and go to his secluded cottage on the beach at Burnmouth. They had been lovers now for more than six months. For a short while after Richard had found them in bed together at the family home in Murrayfield she had accepted his ultimatum to stop seeing David or Richard would divorce her. This state of affairs had not lasted for very long.

Their physical need for each other was as compelling as ever and Polly simply was unable to give up seeing David. He, in turn, wanted and needed her but now he was planning a future for them together.

Following an afternoon of very intensive love-making, they were sitting together in front of a blazing log fire in the tiny sitting room, discussing their situation and whether or not they could or should continue seeing each other. Unlike many affairs which begin with almost uncontrollable sexual passion and end either in acrimony or boredom. David and Polly had become ever closer. Even Richard's threat to divorce Polly, name David as co-respondent and claim custody of the children, after the initial shock and necessary time spent apart seemed to have made no difference to their feelings for each other.

'I've never ever felt like this about any woman before.' David was serious and his voice rang true. 'It's as if we were meant to be together, to make our lives together and, believe it or not, it isn't just about sex.'

Polly felt the tears coming into her eyes. 'David, this started as a fling for me, maybe you too. But I'd never had sex with anyone except Richard and I was flattered and curious too. But now it's different. I don't want to give you up'.

'Then don't,' was his simple answer. His arms held her shoulders. 'Look at me' he urged 'and tell me it's what you want, or don't want too. She looked at him. Yes, he was handsome, yes he was a great lover, life with him would not be boring. Yet, she loved her children, she used to be content with her life, her husband and the comfort of a close, wider family, a position in Edinburgh society where the worlds of law and finance as well as academia were seen as the 'desirable' ways of working and living. David belonged to none of these. He had successfully reinvented himself from his poor upbringing by a single mother in a deprived estate on the outskirts of Edinburgh. Now he was a sought-after interior designer with clients all over Scotland, including the aristocracy.

'Talk to Richard,' he urged 'and soon. We have to make plans.' Though she was still troubled, Polly smiled and said: 'Yes, soon.' He pretended to be content with that for the moment and said 'Darling, come back to bed, We have some unfinished business right now.' She did not need to be asked twice.

Later, as David drove Polly back to Edinburgh and her family in his dashing new Porsche, she was very thoughtful. Life was coming to the point where she either had to try and rebuild her safe, if dullish, life with Richard and her family and settle for that or take this huge chance and start a new and, on the face of it, more exciting life with David. She was torn between these alternatives and yet realised things could simply not continue as they were. Richard was bound to find out again and she knew he would not give her another chance.

As usual when they arrived back in the affluent Murrayfield suburb of Edinburgh Polly was trying to switch back into wife-and-mother mode, and David had to be content with a hasty kiss as she got out of the car at the front door, dashed to her own car to go and collect the twins from their friends' houses and hoped not to have been seen by any of her neighbours. As she found out later her, luck was fast running out.

Whitewalls

Rosie was sitting at her kitchen table frowning over her lists. She had not succumbed to an Ipad or Iphone, preferring still to have pen and paper on which to plan her busy life. She was very tired and, in truth, felt rather old after all the drama of her mother's wedding and the early arrival of her sister-in-law's baby at the end of the reception. Then there was Richard and Polly and the twins. Things were still not right between them. Yet after her earlier attempts at talking with Polly had met such a hostile reception, she was loath to try again, at least at the moment.

A knock at the kitchen door brought her out of her reverie. She opened it to find Michael there, not in his clerical garb but wearing corduroy trousers and a navy blue cashmere sweater. Fleetingly, she thought: He really is very attractive, wonder why he's never married?

'Hello, Rosie, I was passing and hope you don't mind but I thought I would call in and see how you are all getting on. I think the happy couple are due back from Tuscany at the weekend.' She smiled, happy to see him.

'That's right, Molly and I are going to make sure everything is ready at the bungalow. John's had a lot of changes made so that Mum will feel it is her home as well as his. Tell you what, why don't you come with me? Jamie is out on the farm and we can be back by lunchtime.

'I'd be happy to come along with you. Why don't I drive?' was Michael's response. So after collecting the keys to her mother and John's home, and leaving a quick note on the kitchen table, they set off. To Rosie's surprise Michael did not drive a safe, conventional hatchback but a very sporty BMW with a soft top. The car was a stylish silver.

He looked across at her once Rosie had been settled by Michael into the passenger seat. As he leaned across to hand her the seat belt their hands touched. She found that very pleasant and unsettling at the same time.

'This is a very swish car, Michael' she said. He grinned. 'Probably not quite what you expect for a minister? I hope I don't have too many vices, but driving a decent fast car is certainly one of them.' With Classic FM on the radio, they completed the fairly short drive to Stitcholme with Rosie doing most of the talking, telling Michael about her extended family.

'What do you do for yourself, Rosie? It sounds to me all your efforts go in to making life smooth and happy for other people.' She was touched, but only answered: 'I love my garden'. They arrived at the very spruce-looking bungalow and once again Michael came round to the passenger door and helped Rosie out of the car. They both smiled. Rosie thought 'I must be mad, I'm finding him really attractive.' Michael, had she but known was thinking exactly the same.

Rosie led the way to the front door with its trellis porch filled with late-flowering climbing roses. She had keys, so unlocked the door and she and Michael went in together. There were a few letters which she picked up and put on the table to wait for John and Betty's return. But it was inside the sitting room where she got the first clue about how thoughtful John had been.

The bungalow had been completely repainted in a soft yellow which was warm and welcoming. In the sitting room there were a new, comfortable sofa and two equally inviting armchairs. Even the carpet was new.

'Come on Michael. Let's explore the rest of the place.' At first he hung back, but, caught up in her enthusiasm, followed her into the kitchen which was largely unchanged except for the repainting, and the Aga was still safely in place.

'Let's have a quick look at the bedrooms and bathroom.' Rosie was really on a roll now. He smiled and followed her. There was a new double bed in the larger of the two rooms and single beds in the spare room.

'How tactful of John. It means Mum can choose where she wants to sleep. Then she became aware Michael was being very quiet. He smiled. 'Can I get a word in edgeways?' he asked mildly. 'It seems the colonel is not only kind but very perceptive too, as well as thoughtful. My view is only one bedroom will be used!'

'Michael, that's a very risqué remark for a man of the cloth!' He just laughed. 'That's not all I am, Now, do you think we had better make tracks?' In this gentle, happy mood, he drove Rosie back to Whitewalls where they found Jamie in the kitchen stirring the pot of soup on the cooker.

'Come away in, the two of you. It's come to something when my wife goes off with the minister and I'm left to do the lunch!' He was laughing. Rosie took over and shooed the men off to have a glass of beer before they ate. She was, she thought, back in control.

The three enjoyed a companionable lunch when Michael told Jamie some of his plans, which met both with approval and an offer of help.

'I can see I am redundant.' Rosie laughed, 'so I'm going to go over my lists and, if I have time may go into Edinburgh to see Polly and the children.'

'I must go too.' Michael got up and shook Jamie's hand warmly and kissed Rosie on both cheeks as if it were the most natural thing in the world. She felt a shiver, almost a sense of foreboding but smiled as sweetly as she could and waved Michael off from the gravel driveway at the back of the house.

'He's a really good guy,' Jamie remarked. 'I think we're going to become friends and he'll be good for the village too. Right off, to work! I've made time to do some painting today for my next exhibition or I won't have new work to show.' Jamie kissed his wife lightly on the lips and went off whistling.

Chapter 4

Edinburgh

As she drove into Edinburgh with no greater plan than to try and see Polly and the twins, Rosie was going over in her mind the day and the unexpected, though if she admitted it to herself, not unwelcome attention from the Reverend Michael Martin.

As she had felt flustered when leaving Whitewalls, Rosie hadn't stopped to phone Polly to say she was coming. Only as she arrived in Edinburgh did she remember to do so.

'Oh Mum, yes, alright, it would be nice to see you, and the twins are both being brought home from school today so you'll have a chance to see them. See you soon, 'bye'. Rosie reflected Polly had not sounded very pleased to hear of the spontaneous visit. But she didn't know David was at her home and would have to leave very quickly before they were found out again. It was a dangerous situation Polly was in. She had resumed her affair with David even after assuring Richard her choice had been made and she had decided to stay with her husband and family and give up her lover. But she had not kept that promise.

Polly ran upstairs into the main bedroom. David was lying back against the pillows, still undressed and looking smug.

'Quickly David. Get up and go. My mother's on her way to make a surprise visit and this is not the surprise she would have in mind. Besides, the children will be home from school soon.'

'Alright,' he said sulkily, 'but we can't go on like this. How many more times do I have to tell you I love you, I want you to divorce Richard, marry me and we'll look after John and Minty. Simple' But it wasn't.

Just in time, as Rosie turned into Murrayfield Drive, David zoomed out of it in his Porsche. Luckily for Polly, it was another few minutes before her friend Caroline brought the children home.

'Mum, mum guess what? I came top in maths today. Mr Brown said he couldn't believe it so he checked again - and I did come top'. John was always first to get his news out. Minty followed more slowly. Her right leg, broken in the summer in a car accident was hurting today but she didn't want to tell anyone in case her parents made a fuss or in case something was wrong and she had to go back to hospital.

Minty's gait was, though, the first thing that caught Rosie's attention, even before she noticed the flushed and flustered face of her daughter. *Oh no*, she thought *I hope she's not been stupid again.* With Polly and her husband uneasily reconciled after the time she had been found by Richard, naked in bed with David at Murrayfield Drive, everyone had at least tried to pretend all was well. Rosie pushed the thought away and, once Minty had gone slowly upstairs to change from her school uniform and John had gone to switch on his computer, the mother and daughter were alone in the kitchen. Caroline had declined the offer of tea and said she had to get home.

Polly opened the conversation with Rosie. 'Mum, did you think Minty was walking awkwardly just now? She doesn't complain and she's very careful about playing games at school but I wonder if we should take her to the doctor, maybe have an X-ray just to check everything is fine. What do you think?' Grateful for being consulted Rosie agreed. 'You can't be too careful, especially with autumn coming on and colder weather which can make bones and muscles painful. Yes, darling, I think you should do that.'

Polly's next question both pleased and disturbed her mother. 'Mum would you come with me? Richard is very tied up just now, both at work and with the plans for the Lodge?' So, despite her misgivings, Rosie agreed to try and come into Edinburgh once Polly had made the appointment.

Rosie stayed as long as she could and was just about to leave when Richard arrived home, again, on the surface there was nothing visibly wrong about Richard's relationship with his wife. He gave her a peck on the cheek, which she returned and greeted Rosie in his usual fashion with a gentle kiss. 'Hello, mother-in-law. Good to see you. I am relying, or rather we are relying on your expert advice with renovating the Lodge, if you are up for it.' She smiled at the slim, rather earnest young man whom she had loved dearly since he first proposed to Polly over ten years before. The arrival of the twins a year afterwards had, she thought then, enriched their relationship and given her two delightful grandchildren.

The illusion was sadly, for Rosie, shattered when Polly had her affair with David McLean. He had never married, but numerous relationships with mostly sophisticated women gave him the experience and skills to win over the naïve Polly and almost fatally attract not only her body but also her heart.

After agreeing to go with Polly when she could get an appointment for the doctor to check Minty's leg, Rosie did not stay very long but said she was relying on Polly to come down to Whitewalls at the weekend, with Richard, Pixie and Pod, the Norfolk terriers and even Buttons, the tiny Siamese cat David had given to Minty some months before

'I know Jamie wants to talk to you both about the Lodge and to Richard about the horses. Those ponies need some attention too from the twins, so all in all we need a family conference weekend - especially after all the excitement of Great Grandma's wedding and Virginia's baby arriving.' She omitted any mention of Michael Martin and told herself, somewhat unconvincingly, she would deal with any feelings about that later.

Edinburgh's rush-hour traffic held up Rosie on her way back to the Borders, so she had plenty of time to think. In spite of her usual boundless energy she felt tired and burdened again. Still, her mother and John were due back from Tuscany the following week and surely the questions about the Lodge, left by Roddy to Richard, would be answered soon enough. So she decided to concentrate on driving and put Classic FM on her car radio. For once, she had left her own little dog, Empress, the sleeve peke, back at Whitewalls and hoped Jamie had taken her out together with his black Labradors, Tweed and Heather.

Shortly after Rosie left Murrayfield, Richard arrived home. Polly painted a smile on her face,

'Hi, you're early, everything all right at the office?' she said. Polly gave him a peck on the cheek, then remembered the state of the bedroom. If Richard saw the rumpled bed he would know she had been unfaithful again. 'Yes, fine, thanks, We just need to make plans for the weekend. There's a lot to do! I'm really looking forward to getting the Lodge sorted and making a decision about the horses, though that won't be easy.'

'Darling, I just have to go and sort out the bathroom. Back in a minute, I know John wants to tell you about his maths.' It sounded lame but was the best she could manage. Polly raced upstairs. There was no time to change the bed linen but she straightened it and even had time to arrange the cushions on the pillows before Richard came into the bedroom and started to change out of his office clothes. He did not appear to notice anything amiss though there was, he thought, an odd scented smell. It was in fact air freshener Polly had hastily squirted around to cover any trace of David.

After homework had been finished, John duly praised for his maths success and the twins despatched after supper for baths and bed, Richard and Polly were finally alone together at the kitchen table.

'Let's go into the sitting room', said Richard, 'I popped in and lit the fire whilst you were organising the children. I want us to have a proper planning talk and this seems like a good time.' Polly saw no reason to object and decided, at this point, not to mention her concerns about Minty's leg. The log fire was crackling and burning invitingly and

Richard poured each of them a brandy. Polly thought, fleetingly, he looked quite sweet with his rimless reading glasses perched on his nose and the business-like yellow legal pad resting on the coffee table in front of them.

'Right, down to business, he said'

Later, for the first time in many months they went to bed at the same time. Polly had a quick shower, followed by Richard and, on impulse, she got into bed naked. Before he could get into his blue-striped pyjamas she sat up. 'Don't put those on. Come here. Now!' Happily, he did just that.

Whitewalls

As Rosie turned the last corner of the drive leading up to the house she saw the sitting room light was on and two figures sitting on either side of the fire with glasses in their hands. Her heart gave a small flutter. Could it be, yes it was, Michael. Again the small but definite flutter. She parked the car and went into her home.

Both men got up to greet her with mildly guilty expressions on their faces. Jamie took her in his arms, gave her a hug and a hearty kiss on the lips. By contrast, Michael kissed her chastely on the cheek and said,

'Rosie, I do apologise, you'll be thinking I've moved in soon. But I wanted to discuss some plans I have for the church and the manse with Jamie and when he said you had gone to Edinburgh and invited me over, I took the chance of coming. Don't worry I'll be off.'

'No you won't, she said firmly.' I'll have a drink with both of you and Michael, unless you have other plans, why not stay for supper? There's plenty of food, and you can tell me about your plans too.' The men looked at each other for a small moment. 'Well if you're both sure I would love to do that; said the minister.

'Settled,' Jamie said 'glass of wine, Rosie, or a gin and tonic?' Again the flutter 'I think I'll have a gin and tonic. There's plenty of ice and lemons in the fridge.' 'Right,' her husband replied, 'you entertain Michael whilst I go and fix that for you.'

Rosie and Michael were alone with only the crackling of the fire to break the silence, then they both spoke almost at once. 'Really kind of you, Rosie, to be so generous to me'. 'Michael it's a pleasure.' And it was.

Rosie ventured a more personal question. 'Have you never wanted to be married, Michael?' He smiled. *Such a sweet smile*, she thought 'Well, I haven't lived the life of a monk if that's what you're thinking Rosie. Working in inner city churches didn't leave much time for anything other than work. I am sadly a widower. But you never know. Moving to the country may make all the difference.' They looked at each other, then Jamie returned and the moment went.

Later, after a companionable supper and good red wine it seemed only natural for Jamie to say to Michael: 'Look, Michael, we've all had a bit to drink. Why don't you stay over? There's always a bed made up, especially since Polly, Richard and the children stay at the Lodge.' He looked enquiringly at Rosie who said brightly 'Why not? I'll go and get it organised.'

Both Michael and Rosie pushed away the thought they would be sleeping under the same roof and refused even to think of any possible attraction building between them. Rosie returned to the sitting room and Jamie threw some extra logs on the fire.

'Michael, if you want to come upstairs I'll show you your room and bathroom.' These harmless words seemed to her to assume a deeper meaning than a hostess showing an unexpected guest where he was to sleep.

As they went up the spiral staircase Rosie accidentally, though possibly not, brushed against Michael. When they reached the landing, he slowly turned towards her, took her gently in his arms and kissed her deeply on the lips. 'Oh, Michael, no.' 'I'm sorry Rosie, I haven't felt like this for a long time. You're so damned attractive. Admit it, you feel something too.'

'You don't sound a bit like a minister,' she protested. 'I don't feel like one either.' he replied. Then they both laughed. 'It felt very good,' she said, 'but we'd better leave it there.' 'For now,' was his equivocal reply. That was how it began, almost casually and without any conscious planning either by Michael or Rosie.

Later in the night when Jamie, half asleep, reached for Rosie and pulled her close to him to make love, for the first time ever, she pushed him gently away murmuring,: 'Darling I'm so tired. Let's wait until morning.' He was puzzled but tired too and thought nothing of it at the time.

Chapter 5

Stitcholme

With Percy at the wheel, Colonel Prendergast and Lady Betty returned discreetly to Stitcholme and the bungalow where they had decided to make their home. Unknown to Betty, John had left instructions for complete redecoration of the house in soft neutral colours and with new carpets throughout.

'I don't think I'm up to carrying you over the threshold, Betty, but I'll try if you like!' She laughed. 'No my dear husband, I think it would be safer for both of us if we walked in.'

Percy had a smile on his face as he drove away. He reflected that maybe you were never too old to be in love.

'John, what have you been up to behind my back and how did you get all this done from Tuscany?' All this was the redecoration and the new carpets. Again, he smiled at his wife. 'It was easy. Remember, I've spent all my career giving instructions to people. I haven't done anything too radical. I thought you'd have your own ideas, so it's a sort of blank canvas!'

'Come on, coats off! I want to see everything,' she cried. The tour did not take long. In the kitchen, which was largely unchanged was a note from John's housekeeper giving details of the food she had prepared for them realising they would not want to be going out on their first evening back. In fact, she was one of the few people who even knew when the couple was returning.

'I had both bedrooms done and new beds, darling. Just choose which one you want.' Betty hugged and kissed John. 'Don't be silly. Nice thought, the new beds I mean but I'm sleeping with you, unless you have any objection.'

'Hoped you'd say that,' he said and drew her close. 'I've got a new king-sized in the bedroom too.' She smiled warmly at him. They lit the fire in the sitting room, drank a

36

glass or two of champagne and really felt they were at home.

'We'll tell everyone tomorrow that we're back'. This was Betty. 'Or maybe the day after that' was the spirited reply. Both knew there would be a lot to do, family to see, arrangements for the Tower to be finalised, presents given and photographs to be downloaded from John's new digital camera. But that could wait. This night was theirs.

Haute Savoie

The packing was not going well. Alistair realised how really unprepared he was for a more permanent move to Scotland, not to Whitewalls but to a rented Pele Tower owned by his former wife, Lady Betty. He felt badly done by and found it hard not to be bitter. Conveniently, he put out of his mind all the hurt and trouble his past love affairs and scheming had caused the Douglas and Bruce families.

Madeleine too was in a bad mood. She found it, at least for a woman, hard to believe that Alistair's former wife, Lady Elizabeth, had given him the Pele Tower after marrying an army widower, apparently with the approval of both families. To Madeleine, it seemed at the most unsuitable age of eighty. Alistair, for his part, had assured her it was only a temporary move until they took final possession of Whitewalls.

Although she still didn't trust her husband, Madeleine could see no alternative plan to her advantage and decided to go along with the story Alistair had concocted. Certainly, in the short term, the money from the Leseures should tide them over until she was installed as Lady Douglas in the Scottish Borders. She had already had an au revoir afternoon of making love with Henri, her lover in Chambery, and told him she would return to see him again. Madeleine actually had no intention of seeing him again, ever.

Alistair booked their flights through American Express, using his full title. Experience had shown this usually resulted in an upgrade to at least business class and particularly so on the flight to London. As usual Alistair had called upon old friends in Kensington to put him and Lady Madeleine up for a few nights until they were ready to go to Scotland. The MacDougalls, whilst not close friends enjoyed Alistair's company when he was at his best and, besides, were intrigued to meet Madeleine for what would be their first time. So it was settled.

London

In the bathroom of the tiny mews house in London, behind Harrods Department store, Maggie was luxuriating in a steaming bath scented with pine both invigorating and restful at the same time. She had been rehearsing all day for her latest part at one of the lesser-known but still prestigious London theatres.

The door opened and Charles came in wearing his towelling dressing gown, and nothing else. Not that the dressing gown stayed on for long either. With a very cheeky grin, Charles flung it on the floor and said; 'Move over, beautiful. I'll take the tap end, but I couldn't wait to join you, and afterwards I'll tell you my news.'

He sounded so happy, Maggie thought it must mean something good. Promotion perhaps? With the easy familiarity of two lovers now used to each other, they soaped and kissed and eventually, as the water was going cold, got out of the bath and wrapped each other in fluffy white bath towels.

'Come and sit with me next door, Maggie. I want to tell you some news I've just had from HQ.' He didn't need to tell her, instinctively she knew. 'It's a posting?' she asked evenly. Worse than a posting. 'It's Afghanistan. Three weeks' time.' Tears welled up, but she tried to keep them back.

'Darling, we knew this was on the cards. It could be worse.' She cried now. 'I don't really see how and so soon. How long will you be away?' This was even harder,

38

'around seven months, I think. Darling, we could get a special licence and get married before I go if that would make you feel better.'

She tried to pull herself together. 'No, I love you, but I want a proper wedding with a dress and bridesmaids and a marquee and everything and Grandpa giving me away and all your family there. Then I want a honeymoon and babies and a proper family of my own.'

He kissed her gently again. 'Hush, darling. It will all be all right, I promise. I have three weeks' leave starting tomorrow, so let's get dressed, go out and have something to eat and make plans.'

'Yes,' she replied shakily. 'And while you're away, I want to visit everyone in the family once my stage run has finished and spend more time getting to know them all even more. Do you think that will work?'

'Of course it will. They love you already. Come on, put on your glad rags, your man is taking you out to dinner!' She smiled and gave in. Over dinner at their favourite Italian restaurant, they sat very close together and, in the end, didn't talk much about Charles's deployment but about family, the play and Maggie's plans to visit family before going to make the film for which she had already been cast.

It was a happy coincidence the film was to be made at High Wynch Park, and Hughie and Virginia had already asked her to stay in the house with them rather than with most of the rest of the cast.

'But first I want to go to Scotland. I want to see your mother.'

They went back early to the mews house and made love as if it would never to happen again. The next morning they planned their itinerary of visits to the family once Maggie's play finished in two evenings' time. After some discussion they decided not to make the long drive to Scotland but to fly to Edinburgh and hire a car. It was perfectly affordable.

'After all,' Maggie laughed with an attempt at bravado

'think of all the money we'll save not going out for meals. I don't expect there are many Italian or Chinese restaurants in Afghanistan.' There, she'd said the word she dreaded.

'I'm going to ring Ma and tell her to expect us the day after tomorrow.'

Whitewalls

It was early evening and the light was just starting to fade when the telephone rang. Jamie was enjoying a whisky in the company of Michael which was becoming a regular event so, as usual Rosie, answered it.

She came back into the sitting room, looking pleased but at the same time worried. 'What's up love? Come and tell us.' That was Jamie, and she felt mildly irritated at the use of the last word. Michael was hardly a family member, though she was increasingly aware of his presence, usually in a good way. But this was news about Charles. However, she didn't want to say it was private so sat down on the sofa beside Michael. 'Jamie, pour me a gin and tonic please then I'll explain.'

Jamie mixed the drink, put in a slice of fresh lime and handed it to Rosie. 'Now tell us what's happened.' Even shaken as she was, Rosie fleetingly noticed the 'us'.

'It's Charles, well obviously it's Charles. He's being sent to Afghanistan and he'll probably be shot at or worse. And poor Maggie, just when they've got engaged. I don't know what to do.' Michael stood up, drained his glass and, after giving Rosie a brief hug, said 'I really should go. This is a family matter after all.'

To her own astonishment, Rosie reacted: 'No, Michael, Don't leave unless you have to do, you may be able to help with some advice.'

Jamie echoed her. 'Please stay, at least for a while and for dinner if you want to. You've become part of this family.

Rosie continued; 'So they don't intend to get married before he goes as Maggie has decided and, of course,

Charles is so smitten he would agree to anything she wanted. This was said with a smile and was not a critical remark. 'And the good news out of this is Maggie has particularly said she wants to come here with Charles for a few days before visiting her grandparents.' For once Jamie was being the practical one. 'When are they coming?' 'Tomorrow, flying to Edinburgh and hiring a car so they can be independent and see Polly and Richard and the children in Edinburgh and, of course, the newly- weds. We could have loaned them a car but this is how they want to do it.'

At this point, Michael tactfully put down his glass and departed with the words: 'Thank you both so much as ever, but you want some time on your own to take this in. Of course if I can help at all I will. In fact I'd been hoping to meet them both again after the drama of the wedding and arrival of Fleur. I'm safe to drive, so will get off and see you again very soon.' He kissed Rosie on both cheeks, holding her a little too long.

'I'll see you out and give the dogs a short breather too. Back soon, Rosie.' The two men left together with Heather and Tweed, the black Labradors. 'I wish you'd stay, Michael.' 'Thanks, I would like to do, but I think you and Rosie need some space to talk. I'll be here if you need me though.' With that he was gone, still feeling an indefinable pull towards Rosie and, confusingly, to Jamie too.

Michael was still musing on these thoughts when he arrived back at the manse in Stitcholme. It was getting dark and he sighed at the prospect of going back to an empty house, though it had not troubled him before he met the Douglas family. There were lights on in the Prendergast bungalow but he knew the colonel and Lady Betty were newly back from their honeymoon and dismissed the idea of calling on them.

To cheer up himself and his somewhat spartan sitting room, he lit the fire which had been laid by Susan, the young mother from the village who came in to look after the manse and occasionally cook. She had two young children and Michael knew the extra money was a very welcome addition to the family income. Her husband, Brian, was a farm worker on the Whitewalls farm and so knew Jamie and Rosie well. It was, like all the Border villages a tight-knit community. He poured himself a large whisky and sat down to think.

Edinburgh

David found a thick cream envelope on the floor of his entrance hall with the initial H embossed on the flap. It was from his neighbour, Frank Hitchman who had recently knocked on David's front door while he was having sex with Polly on the sofa. He opened it to find an invitation to a piano recital, to be given by Frank in his drawing room together with singing by William Berger, an up-and-coming baritone. Also he was invited to take a guest. Surely he could persuade Polly to get away. Then afterwards she could stay over with him. It was to be a Saturday evening so she could make an excuse she was working and not go to join Richard and the twins at the Lodge.

David's first instinct was to accept at once, but with rare caution he decided he had better sound Polly out first. He didn't want to look too eager in accepting Frank's invitation though he was flattered to be asked. Frank was very well-known in the arts and music worlds in Scotland and a great supporter of many charities. He was a quiet, sweet bachelor with many friends and an honorary doctorate from the University of Stirling.

Polly dashed to pick up her mobile phone which was lying on the kitchen table.

'Hello, darling, it's me',

This was David's usual greeting. She replied: 'I'm a bit tied up just now with the children, and the other phone is ringing. Can you call me later please, or send me a text?' Despite David's at times desperate efforts to get Polly to leave Richard and make her life with him, she could not quite bring herself to make that decision. Richard thought with the death of Roddy, their grandfather, who had left the Lodge and stables to him, there was no question now of their splitting up. As a result, whilst they remained apart, David and Polly were taking more and more risks to see each other. Their relationship, with its high sexual drive and feelings of compatibility, was becoming a rollercoaster.

David did telephone later and explained that Frank had invited him and a guest to a music recital and small reception to take place in his apartment next door to David's. It was to be on a Saturday evening in September.

'Do say you'll come.' Frank is a very nice guy and really well-connected in Edinburgh so there could even be business opportunities for both of us. And if Richard and the twins are down at the Lodge we can spend the night together.'

There was a small sigh then: 'I would love to do, but I'll have to dress it up as a business thing. Maybe I could do the canapés, that would be one way. Yes, I want to spend another night with you. It's like a drug and the more we have of each other, the more I want. But I would have so much to lose if Richard and I split for good.'

'Leave all that for now.' David was learning to curb his impatience though he didn't know for how long. Part of him wanted to give it all up. He had no illusions about who would be blamed in the divorce if it were to happen.

'Anyway, darling, I'll accept and ask if Frank wants you to do the catering which would be a perfect excuse.' Before he hung, up she asked: 'When will I see you?' 'How about Thursday for lunch and afters?'

'Come here and I'll make lunch. That way we'll have more time together.' The eager response was 'Now, there's a brilliant idea! See you around 12 noon.'

Just after David's call the phone rang again. It was Charles, her brother.

'Hi, sister, Surprise!' As ever, Charles sounded cheerful.

'Mum told me you and Maggie were coming up to see us but she wasn't sure when.' The reply surprised her.

'What would you say if I told you we are at the airport, we've hired a car and wondered if we could drop in and see you all before we get sucked into the Whitewalls scene?'

'Of course you can. The children will be home from school soon and Richard shouldn't be late. Can you stay for supper? Anyway, don't decide now. I hope you've remembered how to find us,' she gently teased.

'As if I could forget. Maggie sends love and we'll be with you in about 45 minutes.' After the conversation Polly's doubts about David began to return. But there was no time to dwell on this. The twins rushed in from school, John flung his satchel on the floor whilst the ever-tidy Minty hung hers from the back of one of the pine kitchen chairs.

Polly calmed herself down. 'You'll never guess who's coming to see us, she said. 'I hope it's not David McLean' was John's cross response. Polly ignored that. 'No, uncle Charles and Maggie. They're going to Whitewalls to stay for a few days but they're coming here first, straight from the airport. Isn't that a surprise?'

The bell rang and the twins rushed to open the front door. Charles and Maggie had arrived. 'Uncle Charles, Aunty Maggie it's been a long time since we saw you'. This was John. Charles picked him up and swung him round, 'No it hasn't. Remember Great Grandma's wedding and the baby arriving and everything,' Charles said, laughing. Minty held back but Maggie hugged her and said 'Isn't this nice? We've just come for a short visit but we're going to see you at Whitewalls this weekend and I want to see the Lodge and all your mummy and daddy's plans for it. And the ponies too of course. 'And Pixie and Pod,' John added. Not to be outdone, Minty came in with: ' Chocolate Buttons comes everywhere with us now and the dogs really like her. Do you like her?' 'Of course I do, said Maggie, She's beautiful. Where is she now?' Right on cue the little Siamese cat came gracefully into the chaos and rubbed herself against Maggie's leg, purring loudly.

'Come on everyone. Into the kitchen before we're all squashed to pieces'. So they answered Polly's instruction and were soon in the country-style kitchen complete with its scarlet Aga and the big pine table with chairs and comfy cushions around it.

Richard arrived and, following the noise, came straight into the kitchen. He and Charles hugged and Richard kissed Maggie which made her feel even more one of the family. After tea and cake, Charles and Maggie left to drive to the Borders and, for once, the happy family atmosphere had rubbed off on Richard and Polly so they, and the children, started making plans for the weekend.

Whitewalls

As soon as she heard the car crunching up to the door Rosie threw off her apron and ran outside to meet Charles and Maggie. As ever she was closely followed by Tweed and Heather, with Empress, her little Pekinese following at a rather more stately pace. Charles jumped out of the car and immediately hugged his mother tightly. Maggie was a little more hesitant but Rosie soon drew her in and they went indoors to the kitchen which never seemed to change and to Charles represented all the good things for which 'Whitewalls' stood. Jamie was there already taking a bottle of champagne from the large fridge and Michael Martin was sitting at the kitchen table looking completely at home, which indeed was how he felt.

They sorted themselves out and went to the sitting room, which was also blissfully unchanged and Rosie produced some home-made canapés whilst Jamie poured the champagne, handed round quite unselfconsciously by Michael. *Glad dad's got a new friend* Charles thought, *they're both quiet but seem to suit each other.* Naturally he knew nothing of the growing attraction between Rosie and Michael.

Jamie raised his glass and proposed a toast. 'To our dearest son, Charles, and his lovely fiancée, Maggie. Charles we are all so proud of you going to fight to make the world a safer place and we will all, including Michael here who has been specially recruited for the job, be praying for your safe return.' Michael turned towards Charles and in a very natural way added: 'God go with you.' Rosie felt tears welling up again and it was Michael who gently patted her shoulder before Maggie drew her down to sit on the couch.

'Charles is going to be fine, everyone' she said in as light a voice as she could manage,' and I suggest we all enjoy being together. You have welcomed me into your family and I already feel a part of it, and when Charles comes home we want to be married here.' They had not, in fact, discussed a venue but the thought had come to her and it at once lightened the mood.

Charles said: 'We looked in on Polly and Richard on our way here and the children were just home from school so it was a bit chaotic. We're hoping to see more of them all over the weekend. Richard said they're all coming to the Lodge. Oh, and Polly said she'd bring extra food, Mum. She's going to phone you later.' Rosie was both pleased and slightly annoyed at the same time. Why couldn't Polly just contact her directly? Then she dismissed the thought as unworthy. What did it matter? She was going to have a weekend of family which she would enjoy, despite Charles's impending tour in Afghanistan.

The rest of the day was spent walking the dogs along the river bank and inspecting and sheep and trout pond and also Jamie's studio where he was preparing for his next watercolour exhibition. Once again, Michael was included in everything. He just seemed to blend in naturally. The gardens were already starting to wear their autumn cloaks with leaves turning amber and some already falling. The roses, too, had finished but the plants in the conservatory were thriving and Rosie and Maggie spent a very pleasant hour ostensibly dead-heading but really talking. Maggie wanted to know everything about Charles from the very beginning, why he had gone into the army and his two grandfathers.

'I must ring Betty and invite her and John over for lunch tomorrow so they can see you both' Rosie said 'I know she has this very kind idea of letting old Alistair rent the Pele Tower for next to nothing but maybe John has talked her out of it, though I doubt that. Will you be fine, Maggie if I go off and do that as well as ringing Polly?' 'Of course I will, I'll go and unpack.' 'I've put you both in Charles' old room, no point in pretending you don't sleep together,' said Rosie with a warm smile.

Betty and John were both delighted to accept the invitation to lunch the next day, Saturday. They had not been seen very much since returning from their honeymoon in Tuscany but had been busy arranging Betty's possessions in the bungalow at Stitcholme as well as getting used to living together. John had wanted to build Betty a studio in the garden but she said in the short term she could use Jamie's which was big enough for both of them. Of course Betty and John each had their foibles and preferred ways of doing things but there was nothing major on which they disagreed. As well, the fact they had been such good and close friends for many years made the domestic part of their new life together relatively tranquil. There was now the added bonus of a physical relationship combining gentleness with true love.

For once Richard, Polly, John, Minty and their pets had travelled from Edinburgh leaving early. Certainly on the surface there seemed to be a comfortable harmony in the family. It was a bright late summer's day with just a hint of autumn air first thing in the morning.

The previous evening, after Charles and Maggie had left and the children were in bed, Richard and Polly had sat down at the kitchen table and drawn up a long list of changes needed at the Lodge, to transform it into a family home from a bachelor house having been little changed since the death of Laura, the wife of Polly's late grandfather Roddy.

Although Polly was still heavily involved with her lover David, she did feel she owed Richard and her children the best environment she could help to create for them. They had decided to begin with the kitchen, which in the Douglas tradition was always regarded as the heart of the home.

As well as all the usual paraphernalia, Polly had prepared a whole ham and salads to contribute towards the family lunch and taken a couple of fruit pies from the freezer. Rosie saw to it nobody ever went hungry at Whitewalls but they always had good home-cooked food and with the physical activities in which they all took part in different ways there was no question of anyone in the family becoming overweight in the family.

Richard was in a particularly good mood as the previous night, after large glasses of brandy, he and Polly had made love for the first time for many weeks. 'Darling, I do love you,' she had said, 'Do you? Do you really?' had been his response. In many ways she did, but David was like a drug she was unable to give up. David had, in fact, changed his tactics from demanding she leave Richard, taking the children with her (though he hoped Richard would not let her do this) and was biding his time, pursuing her all over again. Still, she reasoned the Lodge needed doing up whatever the future held.

As usual when they arrived at the Lodge the twins went to see their ponies which had spent the summer outside and were muddy with manes and tails in need of at least some grooming. Butterball, John's Palomino, was well named as he was very round indeed after a summer feeding on sweet grass and Snowball, Minty's pony, was nearly as fat.

They were all tired after a busy week and, once the twins had had their baths and got into pyjamas, an early night was achieved with little or no fuss. Polly had declined having supper at Whitewalls with the perfectly reasonable excuse they would all be together on the Saturday. To Richard's surprise and pleasure, they made love that night for the first time at the Lodge and the second time in two days. Polly's relationship with David had awakened in her the sensual woman hidden beneath the cloak of respectability of the Scottish upper middle-class woman who, as far as her family knew, had always done the right thing. Richard, of course, now knew this, and almost without realising it was now playing her game. He had always been diffident with women and was not a natural flirt.. So, for now they seemed to be sailing into calmer, if not calm waters.

Whitewalls

Rosie had extended the dining table to make room for everyone at the family lunch. Michael was there as well. He was rapidly, almost seamlessly becoming part of the clan since the dramatic events of Betty and John's wedding day. Charles and Maggie were relaxed in spite of what lay ahead, and the twins, especially John, felt very important at being included and were pretending their lemonade was white wine. John was particularly intrigued by the colonel's stories of the World War Two and had already decided like his Uncle Charles, he would become a soldier when he grew up, fight in wars and save his country from the enemy. He wasn't sure who was the enemy but expected he would find out nearer the time.

With her brood gathered about her, good food and a feeling of warmth all round, Rosie smiled and relaxed. Then the crunch of car wheels on the gravel outside the dining room gave them all a start. Jamie got to his feet and looked out of the window as the doorbell rang. He didn't recognise the car but went to answer the door.

'Hello everyone, may we join you? This looks like a really fun party.' Rosie thought to herself *damn why does he have to spoil everything*? It was Sir Alistair, closely followed by Lady Madeleine. On the way from the airport in a hire car Alistair had explained to her tact was needed in dealing with the family, as they would temporarily be staying in the Pele Tower, which Betty had already made over to him pending resolution of the true ownership of Whitewalls. She smiled graciously at the assembled company gesturing to the men to sit down again. 'So lovely to be here at last and I am really looking forward to getting to know you all better.'

Even in extremis, Rosie's manners were impeccable. 'What a nice surprise. Let's all move up and make room for Grandpa and Madeleine.' Though her smile was fixed, everyone, except Michael, knew what she was thinking and moved up. Jamie poured the unexpected guests a glass of wine. We've finished the champagne but this is a rather good Sauvignon blanc. Though I expect it will be rather ordinary for you, Alistair, with your new life as a wine maker.' This was a wind-up as Jamie knew perfectly well the situation regarding the chateau though he had not expected Alistair to leave quite so soon. He was equally determined Rosie should not be put upon by Alistair inveigling his way for himself and Madeleine to stay at Whitewalls.

Alistair and Madeleine both ate what was left of lunch and enjoyed as much wine as Jamie would pour for them. Then came the question. 'Rosie my dear, would it be possible for Madeleine and I to stay here for a few days until we can get the Tower sorted out?' For a moment both Rosie and Jamie were taken aback by the sheer opportunism of the question, after all Alistair had done to try to get Whitewalls into his ownership.

'Out of the question'. This was Lady Betty coming in very firmly. 'I think you will find everything is in order at the Pele Tower and whilst you will no doubt want to add things whilst you are staying there, it's perfectly habitable right now. Why don't you go and stay at the Park Hotel in Peebles tonight? Then you can do your household shopping in the morning. I had a feeling I might see you, so I have the keys with me.' Turning to her husband' she said: 'John dear, could you please be a darling and get them from my bag in the hall?'

Apart from the twins who didn't understand really what was happening the rest of the company wanted to cheer. Betty had certainly come up trumps and in the most firm, yet delightful way. Realising he was beaten Alistair summoned up all the dignity he could muster and took the keys to the Pele Tower from Betty.

'It is most kind of you, Betty,' Madeleine said in a gracious voice 'and we will, of course, look after your home whilst we are there.' 'Oh, surely Alistair told you my home is now with John in Stitcholme. I may eventually sell the Tower.' From Alistair's viewpoint, things were getting decidedly worse so he decided to cut his losses for now and said authoritatively: 'Come along Madeleine my dear. I'll see if they have a nice room at Peebles Hydro, The Park Hotel is not ideal.'

Nobody tried to stop them though they were courteously seen off the premises by Jamie and Rosie, leaving Michael in conversation with the Prendergasts. Michael was delighted John and Betty were interested in his plans to increase the congregation and activities at the little church and they promised to go to morning service the following day.

The trouble began almost immediately.

Chapter 6

Peebles

During a comfortable and not too expensive night at the Peebles Hydro, Alistair spent some time thinking of his next move and how to persuade Madeleine they should live in the Pele Tower. He thought she would hate it. He was right.

Laden with supermarket shopping bags, in itself a new experience for Sir Alistair, they drove up the winding hill to the Pele Tower overlooking the surrounding countryside. It looked grim and forbidding from the outside, which he hoped Madeleine would not immediately notice. He was disappointed.

'Mon dieu,' she screamed as the car crunched to a halt in front of the old oak door. ' This is terrible-like a prison.' 'Patience, my darling. It's lovely inside.' He struggled with the big brass key which opened the door. Madeleine followed him inside, screeching as she did so.

'This place is awful. It is dark and dusty- and the kitchen! How could I make meals in there on the old stove? An antique, it is so old.' Alistair was partially prepared as he had bought a bottled of chilled champagne in the supermarket, so he managed to soothe her a little, put on the central heating and find two clean glasses. Lady Betty had not troubled about such trivia as the correct ones for different drinks but he found two wine glasses, persuaded Madeleine to sit down at the ancient kitchen table and he poured two generous glasses of what turned out to be a half-decent champagne.

Madeleine was a good actress, and the Pele Tower was exactly as she had imagined it to be. Sometimes, for a clever and devious man, Alistair was very easy to deceive.

In fact, Betty had left a comfortable, if somewhat shabby, home when she left to start married life with John Prendergast. Most of the furniture though old was in good condition and Molly, who despite taking a dislike to the 'Frenchie woman' on one of the few visits Madeleine had paid to Whitewalls, had given the whole place a really good cleaning out from top to bottom. This, in itself, had not been an easy task owing to Molly's comfortable girth and the steep staircases which were a feature of the Tower. One thing she had done was to make up the beds in both rooms with the best linen she could find. Molly was not having the Frenchie woman criticise Lady Betty or her housekeeper.

The food they had bought from the delicatessen in Peebles, together with more champagne, got them through the evening. Madeleine was slightly modified by having a hot bath but just when Alistair thought he had won and they were in the same bed together, she said, 'Cheri, we cannot stay 'ere. Maybe for the weekend, but we must get an apartment in Edinburgh.' *Damn,* he thought. He had some money thanks to the Leseures' generosity but it would not last long if he had to pay rent for the kind of apartment Madeleine would consent to live in. He wished now she had stayed in Chambery.

Still, he managed to make love to her, albeit she was imagining Henri throughout the short engagement and, Alistair's mood was somewhat improved.

They were both tired and slept for a while, though by 4 am his brain was already working on a scheme to get hold of some money. This included the possibility, unlikely as it seemed, of Madeleine getting a job! She had worked before, and Edinburgh had a number of high-class boutiques. It would be worth a try. Although he tried to get up and dressed before his wife she was too quick for him. So, after a cursory breakfast, she pronounced herself ready to be driven to Edinburgh.

Chapter 7

Yorkshire - Manor House Farm

After very fond farewells with the whole family at Whitewalls, with the exception of Sir Alistair and Madeleine who had disappeared into Edinburgh, Charles and Maggie drove their hire car back to the airport to catch a flight to Leeds/Bradford airport, for the next stop on their itinerary to see Florette, her grandmother, and Nigel, her dear step-grandfather at Manor House Farm where they lived and worked. Nigel's farm was successful in spite of challenging economic times and Florette ran her business, selling cashmere clothes and blankets online so they were very comfortably off.

Charles and Maggie didn't talk much during the short flight but held hands and felt at ease and at peace with each other. When they arrived at the small airport they were both delighted to see Nigel and Florette waiting for them.

'My darlings, it's so good to see you', Florette exclaimed. 'We could not let you hire a car to come to us so we have come to collect you!' Nigel in his quiet way hugged both of them and said 'It's only a short journey home then we can all relax. I'm so happy to see you.'

They were soon back at the house with the usual collection of dogs rushing down the steps to greet them. 'Now, I've put you in your usual room and you might want to go and unpack before lunch, Florette said.

Unpacking did not take long and though they both wanted nothing better than a shared bath and bed, they knew Nigel and Florette were waiting for them downstairs. So after a quick tidy, Charles and Maggie went hand-in-hand down the wide staircase and out to the terrace which, as Florette had said was warm enough for a brace of strong gin and tonics generously as ever poured by Nigel. There were tiny, home-made, still warm cheese biscuits to nibble and Charles thought how much the rhythm of Whitewalls Maggie's grandparents' way of life resembled that at Whitewalls.

After a very pleasant and relaxed lunch Florette suggested Maggie have a 'toes up'. With all the drama of the last few days Maggie, was grateful for this idea from her grandmother, who understood her so well.

'I really feel rather feeble but, yes, I think I would like a short rest, but don't leave me too long. What are you going to do, Charles, darling?'

'Oh. don't worry about Charles. We're going to have a drive around the fields and talk boring things like agriculture.' This was Nigel's answer and Florette, in turn, announced she was going to check on despatches of the cashmere collection she successfully sold direct from her elegant website.

Maggie soon dozed in the quiet, comfortable bedroom which Florette had made Charles's and hers. When she reappeared downstairs, she found Charles and Nigel deep conversation in the library.

'Darling, Nigel and I have been having a closer look at the partnership proposition and I am getting rather keen on it,' Charles enthused. 'Don't look so worried' Nigel seeing look of doubt crossing Maggie's face. 'There is still a lot to be gone through, and Charles would need to finish his army tour and then go to Agricultural College, maybe Cirencester, for a year to learn the ropes.

Maggie pulled herself together as Florette came into the room.

'Did you have a nice-toes up darling?' her grandmother asked. 'Yes thanks, I didn't think I was tired but I must have been.' 'Well,' Florette continued, 'I've asked Gillian and Peter Morris to come over for supper this evening. I'm sure you'll get on very well together.' Seeing Maggie was still concerned, she added 'Yes, before you say anything, Peter does farm but runs a farm machinery hire business as well and Gillian is an artist and an author, so you may find you have things in common. More fun than just the golden oldies.' This was all delivered with a charming smile but Maggie knew when she was defeated. She would much rather have spent the evening just with Florette and Nigel but gave in gracefully.

'They sound interesting. I'll look forward to meeting them. Right now I think I'd like some fresh air. Do you want to come, Charles? Maybe we could take the dogs?' So it was agreed and accompanied by assorted canines the couple went out into the immaculately kept gardens.

Once the dogs had settled down Charles and Maggie, by common consent, sat on the teak bench placed in a corner of the garden, out of sight of the house. The animals were well-behaved and settled at their feet.

Maggie spoke first, 'Charles, darling, isn't all this a bit premature? You haven't done your tour in Afghanistan yet, let alone seen about resigning your commission. Anyway, I would have thought you would want to join your dad if you were opting for the country life.'

He took her gently in his arms and hugged her. 'Nothing's decided but when we're married it will be much easier for your career if we are living between here and London. Besides, it looks as if there will be more films for you being done at Uncle Hughie's and you've really been a hit with them. And believe me, Virginia is not easy to please!

'Anyhow, as you know, I love my family but I want to make my own way too and the more I see of Nigel and the set-up here the more I like the idea.'

'Well, I suppose we could agree in principle and see what happens next. Darling, if you agree I want us to get married at Whitewalls after you come home from Afghanistan a proper wedding with Minty and John as bridesmaid and page-boy, oh, the whole works if your mum and dad agree!'

Once again, he took her firmly in his arms and gave her a long. lingering kiss which left both of them not only breathless but also aroused. By now, the dogs were getting restless and this broke the spell for the moment. They made to go back to the house, holding hands, with the dogs jumping around them.

Florette and Nigel watched them approach from the terrace and smiled at each other. 'I think you have your answer, Nigel, darling, and hopefully meeting Peter and Gillian this evening will let them see it's not just old people like you and me who enjoy this part of the world.' Now it was Nigel's turn to kiss his wife. 'Old? You? Never.'

By the time Peter and Gillian arrived both couples were very much at ease and the champagne ready to be opened proved a good ice breaker. Peter was tall, like Charles but with fair hair and blue eyes, and Gillian, small and bouncy with a shiny black bob, was very chatty from the start. They had brought with them their border terrier Dandy who was well used to coping with the home team of dogs and they were all allowed to stay in the library whilst the human beings enjoyed their champagne and home-made cheese straws.

Dinner that evening was a very relaxed occasion. Joan had done a chicken pie preceded by a starter of salmon with wafer thin brown bread. Peaches poached in brandy with thick cream on top rounded off the meal, which was finished by everyone, including Florette who usually didn't eat a great deal. Nigel had produced some very palatable Sauvignon Blanc and that went down easily too.

'I really admire you for becoming a successful actor.' Said Gillian. I know it's not easy for anyone in the arts world right now but you seem to have cracked it!' Maggie was warming her already, but being given such a spontaneous compliment reinforced her feelings. Maggie agreed to go the following morning and look at Gillian's studio and the kind of work she produced.

Glancing across at Charles and Peter, already in deep conversation over the kind of modern farming methods he was introducing to his farm, right next door to Manor House Farm, Nigel awarded himself a small inward smile of satisfaction. The plan was working. He looked at

Florette who gave him one of her sweetest smiles. She, too, was good at reading people and situations.

The evening concluded quite early as Peter and Gillian needed to get back both for their baby-sitter and an early start the next day.

'Will you show me round your farm tomorrow whilst the girls are talking about what girls talk about, Peter?' 'Of course I will. I think you'll find it interesting.' With much waving and 'see you tomorrow' they drove off in their rather battered LandRover.

Later that night after delightful lovemaking Maggie snuggled up to Charles and whispered: 'You know there might be something worth thinking about here.' She drifted off to sleep again but Charles lay awake for a while trying, and mostly succeeding, to visualise a future here after the army. It felt good and very possible.

Maggie woke early the next morning and glanced across at her still sleeping lover. His dark hair was ruffled and he looked very young and boyish. She loved him.

They got up early and both of them went downstairs together and ate a good breakfast of scrambled eggs, bacon and sausages. This was not Maggie's normal food but she felt energised and was looking forward to visiting Peter and Gillian and seeing a little of their lifestyle for herself. Charles too was in a very good mood.

'Could we possibly stay another night?' he asked Florette. 'I think Maggie would like to see some more of the countryside and we don't have to be at High Wynch Park until the day after tomorrow.'

'My darling Charles, stay as long as you wish. It is giving Nigel and me so much pleasure to have you here, and Joan has also fallen in love with you!' She said this with a huge smile. Joan carefully kept her age to herself but Florette reckoned she was a least seventy but had all the strength and tenacity of the typical Yorkshire woman.

One of the border terriers, Dandy, had firmly attached himself to Maggie and jumped into the car as they set off for the farm visit. Nigel and Florette waved them off happily. 'Stay as long as you like, we'll be here when you get back. Just the four of us this evening, so we can have a good gossip' were Florette's parting words.

It was a short drive to Peter and Gillian's farmhouse. The grey stone house looked solid and homely without the grandeur of Manor House Farm but the drive to the front door was well kept and there were late flowering roses lining the beds immediately in front of the house. Peter flung open the front door accompanied by two golden Labradors Gelus and Romy. Little Dandy lived up to his name and barked with the best they could come up with. Gillian and the two children appeared from round the back of the house.

'This is the only time you'll come to the front door. Friends come round the back to the kitchen door', she said with a wide smile. So the friendship began. Peter took Charles off to look round the farm and Maggie stayed in the kitchen with Gillian.

'I'll just put this roast in the bottom oven for now, then show you over the house. Not that it's as grand as the manor but it's comfy and it's ours. I even have my own small studio at the back which you might like to see?'

'I'd love to do', said Maggie and, accompanied by the two children and three dogs, by now all friends, they went round the house. Alexander and Jessica, Peter and Gillian's children, were polite and Jessica offered to show Maggie her pet lizard. Not to be outdone Alexander's ferret had to be shown off too.

'Right, you two, leave Maggie in peace, I want to show her the studio.' Laughing, the two women went off down the garden to the wooden studio built in the shade under a beautiful old oak tree. The early autumn sunshine was filtering through the leaves which had not yet begun to fall and Maggie became filled with a new feeling of lightness and tranquillity she had not had for some time. This lack had been especially noticeable due to hearing Charles's news but it was more than that. Gillian broke her reverie. 'Are you coming in, Maggie, or going to stay there in a world of your own for the rest of the day?' She laughed as she said this. Maggie smiled at her new friend and the moment passed.

The garden studio was full of colour with a painting in progress on the easel and more finished works stacked against the wall waiting to go and be framed. There were family photographs pinned up everywhere and Jessica and Alexander had their own corner where they were making a papier mache dog over a wire frame.

They re-joined the men over tea and scones at the kitchen table, after which Maggie and Charles went back to Manor Farm with exhortations to return whenever they pleased.

Over supper that evening, which they had in the kitchen as it was Joan's night off, Nigel and Florette tactfully did not bring up the subject of the future plan. It was, in fact, Maggie who broached it. 'Peter and Gillian are so nice and the children are great. They all seem so relaxed yet they're busy too with the crops and the animals. It's almost like another life!'

'Well, my dear, there's a lot to think about before you begin to make definite plans,' was Nigel's only reaction. In fact he was delighted at these positive comments. He and Charles had already had a discussion and Nigel was going to work on some figures whilst Charles was away. Florette, naturally, was delighted even at the thought of having her beloved granddaughter close by but she also talked of films and plays and clothes before by comment consent, and all now yawning after a long day they went off for the night.

Charles was not even thinking about what was ahead of him and Maggie was feeling deliciously loving and mellow at the same time. The owl outside the window was particularly vociferous that night and in the oddest way made Charles and Maggie feel even closer as the couple cuddled up together in the small hours.

They were up early in the morning ready for the next stage of their journey. Nigel drove them to Leeds/Bradford airport for the next stage of the tour round the family, to High Wynch Park, before Charles and Maggie returned to London and what lay ahead. The farewells were warm but, by common, though unspoken consent, were not emotional as they all wanted to be positive and keep their spirits high. Florette had been rather tearful hugging both of them as they left Manor House Farm and she wished them 'bon voyage'.

Checking in at the airport, which was small and friendly, was simple and quick and the plane took off on time. They were both tired and snoozed for much of the short journey to East Midlands, the nearest airport to Charles' uncle Hughie and the new set-up there with little Fleur now part of the family after her dramatic birth at the General Hospital at the end of Colonel Prendergast and Lady Betty's wedding.

Maggie was delighted to see Hughie waiting for them as they came through arrivals at the airport. So was Charles, though not surprised. This kind of thoughtfulness was simply typical of the family! Hughie was positively beaming. He'd lost some weight which suited him though he still wore his favourite old checked jacket and yellow cashmere pullover.

'Great to see you both,' he boomed, kissing Maggie warmly and grasping Charles by both arms. 'Bit of a change at home since you were last here but Fleur is, I have to say, a very good baby. You'll love her. But come on, let's get out of here. You must be sick of travelling but we're really pleased you could find time to come and stay even for a couple of days.'

As High Wynch Park was now almost permanently in use as a film set Hughie drove them to the back door, unheard of in the old days. Virginia coming out to meet them holding a very pretty, dark-haired baby in a sling across her front. Maggie was used to the reserved, elegant and rather haughty Virginia but this was quite different. Her hair was as blonde as ever but now caught up in a pony-tail and she wore jeans and a long shirt, tucked in with a smart belt but still more casual than she had ever looked before. Even Charles noticed. 'Wow, Virgie, this motherhood lark really suits you. You look fantastic.' And for the first time in his life he kissed her.

'Come in, come in and do excuse the mess.' As mess and Virginia were hardly synonymous this was a new feature too. The kitchen was cosy with the inevitable Aga, a tasteful shade of blue, and evidence of baby things but also and more usual signs of food preparation for supper. Charles found this reassuring after all this baby stuff. Maggie found it all fascinating. This, after all, would be her home for part of the time Charles was away in Afghanistan when she would be taking part in her next film, thanks to Piers Romayne but also to her own increasing confidence and talent in front of the camera.

Hughie took them up to the guest room. 'Hope you'll be okay in here. I think there's everything you need, and I've popped a bottle of champagne over there in case you feel like some bubbles before dinner. And, you remember the bathroom is through the door! There was now no pretence of separate rooms and Maggie flopped on the comfortable bed and held out her arms to Charles.

'Let's open the bubbly first', he said, which is what they did. Later they were sitting up in bed, wearing the white fluffy dressing gowns after sharing a relaxing bath, when there was a discreet knock at the door. It was Roberta, who was visiting for a few days. 'Hi you two. Mum says not to disturb you but drinks downstairs in half an hour or so then supper. Okay?' and without waiting for an answer she was off.

'Does all your family eat so many meals at set times?' Maggie asked. Charles grinned, 'Never thought about it, but yes, I suppose we do. We had that very traditional upbringing where you had morning tea, usually in bed if you were female, lunch around one o'clock, sometimes afternoon tea about half past four, pre-dinner drinks at seven and dinner after that!' 'Why aren't you all as fat as pigs then?' This question was accompanied by her running her hand over his naked and very trim stomach. 'Don't worry. Whilst I am away, you can go back to living on microwave meals.' As soon as he said it, Charles knew it was the wrong thing to say. He wasn't very good at tact so quickly changed the subject. 'Just one more family dinner to please me, darling, and I promise you will never be fat. I love you just the way you are.'

It turned out to be another very enjoyable family evening and even Roberta, not known for her good nature, played a lively part. Not only did she help her mother prepare supper, she volunteered to put Fleur to bed whilst the rest of them caught up over some of Hughie's famously strong drinks in the drawing room. Even here Virginia had relaxed her usually exacting standards of tidiness and order, though the squashy sofas and cushions were still very much in evidence.

'What's the next film called?' Virginia asked Maggie. 'Well, Piers says the working title is "Mysterious Death in the Commons" so it's carrying on with the political mystery theme as the last one did very well. Only this time I have a much bigger part. I'm the much younger wife of a cabinet minister! But I'd better not give too much away. Though High Wynch is again the house in the country where I spend most of my time, not always behaving well. The scenes in London are meant to be in Parliament, where my husband is also not behaving well! So I'll be staying in London for those scenes.'

'Then you are definitely staying here for the filming in this part of the world.' This was Hughie, but Virginia was very quick to agree. 'That is, if you don't mind the baby!' 'Of course not,' Maggie replied 'I think she's gorgeous and hope to see much more of her. Not sure who she looks like, though she's definitely got Charles's lovely dark hair and blue eyes.' As Virginia still didn't know whether Fleur's father was Hughie or Anthony Goodman, Piers Romayne's financial backer, she made no comment.

Around eleven o'clock, everyone was yawning. Roberta had again volunteered to feed Fleur and put her into her cot, which was now in what had been Hughie's dressing room and where he had previously spent more time than in the big double bed with his wife. That, too, had changed and, whilst not exactly full of passion for her husband, Virginia had reached a point, which happens so often in a long marriage where she had decided to settle for what she'd got. She had put off love-making for as long as she could claim it was bad for her after the birth but now she relented because of seeing Charles and Maggie so much in love and at the start of a life together, or her own older daughter's change of attitude. This was the night she admitted Hughie not only into her bed but into her body. It was quick and unbidden images of the brooding features of Anthony that saw her through the experience. For his part Hughie was euphoric. 'I say, old girl, that was amazing, wonderful.' Then he fell asleep and snored but Virginia lay awake for some time thinking of what might have been.

For their part although they were tired after a long day Charles and Maggie were not too tired to make love again before they too fell into a deep and dreamless sleep.

Next day Charles and Maggie left to go by train to London and, once again, Hughie took them to the station. 'It's been marvellous having you to stay, even for one night. And Maggie, we meant it about your staying when the filming is going on here.' As they got out of the car, Hughie grasped Charles's arm, his face serious for once, and shook his hand warmly. 'You're going to be fine in Afghanistan, I know you are, and we'll have a big party when you get back!' He kissed Maggie and hugged her. It had been such a happy and memorable visit.

Chapter 8

London

Both Charles and Maggie were tired when they returned to the mews house and decided to go out for supper at Ping Ho's, their favourite Chinese restaurant in walking distance. They were greeted by Mr Chan with smiles and questions about why he had not seen them lately and whether they no longer enjoyed his food! This was said with more smiles and the explanation was given that they had been away visiting family. For no logical reason, except perhaps tiredness, Charles said: 'I'm afraid I will be going away again soon with the army and Maggie here is going to be making another film'. At once Mr Chan realised the sensitivity of the situation and only said 'But I am neglecting my duties. Would you like your usual table'? They said they would.

Champagne was not their usual drink with Chinese food, but this evening was special and a bottle of Tattinger, dusty but nicely chilled, was produced to be drunk with the steamed dumplings, crispy prawns and beef with chilli and green pepper accompanied by egg fried rice and noodles. Whilst this may not have been a choice for a light meal, they were both hungry and after eating British food on their travels round the country were ready for something more exotic.

So it was they sat very close at their candlelit table and enjoyed an excellent meal. Mr Chan shook hands with both of them and rather unexpectantly said as they left: 'Have courage, my friends.'

They walked back together under the now darkening sky, arm in arm and feeling as if they could cope with anything the world decided to put in front of them. This feeling of complete happiness lasted right through to the next morning and a telephone call from Charles's colonel.

Whitewalls

Jamie had driven into Edinburgh to see his friend gallery owner Henry Duncan to talk about his forthcoming autumn exhibition. It was midweek and Richard and Polly were both in Edinburgh. The manager, Tom, and his new young assistant Katie had seen to the horses and there was an air of peace and tranquillity in the house and garden.

Molly had categorically refused to go to the Pele Tower to help Sir Alistair and Madeleine. 'I'm sorry, Mrs Douglas, but I am not going to put myself out for that Frenchie woman. She'll either have to do it herself or find someone else, though I doubt she'll be able to do that.' She sniffed loudly and Rosie, wisely, simply replied: 'It's up to you Molly. I really don't mind but I don't want you to be overworked.' 'Settled then. I stay with you and do for Lady Betty and the colonel. I might-only might, mind you see if that nice minister would like a half day a week. Living there all on his own. He needs to get himself a wife, that's what I say.' At this, Rosie firmly changed the subject and said 'I'm going out into the garden so I'll leave you to get on.'

The truth was the mention of Michael's name had made her feel curiously stirred. What on earth was going on? She asked herself. Then with a little mental shake she picked up her trug and secateurs and went into the walled garden to dead-head the late flowering roses.

As often happened when working in her garden Rosie lost track of time and it was only when Molly came round, clearly ready to go, she looked up from the rose beds. 'I'm off now. Mrs D, but you won't mind if I offer to help the minister with the housework, will you?' 'What was that, Molly?' Rosie was only half-listening. 'Oh, no, of course not, if you think you can manage all of it.' Only after Molly had bustled away wondering what was up with Mrs D, did Rosie realise she had just encouraged even further contact with Michael. Given Molly's incurable love of gossip Rosie had no doubt there would be regular bulletins from that source. *Damn, she ought to have made time to discuss this more with Molly but it was done now and didn't mean anything. Did it?*

Rosie went back into the house, leaving her boots in the porch to enter an empty and very tidy kitchen, silent apart from the ticking of the clock. Her immaculately written list was in its usual place near the Aga but, for once, there seemed to be little on it. Her mother's wedding was over, her sister-in-law's baby was thriving and had brought Hughie and Virginia closer together and even Polly seemed to have settled down. Certainly, the arrival of Fleur had given Virginia both a new lease of life and brought out the best in her, which was a vast improvement!

Jamie was very keen on his painting again, which had taken a back seat during the dramas of the summer months. They had talked about going away for a holiday - something they rarely did - but there didn't seem to be time. So they had decided a winter break would be a good idea when the harvest was in, a cruise maybe but certainly something which would give them a real holiday where Rosie, in particular, would be able to relax and be waited upon. Musing on this and unable to be idle, she set about changing bed linen and generally sprucing up Jamie's and her bedroom. Molly was a good cleaner but never put things back exactly where they ought to be! A maddening habit of hers was sometimes to arrange photographs and ornaments how she wished. Over the years Rosie had tried to dissuade her from doing this, without success.

Edinburgh

After a long and highly enjoyable lunch at the Alba Club Jamie and Henry discussed the dates and details for Jamie's autumn exhibition at the gallery. They had walked up to the club and back again to the gallery where Jamie had parked his car in the small car park behind the old stone terraced building. Time had passed very quickly and, looking at his watch, Jamie saw it was after four o'clock. He realised that he had consumed far too much wine and now brandy to drive safely back to Whitewalls that afternoon. Then he had an idea.

'Haven't seen much of Polly and the grandchildren in the last couple of weeks, Henry, so if she can put me up this evening, I'll take a taxi to Murrayfield, leave the car here and come back in the morning to collect it and get on out of your way!' 'No trouble at all, old boy, and I think you're right not to drive. Anyway, do you good to get away from your country seat, lovely as it is. We wouldn't have so many good pictures if you lived in the city would we? On the other hand, perhaps we would have. What about trying some landscapes of the city from different perspectives?' 'H'mm, I'll certainly think about it, but I've got enough of the traditional ones for this exhibition.'

Polly had just spent a very hectic and highly satisfactory afternoon in bed and was shooing David away before the children came home from school. She had tried to give him up but couldn't, or wouldn't. The more she prevaricated about making a decision to be totally honest with Richard and live with David, the keener he became. The telephone in the hall rang. 'Hello, darling.' It was her father. Genuinely surprised, she blew a kiss at David as he left. Dad didn't often ring out of the blue. 'Are you there, Polly? 'Yes, yes, I'm here. How are you, there's nothing wrong I hope?' 'Nothing at all,' was the cheery reply from her mildly inebriated parent. 'I'm in Edinburgh, been out with Henry and organising my next exhibition. Quite honestly, had a bit too much to drink and wonder if I could stay the night at your place. I don't think I should drive home and Mum will be fine.'

She tried to inject more warmth into her voice. 'Dad, that would be lovely. Where are you? Do you want me to come and collect you when the children arrive back from the school run, or can you take a taxi?'

'I'm still at Henry's. I can leave the car here and get a taxi. Be with you in around twenty minutes if the traffic's not bad,' he said cheerily. *Damn*, thought Polly though she wasn't really cross with her father. In fact she spent so little time alone with him it would be good to see him. Also, he and Richard liked each other very much and would be a buffer between the spouses in what was becoming once again a tense relationship.

One more call for Richard to make. 'Hello, Rosie, it's me!' She was genuinely surprised. They were almost always together at this time of day. 'The thing is I had a very good lunch with Henry, drank a bit too much and don't think I should drive back, so I'm going to stay with Polly and Richard.' Another surprise. More was to follow. 'Why don't you give Michael a call and ask him to have supper with you if he's not doing anything else? I don't really like the thought of you being at Whitewalls on your own.' In spite of herself she felt a rush of excitement. 'I might just do that,' she replied airily. She wanted to add 'if you don't mind' but Jamie would not have suggested the plan if he did mind. 'See you tomorrow morning, darling' Jamie's voice brought her back to earth. Rosie went into the kitchen for a moment or two and sat at the table to think. Then she.picked up the phone. Michael answered quickly in his low, modulated voice.' The Manse, Michael Martin speaking.'

'It's Rosie, Michael. How are you?' Without waiting for a reply she went on: 'The thing is, Jamie is spending the night unexpectedly with Polly and family in Murrayfield and he has just phoned and suggested I invite you over for supper and, in fact, stay the night. We've plenty of spare bedrooms.' There the die was cast. 'Rosie that would be lovely? Can I bring anything?' 'Just yourself, it's only a kitchen supper so old clothes and no dog collars.' He laughed, 'I think I can manage that and a bottle of champagne. In around an hour all right?' *It was very all right* Rosie thought.

Looking back to that evening and night, Rosie could never work out exactly what trigger set in motion events that meant life would never be the same again.

True to his word, Michael arrived promptly. Rosie had spruced up for the occasion, even changing from her inevitable uniform of shirt and trousers into a soft, longish skirt and top. They were a particularly attractive shade of blue. She had tied a deeper blue cashmere cardigan from Florette's collection round her neck and set the kitchen table with a cloth, crystal glasses and a little more attention than usual.

She heard Michael's car crunch on the gravel and went out to meet him. He was carrying a small overnight bag and a bottle of champagne. 'This is very kind of you Rosie. I'm not really used to impromptu lovely invitations'. He kissed her lightly but with warmth. 'It's so good you could come. Jamie for some silly reason didn't want me to be on my own.' There, that set the parameters. Or did it? She returned his kiss and they went together into the house.

'Shall we have a glass of champagne whilst it's still cold? I've had it in the fridge since you called.' 'Yes. Come into the sitting room. I lit a fire as it's getting quite cool now. Supper is just a casserole so it will be ready to eat when we are.' He laughed. 'Stop trying to live up to your reputation as the perfect hostess. Let's relax and you can tell me all about the real Rosie.'

Feeling light-hearted and somehow expectant, they went to the sitting room. Rosie had put out some of her home-made cheese straws and two champagne glasses. Michael laughed. 'Still the perfect Rosie.' he teased. Matching his mood, she smiled. I do my best.' Two glasses of champagne each later they wandered into the kitchen where Rosie cut up some baguette and took the pheasant casserole and vegetables out of the Aga. She gave him a bottle of Merlot to open. 'Red all right for you?' 'Absolutely'.

Over the relaxed meal, followed by fresh blackberries and cream, then some ripe brie they talked. Michael had the gift of getting people to open up about themselves and here Rosie was no exception. 'It sounds very dull when I talk about my prosaic life.' she said ruefully. 'It sounds very contented without being at all dull,' returned Michael, you're the centre of this family, you and Whitewalls, I could see that soon after we met.' 'Let's go and have a glass of brandy and you can tell me all about your life as a bachelor minister,' his hostess suggested. Michael surprised Rosie by smacking her lightly on the bottom and putting his arm casually round her shoulder. 'Well, I felt this calling to the church after working in Africa, in some of the poorest countries which are also some of the most corrupt I travelled quite a lot then I met Charlotte, a lovely girl working for Save the Children. I've no idea why but she fell in love with me too and we intended to marry, then come home for a while before carrying on our work.'

Softly Rosie asked 'What happened?' A bleak look crossed his face. 'She caught an infection. Conditions were very primitive and in spite of the best the local doctors could do, which wasn't much, she died. There have been other women since then, for some reason it's always there for ministers if you want it-but only rarely did I have an intimate relationship.' They sat in silence for a while then Rosie kissed him on the mouth. 'Let's take the dogs for a quick run in the garden, then go to bed.' 'Are you sure, about bed I mean?' 'I'm sure.' In a dreamlike state they took the dogs out, settled them in the kitchen, including Rosie's rather indignant Pekinese, Empress, who was more used to sleeping in the master bedroom.

Rosie had half-expected Jamie to phone again during the evening but he hadn't done so and had realised it was probably too late at ten o'clock as he ended his happy evening with Polly and Richard.

She had quickly gone into the bedroom, put on a soft bedside light and turned back the bed after a quick trip to the bathroom. When Michael came in-wearing highly respectable pyjamas she laughed again. 'Oh, you can't wear those-far too elegant.' He pushed her gently on to the bed, took off her equally respectable dressing gown and pulled her towards him.

Their bodies fitted perfectly. Rosie ran her fingers

through Michael's silvery curly hair and he caressed her, seeming effortlessly to find erogenous zones she did not know she had. There was a moment when both of them stopped and looked deeply at each other. 'Are you quite sure?' he asked. 'Quite sure' she replied. Outside, in the dark an owl hooted. They laughed and soon brought their love-making to a mutually and highly satisfactory conclusion.

During the night they came together again. There was no need for words, that could wait. Their hunger for each other was satisfied again and again before Rosie finally went to sleep in the crook of his arm. All too soon it was morning. Michael was still sleeping peacefully. It was 7.30 am. Rosie eased her naked, aching body from the bed and slipped silently into the bathroom. He was still asleep, snoring gently, when she returned and just as quietly dressed. She knew Jamie would telephone in the next half-hour.

Downstairs she let the dogs out into the garden, as well as a very cross Empress, put the kettle on the Aga to boil and began to contemplate what she and Michael had just done. He was a minister and she had been, until now, a completely faithful wife who had only ever had a sexual relationship with her husband from when they married at the age of 21.

The phone rang and Rosie quickly picked it up. Exactly as she had thought, it was Jamie. 'Hello, darling, I had a great evening with Polly, Richard and the twins. How did you get on with Michae?' She hated lying 'Oh, we were fine. We had your favourite pheasant casserole and he brought champagne!' 'What were you celebrating?' 'Oh, I think it was a bottle some parishioner had given him,' she laughed. 'Well, how is our favourite minister this morning?' She lied again, 'I don't know, I had better make some tea and give him a shout.' 'Well, I should be with you about half-past-ten. I'm going to call in at the corn merchant on the way. Love you, darling,' 'Love you too!' and she did.

Then Michael appeared He kissed her with affection and not with last night's passion. 'Is that the best you can do?' 'Darling Rosie, if we are going to take this any further I want you to think very, very carefully about where it might lead. I like Jamie and have betrayed him, but I am drawn to you in a way which is hard to control. Does that make sense?' 'Yes, yes, it does and I am not going anywhere else in a hurry and I hope you're not either.' So Michael had breakfast and they avoided further physical contact.

Then, Jamie, in very good form, came in through the kitchen door with a box of Polly's home-made dishes. 'You two are a lazy pair. I've normally done a day's work on the farm by now!' 'And I've normally gone right through my prayer list and started a sermon,' Michael interjected, smiling. 'Rosie, could I have some coffee? Then I'll go and check on the sheep.' 'Shall I come with you?' Michael offered. Rosie stiffened. Was this how it was going to be? 'Why no?, glad of your company and I'm sure we've got rubber boots to fit you. It's probably going to be quite muddy on the hill.' So, after giving her husband coffee, Rosie watched them both as they left the kitchen apparently very happily together. Her own thoughts were very complicated. She could hardly believe what had happened the previous night and how much she had enjoyed making love with Michael. She gave herself another mental shake and resolved to get on with her day, whatever it brought with it.

The Pele Tower

'Alistair, this place is a dreadful dump, I really can't spend much more time here. There is nothing to do, the furniture is awful and your family seem to have decided they want nothing to do with us. You have to do something about this or I may as well go back to France!' Clearly, Madeleine was unhappy. Alistair mused as to whether or not it would, indeed, be better to be rid of her and let her go back to France. On the other hand, she was very pretty and he was still fairly determined to get back into Scottish society. Also she didn't know that far from giving Alistair the Tower Betty was only leasing it to him at a peppercorn rent.

'Darling, I'm still working with the lawyers regarding my claim on Whitewalls. We have enough money to live on in the meantime, so be a darling girl and be patient.' In order to shut her up, he kissed her as lovingly as he could manage and persuaded her to climb the stairs to the bedroom at the top of the tower where, at least, he had bought a new double bed and fresh bed linen. It did work but not for long.

Afterwards Madeleine went back on the attack. 'Cheri, why don't I go and speak to Betty? Now she has remarried, she really has no need at all to keep this place. We could sell it and buy an apartment in Edinburgh. I could even get some work to do in one of the fashion boutiques!' Inwardly, Alistair groaned. 'Please my darling, leave Betty and John alone for the present. I know it was not appropriate for us to be invited to their wedding but I am sure they will come round to us before very long.'

Alistair had an idea. 'My darling would you like to take a drive to Stobo Castle, have a look at the facilities and maybe enjoy a glass of wine? Hopefully, the owner, Stephen Winyard will be there and he is well known to the family. It really is time you got to know him too.' She perked up at this. 'H'mm, all right, why not. There is really nothing else to do and it's still raining!' So, with Madeleine temporarily mollified, they went down to the car and set off to Stobo. Alistair had, in fact, taken the precaution of telephoning ahead to make sure Stephen Winyard would be there

She was very gratified, after they had driven up the long, winding drive to the castle standing on its hill to find as they drew up the owner coming down the steps, hand outstretched to meet them. 'Sir Alistair, Lady Douglas, It's really good to see you both. So this is the lovely Lady

Douglas, come in please.' This was all rather flowery but Stephen knew his market and how to flatter. He did not, of course, know of the precarious state of this branch of Alistair's family finances.

As they toured the magnificent facilities, saw into some of the state-of-the-art treatment rooms, the lovely drawing room and dining rooms, Madeleine started to formulate a plan in her head. She kept this to herself for the moment. 'Oh, Stephen, may I call you Stephen?' She didn't wait for an answer 'This must be one of the most luxurious spas in the world.' He smiled and thanked her profusely. 'Well we do pride ourselves not only on our past reputation but also on being the most up to date with our treatments and nutrition for our guests who do, in fact, come from all over the world.'

'Is it true you have film stars and important politicians coming to this lovely place?' Stephen smiled enigmatically. 'Oh, I couldn't possibly say. Our guests welcome the fact we treat everyone confidentially. It's worked pretty well for the past twenty-five years, so I don't propose to change the policy. People find it very liberating to wear a dressing gown all day, even for lunch, though most people do like to dress for dinner in the evening.' Madeleine decided not to push her new idea at Stephen and after enjoying a couple of glasses of wine with him, they left to return to what she had begun to call the prison tower.

Edinburgh Murrayfield

'Mummy, my leg is really aching today. I just couldn't do PE and Miss Wilson said I was to be sure and tell you. Polly felt momentarily distracted. She had so much on her mind and was not really listening to her children's after-school chat. But this did bring her up short.

'Do you remember falling or hurting it?' 'No, it's been getting sore for a long time now, but I thought it would just get better by itself and it hasn't done.' Polly sighed-silently, she thought. 'I'm sorry, Mummy, but maybe we should get it looked at. Could we do that, please?' Overcome with remorse, Polly hugged her brave little daughter, kissed the top of her head and said; 'There's nothing for you to be sorry about, darling. Your health is more important than anything.' She really did believe this to be the case - at that moment. Polly picked up the phone and made an appointment to see Dr Cluny who had taken a great interest in Minty's case from the outset. He would be able to set up an appointment with the consultant. Then she tried to call her mother. To her surprise she got the answering machine message. She was not to know at that moment Michael and Rosie were stealing a few amorous moments together, ironically as she herself had done so many times with David.

The phone rang again. It was David. 'Hi honey, is this a good time? Or shall I call later? This was showing some sensitivity as the late afternoon was hardly ever a good time, unless they were alone together. 'No, Richard will be home soon and I'll see you tomorrow morning anyway. We have to sort out the recital at Moray Place. So I will be round by half-past-ten. Be good! She heard him sigh in a rather exaggerated way. 'If you're not there, what else can I be? Love you.' The children were still there so the best she could manage was 'me too, you.'

Soon afterwards Richard arrived home. Things were better between them but they were wary with each other. Polly had good reason to be careful when describing her activities. For the moment, Richard did not want to cause any further ripples in case their fragile relationship snapped. So it was with a peculiar sense of relief once the children had done their homework, had their baths and gone to bed, Richard and Polly discussed what should happen as far as Minty's leg was concerned. They, as well as Minty, had hoped it would get stronger of its own accord and felt a shared guilt about leaving it longer than they should have done.

'Mum says she'll come with me to Dr Cluny'. 'Wait a

minute, Polly I am going to come with you. Minty is our daughter and I need to be there too'. Oh, sorry, Of course you do.' He looked pensively at her but left the conversation at that.

Polly, feeling vulnerable again, answered in a conciliatory voice: 'Of course. I wasn't thinking straight, a bit shocked really. Mum will understand. Just you and I will go. I'll call her and explain. Fortunately Rosie said she did understand. Polly was a little surprised her mother had given in so easily, but then she didn't know about Michael. The appointment was made for the following week and the couple decided together to take the children down to the Lodge for the weekend to take everyone's mind off the problem and make plans for the refurbishment.

Moray Place

Frank was delighted with the number of acceptances for his drawing room recital to hear him play the grand piano, dressed in his white tie and tails and accompanying baritone William Berger whose third solo disc was due to be released the following year.

As expected, he had asked Polly to do the catering. She was happy to do this because she was very fond of Frank, a retired bachelor who did a great deal of good for various charities, always discreetly and often unrecognised. As well, it would mean she and David could both be there and she could stay on, in David's apartment afterwards. Polly knew she was taking a huge risk here, especially with the possibility of Minty needing more surgery, Richard nagging her to get going with the Lodge restoration and the day-to-day running not only of her business but also the house in Murrayfield.

The drawing room would comfortably seat 20 people and the dining room would be used for the champagne and canapés so it would not be a difficult assignment, once she had persuaded Richard. He didn't know about David's apartment being on the same floor and there wasn't really anything to arouse his suspicions, or so she thought.

Frank felt good. He was not a man prone to drawing personal attention to himself. Yet he had a dream of wearing white tie and tails, playing a Bechstein piano and also accompanying William singing. It had come to him it would be absolutely ideal to have this occasion in his large apartment in Moray Place giving pleasure not only to himself and William but also to some of his closest friends. The arrangements were made and the invitations had been sent. The soiree would take place the following Friday evening.

Polly had agreed to do the catering and promised the canapés would be elegant and bite-sized. David had accepted the invitation as a guest and he and Polly had agreed to spend the night together in his adjoining apartment after the party had finished.

It was a cool but calm early September evening and the guests arrived promptly at six o'clock, intrigued and looking forward to the evening. Most of Frank's friends knew of his great love of music and his habit of travelling all over the world to hear the concerts and operas he loved so much. Very few, however, had heard him play the piano and, indeed, thought perhaps it was there in his apartment just to fill up a corner. If it had not been for his desire to let his friends hear William sing in the intimate setting of Moray Place, it was doubtful if he would ever have played in public, even to a small invited audience.

Champagne was handed to the guests as they arrived and soon Polly, discreetly dressed for the occasion in a little black dress, was handing round tiny canapés and small napkins so people could mill about and talk to each other for the half-hour or so before the recital was due to begin.

Frank became a little nervous but a final glass of champagne steadied him before he sat down, flicked the tails of his jacket over the back of the tapestry-covered piano stool and ran his fingers lightly over the keyboard.

William, who was not nervous, stood beside his guide

and mentor and prepared to sing. His voice was spell-bindingly beautiful. He had chosen to sing Lieder by Schubert and Schumann. Frank had explained the make-up of the audience and together they had chosen well. After four encores, sung with the same grace and charm, Frank insisted the party was over!

The guests gradually left and David, one of the last to go, whispered into Polly's ear: 'See you next door as soon as you can get away.' In the event, it was sooner rather than later as Frank, with typical thoughtfulness, had engaged his cleaning lady to do the clearing away and wash the glasses.

Although he had already drunk a fair amount of champagne David just had time to put a bottle of Tattinger in the wine cooler when Polly let herself into the apartment and into his arms.

Back in Frank's apartment he and William were relaxing after their joint efforts. 'Until we started rehearsing I didn't know you were such a good pianist, Frank. We should perform as a duo more often! Your friends were very encouraging too and I thought Polly was really sweet. Is there something going on between her and David McLean?' Ever the soul of discretion, Frank smiled enigmatically and poured them both more drinks.

Chapter 9

High Wynch Park

Hughie and Virginia were deeply embroiled in all the arrangements for the next film to be made by Piers Romayne, which was a political thriller provisionally entitled 'The Minister Who Lied'. Maggie, Charles' fiancée, was going to play a leading role in the production and had gone to stay as a house guest soon after her Charles had been deployed to Afghanistan.

His departure for the notorious war zone had been sudden though not unexpected and Maggie was grateful for the chance to get away from their London mews house as soon as possible. She was trying very hard to stay positive and not think the worst could happen. They had so far managed to stay in touch with mobile texts and a telephone call when he assured her all was well with him and begging her not to worry. In turn, Maggie had said to him: 'Darling, I can't promise you but I will try very hard and I'm going to throw myself into work. Everyone here at High Wynch sends you lots of love and are all thinking about you.'

Rehearsals were due to start at the beginning of the following week, so Maggie had a very pleasant weekend helping Virginia with little Fleur and listening to Hughie's plans. Roberta and Alexander arrived on the Saturday and took Maggie out to the local pub, The Red Lion, for a very convivial bar dinner.

'I never in a million years thought Mum would produce a sprog again and still less did I ever think I wouldn't mind too much. In fact little Fleur is quite sweet, especially now she is starting to take notice of what's going on around her.' Coming from Roberta, this was an unusual comment and Maggie reflected how much nicer she was than when the two of them had first met.

Alexander was not quite so fulsome about his

immediate family but with a captive audience talked about his career ambitions to work in the financial field. This film lark is okay but you never know where the next deal is coming from and Dad has never been good with money. It's a good job the house isn't mortgaged or I think he might have been in a load of difficulties.'

They shared a bottle of Shiraz, tucked into steaks and generally relaxed and enjoyed themselves. This was exactly what they all needed, for different reasons. Maggie kept up a bright face during the evening but declining coffee then asked 'Do you two mind if we go back now? I'm feeling rather tired. I think the reality of Charles being away and where he has gone is beginning really to sink in. If you want to stay I'm sure I can find my way back.'

'Don't be an idiot, Maggie. Strict orders not to let you out of our sight.' This was Alexander who then went off to pay the bill whilst Roberta and Maggie visited the ladies' loo. 'It's easy for me to say this, Maggie, because I haven't even got a man in my life, but try not to worry too much. Your Charles is a star and he'll be fine.' Maggie managed a 'thanks, Roberta' and they had a quick hug before joining Alexander for the short walk back to the big house. It was a clear starlit night and Maggie thought of Charles under the same starry sky and the three linked arms.

After a glass of brandy once they got back, Maggie excused herself and went off to bed. Virginia and Hughie had already gone. Piers Romayne and his financial backer Anthony Goodman were due to arrive the next day for final discussions about which parts of the estate to be used as film locations.

Although her bedroom with its en-suite bathroom was comfortable and warm Maggie found it very hard to get to sleep. She tried Charles's number on her mobile but it went straight to voice mail so there was no help there. She tried to read but found it impossible too. Eventually, though she dozed into a troubled sleep, filled with dreams. Thankfully, she did not remember them in the morning.

Virginia also found it difficult to sleep. On the surface

there was no reason. Hughie was snoring gently beside her, she was used to that. Fleur, too, was asleep in her bassinet at the side of the bed, making little contented snuffling sounds. The problem was the arrival of Anthony Goodman the next day. Her brief affair with him might or might not have been when Fleur was conceived. There was absolutely no way she could ask him to take a DNA test. She did wonder about sneaking a few hairs from his head, but didn't know how. Maybe it was for the best all round, Hughie being the proud father, her grown up-children not only accepting their baby sister but actually liking her and happily coming home more. Eventually tiredness overcame her and she too slept.

Little Fleur had slept peacefully until around six in the morning when she woke up and demanded to be fed. Virginia had fairly early abandoned the Mother Earth image of breast-feeding, and bottles were always prepared the night before, ready to heat up. Even the chaos of becoming a late mother had not entirely caused her to stop being highly organised.

Eventually Virginia woke from her fitful sleep and tried to compose her thoughts to meet the forthcoming day. Her brief, very liason with Anthony had been a mistake. She now realised that. It had coincided with a bad patch in her long marriage to Hughie, when she had been more than usually bored with him and the suave, dark-haired, moody Anthony seemed to be glamorous and from a more exciting world, financing films and other fascinating projects. It was just as well Piers Romayne, the film director, was coming now too. She thought this would save any awkwardness and was determined Anthony should not see Fleur, just in case. In case of what she wasn't sure, because Fleur had blonde curly hair and blue eyes and looked nothing like Anthony.

With all the hustle and bustle of getting the day underway with at least a semblance of her usual efficiency, almost mirroring her sister-in-law Rosie at Whitewalls, Virginia didn't have time to fret any further. Maggie proved to be an excellent choice for taking care of Fleur and, as it was a sunny morning, volunteered to take her out in the pram for a walk in the grounds. 'It won't be any trouble at all' Maggie said, 'and it gives me a chance to get a feel for the gardens again, though I don't know yet how much filming will be outside. It's so good of you to have me to stay whilst we're filming here, and the chance to work with Piers again will take my mind off what's happening to Charles.'

'I'm so sorry, Maggie. We've been so wrapped up with everything going on here I haven't asked you very much about how you're feeling.' Maggie gave Virginia a hug and said 'I try not to imagine too much and at least we are able to be in contact, but thanks anyway and I'll come and cry on your shoulder if I need to do.' This was a new side to Virginia whom she had always thought of as cold and calculating. Clearly, the arrival of Fleur had changed her for the better.

Although Virginia had felt very nervous at the thought of seeing Anthony again when he arrived, accompanied by director Piers Romayne, some of her old, steely personality returned. She had suspected at least some flicker of acknowledgement of what they had done together but, in the event, it was like making the acquaintance again of someone who didn't really matter to her at all.

His voice was deeply resonant. 'Well, Virginia, my dear, motherhood seems to suit you even at this later stage in your life!' Inwardly she seethed as he kissed her on the cheek. 'Good to see you, too, Anthony and of course Piers'. She deliberately made a fuss of the latter and threw her arms round him and kissed him warmly. Fortunately, Piers was gay, so there was no question of any frisson on either side though he returned the hug with enthusiasm.

Hughie arrived slightly breathless from the garden and greeted the two men enthusiastically. 'Good to see you, Anthony and you too, Piers. Come away in and we'll have some coffee and discuss what you plan to do.

'I'll leave you to it, then', said Virginia. I need to go and see to Fleur. But do stay on for lunch, won't you?' As she looked at her little daughter sleeping peacefully in the crib, Virginia put out of her mind any thought of a DNA test for now.

There had an unmistakable look of what could only be described as lust on Anthony's face. In fact, he didn't understand why on earth he should still fancy Virginia except that motherhood had made her somehow just as sexy as when he had met her. Then she had been cool, haughty even, and apart from sexual passion, showed no sign of tenderness. For all his sophistication, Anthony had found little of the latter quality in his life thus far. His wealth and suave good looks attracted a certain type of woman, usually after all she could get. Yet what he subconsciously craved was a warm and loving relationship. The two types of personality tended not to go together.

Piers interrupted this brief reverie. 'Maggie, I think there is a bigger part for you than I had thought. How do you feel about playing the minister's mistress?' 'Well, that's such a surprising thought, what would be involved?

'Come into the garden and we'll have a walk and I'll tell you about it whilst Anthony here goes over the figures with Hughie'.

Edinburgh - Murrayfield

Polly was busy getting the children's school uniforms ready for the start of the new term and buying all the other items they seemed to need. John's satchel would probably not last until Christmas so it seemed a good time to get a new one. Minty, who looked after her things rather better than her twin brother, didn't need a new satchel but did need a new hockey stick. Polly was reluctant to buy this as she did not believe Minty's leg, broken in the car accident, was ready yet to take part in sport, especially such a physical one. However, Minty asked for so little and perhaps she could have a word with the games mistress

84

and get her to introduce her back into the game as gently as possible. So the stick was bought. It was some time before it was used.

With their marital problems unresolved, Richard and Polly continued to be polite to each other but the intimacy in their relationship had gone. They both knew it was only a matter of time and choosing the right way for their marriage to end. This was unless a miracle happened! So far Richard had not retaliated after discovering Polly had been unfaithful with David throughout the spring and summer. He suspected, though because she was being very careful the relationship had not yet ended. If Richard had not attempted to 'get his own back'. This was partly because sex was not hugely important to him and partly because, as a newly appointed-partner in his law firm, he could not afford any scandal being attributed to him.

The children were a blessing, providing the couple with conversation and planning. Also, Richard was genuinely enjoying his weekends, sometimes with his wife and children, at the Lodge at Whitewalls. The stables went with the property and Richard was looking into the possibility of getting a licence, called a Training Permit, to carry on in a small way where the Jamie's late father had left off. In fact, in his rare dreamier moments, Richard felt he could be very happy living the kind of life associated with Whitewalls and all the country pursuits. He resolved, in any case to try and have a confidential chat with Polly's father who seemed to manage to farm, paint as a reasonably lucrative hobby and live a life only marred earlier in the year by a prostate gland cancer scare. The two men got on well together though usually they were surrounded by other people, whether it was Rosie, the children, neighbours or friends. So a talk in the studio or maybe after everyone else had gone to bed at the main house, over a glass of brandy, could be very productive for both men.

The most pressing issue, though, was Minty's mobility about which they had made an appointment with Dr

Cluny, their kind and friendly GP who had children of his own and seemed to have a particular empathy over issues concerning other people's offspring. Rosie had offered to go with Polly to take Minty for the consultation. But here Richard had been firm. He was Minty's father and he and Polly would go together. He was very fond of his mother-in-law, but sometimes he felt she wanted to run everyone's lives.

Dr Cluny carefully examined Minty's leg, then made a game with her of walking round the surgery. 'Does it hurt to walk?' he asked. 'Not exactly, but my leg, the one that was broken, aches a lot and I can't run very well.' Polly and Richard exchanged glances. This didn't sound good, but Minty had not complained at all.

'Minty, do you remember the kind surgeon at the hospital who put your leg right after the accident?' Dr Cluny said this in a gentle, sympathetic voice. She nodded. 'Well, I think we should let him have another look and take a picture of your leg to see how it's getting on. Would you be willing for us to do that?' Minty gave him one of her lovely smiles, reminding her parents of how truly pretty she was and, lately, how infrequently she smiled. They both felt guilty, for different reasons. 'No, I wouldn't mind as long as Mummy and Daddy come with me. You can come too if you like!' Dr Cluny smiled again and said tactfully 'I don't think I need to come along but Mr Robson will let me know what he thinks we need to do, if anything, after he has seen you.

They left the surgery each with their different thoughts. Minty saw and knew more than she ever said and she was a little bit afraid. She so much wanted to run and play hockey with the other girls in her class, then maybe tennis too. Swimming, which she was allowed to do, was a bit boring.

Both Richard and Polly felt sad. It seemed so unfair. Minty was such a good child and had already been through so much. In Polly's case, this feeling was made worse by the fact she had been late to collect Minty from school the day she was knocked down and the reason for not being there on time was because she had been in bed with her lover David. She had tried to justify herself by the thought it could have happened anyway. But Polly knew, in her heart, this was unlikely.

After they returned home to Murrayfield, Richard said; 'I have to go back to the office, but this weekend I want us all to be at the Lodge and make some solid plans for the future. We really can't go on the way we have been doing for the last few months and it will be easier to talk there. Do you agree?' How could she not consent to what was, after all, a perfectly reasonable proposal from her husband? So she agreed. 'I'll ring Mum and tell her we are all coming.' 'No need,' he replied rather smugly, 'She already knows.'

The Pele Tower

Madeleine was definitely not enjoying life in the 'wilds of Peeblesshire and particularly not living in the Pele Tower which, Alistair had told her, his ex-wife Lady Betty had made over to him. It was getting colder, the evenings were starting to get darker and she was bored. There was nothing for her to do. The house was cold and damp. She resolved to do something about it and took the opportunity whilst Alistair was away in Edinburgh seeing his lawyer - or so he said.

She easily found John Prendergast's telephone number and he answered the phone. 'Oh hello colonel' she gushed. 'Sir Alistair and I were wondering how you and Lady Betty were getting along.' *What does this woman want* John thought 'So, I, we wanted to ask you round here for drinks tomorrow lunchtime.' 'How very kind of you. I will just speak to Betty if you could wait a moment'

Betty shared her husband's view the scheming Madeleine wanted something. 'I know, let's ask them round here instead.' 'Meet them on home ground you mean?' They smiled at each other. 'I imagine Alistair has no idea she has been in touch.' This was Betty 'But it should be interesting. Please ask them to come for twelve noon. Then we won't have to give them lunch.' So he did. Madeleine was disappointed as she had expected they would be asked to Stitcholme for lunch, not just drinks. However, she graciously accepted, then thought how to get Alistair in a good mood to agree to go along.

Alistair was furious. He had gone through another frustrating meeting with the lawyer, Christian Hookey, trying to find a way of getting the whole Whitewalls Estate back into his hands. Now it transpired he couldn't even get The Pele Tower which, he knew, Betty really didn't have any further plans for, and now Madeleine had contrived to get them an invitation to drinks with his ex-wife and her new husband in their no-doubt boring bungalow at Stitcholme.

'What on earth possessed you to agree, Madeleine?' he asked angrily. 'Wait a minute, did you phone them or did they phone us?' 'Does it matter?' 'Of course it bloody well matters. Why did you do it? Do you really think I want to see my ex-wife again gloating with her new military husband whilst we're stuck here?' This was developing into a real row. 'That's just the trouble. We're stuck here. She's given us the property, why don't we sell it? Someone would be crazy enough to buy it for, oh, I don't know, a holiday house.' Inwardly, he groaned. *If only she knew.* Then he regained his outward composure.

'Alright, but don't ever do anything like this again without consulting me. Let's have a gin and forget about it until tomorrow.' They ate their dinner in almost complete silence at the kitchen table. In fact, the kitchen was the warmest room in the entire house, if you didn't count the attic studio which, being at the top did borrow heat from the rest of the tower. Then Alistair had an idea. 'Darling, I'm sorry I was cross with you. It was just so unexpected and I had really intended to ask them here first.' She smiled at him, a little placated. Alistair was going over in his mind whether or not he could sublet the property and get enough rent to cover a flat in Edinburgh. They wouldn't necessarily need a car as they could hire one or get lifts to visit the Borders. Maybe Madeleine could get a job in one of the smart boutiques, bring in some money and this would keep her occupied whilst he tried to challenge, once again, the divorce settlement.

Despite the thawing in the atmosphere, when they went to bed early they ended up sleeping as far apart as they could in the lumpy double bed. Alistair's age was catching up with him and his bones ached with arthritis, becoming worse in the Scottish climate, even though it was a dry late summer and early autumn. He couldn't even summon up the energy to make love to Madeleine despite her efforts to arouse him and he pretended to be asleep.

They arrived in their hire car at the Prendergasts's bungalow just after noon. Alistair explained patiently to Madeleine: 'It's not polite to arrive too early, or too late for that matter. We won't stay too long and I'll take you out for lunch in Peebles afterwards. There's the lovely place Osso near the Park Hotel. It's ideal for a light lunch.' This did not particularly suit Madeleine who had wanted to go into Edinburgh to look at the shops, but, wisely, she didn't say anything. If Alistair could pull off his plan, she wouldn't have to put up with the horrible Tower for much longer.

'Come away in,' John greeted Alistair and Madeleine cordially. Betty was in the very attractively decorated and well-furnished sitting room. Madeleine looked round enviously but greeted Betty in as charming a way as she could. 'It's so good of you both to ask us around,' she said. John and Betty smiled at each other. Madeleine had wangled the invitation and, with Alistair involved Betty knew there must be an ulterior motive.

'Gin and tonic all right, folks? Or would you prefer wine?' John was a good host and they settled for gin and Betty produced some very good canapés. The conversation ranged round the family. Alistair and Madeleine talked about France. 'We may, of course, go back to the chateau,' she said, 'but not at the moment. Scotland is so charming and people are being very kind.' She gave a little laugh and moved in for the kill. 'Betty, I am relying on you to introduce me to people. John, you and Alistair are old friends are you not?'

Even Alistair, with his lack of morals, felt a little shame at this. For John knew all about his past and, thank God, was too much of a gentleman to enlighten the avaricious new Lady Douglas. Betty knew Alistair wanted to talk to her alone so she turned to her husband. 'John, darling, why don't you take Madeleine to look at the conservatory and the garden?' He got the message, and Madeleine had no choice but to accompany him, leaving the other two together.

'Well, Alistair, what is it you want.' Betty had found over the years the best way to deal with Alistair was to be very blunt with him. 'And don't try your legendary charm, you should know that by now.'

'All right, Madeleine thinks you have legally made over the Tower to me and I should be most grateful if we could keep letting her think that. She's not happy and wants to live in Edinburgh. So I wondered if I could sublet, perhaps for a weekend place and we would move out until such time as everything to do with France and the money side is sorted.' For a moment Betty felt pity for her ex-husband. She was now so happy with John. He was apparently on his uppers yet again. What harm would it do to play along with Alistair's seemingly harmless suggestion? She doubted whether or not anyone would want to rent The Tower, but you never knew. She'd had enough unpleasantness with Alistair over the years and did not relish any more.

'Well, I can't say I am happy about it,' she responded 'but I will keep your little secret and you can try to sublet but I would want John and myself to see and approve any tenants.' He smiled, telling himself. *You've won again for now, old boy.*

John and Madeleine returned from the garden and Alistair said 'Now, my darling, we must go and leave these good people in peace. He waited in vain for an invitation to stay and have lunch, so they shook hands rather awkwardly and Alistair and Madeleine left.

Alistair was smiling, so she tried again. 'Sweetheart please take me into Edinburgh. We can have a nice late lunch in George Street and look at the shops. There are some lovely boutiques and, who knows, there might be a chance for me to find a job.' He gave in and they drove to the city in a degree of harmony.

After getting rid of their guests, John and Betty decided they would have another gin and tonic whilst Betty filled him in on the details of the conversation she'd had with Alistair. 'Wasn't that a bit risky, my darling? Who knows what the old devil will get up to next?' She smiled sweetly. 'Ah, but he's told Madeleine I have given him the Tower and this way I have a greater hold over him,' she laughed. 'You wicked lady, this sounds almost like a blackmail situation in the making.' It was. But who was doing the blackmailing?

The Lodge

Polly had decided to make a special effort for the planned weekend at The Lodge. She was still torn between staying with Richard and trying to make a go of their marriage and leaving him for David, with all the unpleasant consequences and undoubted upset to her whole family. Sometimes she wished she had not married so young, had instead travelled and made her own way in the world in her twenties. Was it too late? If she left Richard for David, was it just going from one all-enveloping relationship to another. Then there were her children whom she loved dearly.

The children, dogs and even Buttons, the Siamese kitten, were all excited on the journey from Edinburgh. It was as if they had picked up something of the determination of their parents to reach some decision, though they had no idea what it might be. Polly, for her part, felt she held all the cards but maybe she did not. Richard had been doing a great deal of thinking about his marriage, his children, his job and the future direction he wanted his life to take. He felt he had given Polly and their marriage every possible chance but she had hurt him dreadfully and even Richard's calm and loving nature had limits to what it could take!

The departure from Murrayfield to Whitewalls was the usual melee of finding things needed there, the cat basket, getting Pixie and Pod, the Norfolk terriers calmed down before the journey and generally getting everything together. Polly had not yet stocked the freezer at the Lodge so a greater amount of food than usual had somehow to be squashed into the Rav.

A surprise awaited Polly as Richard drove straight up the long drive to the main house, past the Lodge. 'Where are we going?' Polly asked. 'You've driven straight past the Lodge.' 'Your mother has very kindly agreed to have the twins and Buttons overnight so you and I can really sit down and work out our plans' 'Well, you might have consulted me' Polly was cross. The last thing she wanted at the moment was to be alone at the Lodge with Richard. She was still torn between her husband and her lover, and both were pressing for a final resolution.

The twins saw nothing unusual in the plan for the weekend. Indeed they were very happy as Granny always spoiled them and she and Grandpa had a new friend, who was a minister. This had sounded very boring until they met Michael Martin and discovered that, far from being boring, he could do conjuring tricks and could tell them stories about Africa. So John and Minty piled out of the car. Minty scooped up her little cat and the Norfolk terrier had to stay in the car to go to the Lodge with Richard and Polly.

After Polly had unpacked and made coffee, they sat down in the still sparsely furnished sitting room to try to plan their future. Polly was not sure they had a future but for the sake of the twins and the rest of her family, she decided she would at least listen to Richard and respond in as positive a way as she could. He poured them both a generous gin and tonic. Richard knew more about Polly's doubts than she realised and he very much wanted the new arrangement to work. Not absolutely certain she had got over David McLean, his plan was to have life concentrated much more in the country and away from temptation.

She looked at her husband as he put on the half-rim spectacles he had taken to wearing when tackling paperwork, and felt a flicker of something she hadn't experienced for some time. When he got out a yellow legal pad, though, she realised he was deadly serious. Once they began to plan the necessary changes to make the spartan Lodge into a comfortable home, Polly found herself drawn in and even becoming enthusiastic. They agreed to start on the kitchen and make it bigger by taking down the larder wall and creating a living area. Next on the list was the dining room, unused for years. 'We don't need a dining room,' Polly said 'Why not a study instead, then the sitting room sort of for "best" and the bedrooms will do for now.

'Perhaps we could make an en-suite off our bedroom'. Richard used the word 'our' quite deliberately. She hesitated, part of her knowing she might not be there to see all this through. 'Oh, yes, why not?' This seemed to be a safe answer. 'Fine, I think that's probably enough for now, Polly. Your mum is expecting us for lunch.' Polly was relieved and got up with alacrity. 'Shall we walk and take Pixie and Pod with us?' 'Good idea. Let's go'.

Over lunch, which was also attended by Michael, Richard and Polly began to feel like a couple again. They found, like Jamie and the twins, that Michael was very good company with a charm and warmth about him drawing everyone in. For once, Rosie was very quiet. She was becoming not only increasingly fond of Michael but also physically more and more attracted. Little did she know at this point about her own daughter's similar dilemma. Jamie was in sparkling form. 'Minty and I are going to be painting in the studio this afternoon, folks.'

'Yes, Grandad is going to start me on watercolours now I've learned how to draw.'

'Dad can we go to the stables please, and I want to ride Snowball. I suppose I'll have to ride Butterball as well!' They all smiled at this, knowing John was keen on his riding and becoming more and more expert even on the sturdy but fast ponies which really didn't get enough exercise, Kate, Richard's new assistant, did her best but she was really too tall, though very slender, to ride the ponies.

Michael tactfully excused himself, saying: 'I've got to go and write my sermon for tomorrow and hope a few people come along'. 'Well, you can count on Rosie and me and as many others who can be persuaded. I think John and Betty intend to be there with two of their neighbours,' Jamie's answered. As Michael left he whispered to Rosie: 'I may need some help with my sermon this afternoon if you are free?' She whispered back: 'Maybe, I'll see.'

They went their separate ways and Jamie and Minty spent a very happy and peaceful afternoon in the studio, where, to his great pleasure, Jamie found Minty very quickly picked up the initial techniques of watercolour painting. 'Do you really think I can do this, Grandad?' she asked, a little anxiously. 'You, my darling granddaughter, are picking this up amazingly quickly. I really think you might grow up to be an artist yourself.' 'Well if I do, it's thanks to you, you've taught me everything so far.' So as they walked together, slowly back to Whitewalls both of them felt very pleased with the afternoon's work.

John was in his element. He loved the ponies and horses and just being on his own with his father, just the two of them was great too. 'Dad, when I grow up I think I'd like to be a horse trainer, like Grandad Roddy was. Do you think I could do that?' Richard smiled and ruffled John's hair. They were both pretty muddy and sweaty from dealing with the horses. It was Kate's afternoon off, so it took quite some time to get all the horses and ponies settled. The ponies were still out in the field with their shelter and hayracks in one corner, but Border Prince and Border Princess, the only two racehorses left in the yard, were in their loose boxes in the stable block.

Rosie drove the short distance to Stitcholme and the manse with her head in a whirl. She knew she should not be going near Michael, and yet she couldn't stop herself. He was waiting for her. 'Well, what about this sermon then?' she asked. Gently, he took her hand, led her into his study and showed her the neatly printed pages of the next day's sermon on his desk.

They kissed with a deep, wordless passion and, still without speaking they went upstairs. It was as if saying anything at all would break the magic spell. The magic continued into the early evening. Then without very much conversation they parted, only to meet again later over another dinner at Whitewalls. Both of them felt they passed the test of pretending to be hostess and family friend well, but Richard at one point saw Michael looking across the table at Rosie in a way suggesting something more.

Richard and Polly were going back to the Lodge to spend the night there together without the twins who were already in their pyjamas having eaten their favourite supper of macaroni cheese earlier. They walked the short distance back and Richard said, almost casually: 'Did you see the way Michael was looking at your mother? If he weren't a minister, you could almost think he fancied her!' Polly laughed 'Well he is a bachelor and just because he's a minister it doesn't mean he can't appreciate a good-looking woman, which Mum certainly is.' Later, quite a lot later in fact, they were both to remember this brief conversation for different reasons. For now, though, they were both feeling relaxed and even Polly was feeling in the mood for making love.

The whole family was going to go to church at Stitcholme on the Sunday morning and Michael had promised John and Minty he would show them some more magic tricks afterwards as a reward for being good at the service. So the family were all happy again, for now. Even the Sunday church visit was a success and the little church had already gained a new following, thanks in part to the support of Colonel John Prendergast and his new wife, the former Lady Alistair Douglas. It was a memorable weekend for many reasons and would be fixed in the memories of each generation for many years to come.

Chapter 10

London - the Mews House

Maggie was feeling restless. She was at the point where rehearsals had not yet properly begun for her role in the film 'The Minister Who Lied' and whilst she knew she was more than welcome to stay with Charles's uncle Hughie and aunt Virginia at High Wynch Park, where the film was being made, she needed a break.

When she arrived at the mews house, bought for her by her grandmother Florette it had an unlived-in look and all the electricity had been turned off as both she and Charles had thought neither of them would be back for some time.

However, after a brief trip to buy some essential supplies, including a bottle of dry white wine, Maggie was on the sofa in the sitting room when her mobile phone rang. She eagerly pulled it out of her handbag, hoping it was Charles. It wasn't. Instead the deep mellifluous tones of Adrian Phelps, who was going to play the lead in the film came through.

'Maggie, my dear I've tracked you down. Virginia was a bit vague, she thought you had gone to Yorkshire to stay with your grandmother but Florette said you had come to London for a few days before we start rehearsals.' She felt a little flustered. 'Oh, Adrian, how nice of you to call. Where are you?' There was laughter in his voice as he replied: 'Just around the corner and hoping to take you out to dinner.' Oh, what was the harm, she thought. Charles would understand and it would give both her and Adrian a chance to get to know each other better. 'Are you still there, Maggie?' 'Yes, yes, I'm still here You know the address, why not come round and we can decide where to go.' So he did.

'I hope you like Italian food, Maggie. There's a great little restaurant just an easy walk from here called La Piazza? Adrian had come up to the small sitting room. He

97

was taller than Charles and seemed to fill the place. 'Yes, I know the one you mean, though I haven't been there for ages'. She felt a little uneasy but, she told herself, Adrian was her leading man in the film and they needed to get on together. Nevertheless, she was relieved when he declined a drink and they set off together amiably enough.

Although she and Charles had spent a good deal of time at the mews house, the restaurant was new to Maggie. Adrian had chosen well. La Piazza was small, softly lit and with the charming, flirty staff so much a hallmark of Italian restaurants. Clearly, Adrian was no stranger to them and the owner greeted him warmly with bear hugs and kisses. Maggie escaped with a kiss on her hand from Giuseppe.

Maggie started to relax. After all, what was the harm in getting to know her leading man? He was a much more experienced actor than she was and knew she would need to rely upon him to bring out the best in her own performance. Adrian was very sensitive to her mood and after a starter of antipasti and some good red Italian wine, she was not nearly so tense. 'Maggie, I won't pretend I don't find you damned attractive and as we're going to work together we need to know each other and relax. Also I know you're about to get engaged and your fiancé is probably going to Afghanistan so I promise to be gentle and make sure we work together as real professionals. This film could be very important for your future career as well as mine and you have your family supporting you.' Just before the main course arrived she gave him a dazzling smile, which made him realise how easily he could be aroused by her. 'Thank you, Adrian, for being so sweet and understanding. I do appreciate it and I will be relying on you to bring out the best in me!'

They walked back the short distance to the house together and Maggie felt comfortable arm-in-arm with her temporary leading man. When they reached the door he asked, teasingly: 'Are you going to invite me in for coffee?' Lightly, she replied: ' Not a good idea right now,

Adrian. Early start tomorrow, but we'll be spending a lot of time together, won't we?' He didn't persist. There would be plenty of time later on.

Thinking she had perhaps been a little dismissive, Maggie thought she had better sweeten the pill. 'It's true, Adrian. I am driving up to High Wynch Park tomorrow. As you know, I'm staying there. Hughie is Charles's uncle. I could give you a lift if that's in your plan too!' 'That's very sweet of you but I've things to do in London before we start rehearsals and I'll need my car to get to Gloucestershire. After she had unlocked the house door, he gave her a very satisfactory kiss on the lips and departed 'See you very soon, lovely Maggie.'

She found it difficult to sleep and spent some time tossing and turning, then her mobile phone bleeped. It was a message from Charles. 'I love you, my darling girl, can't say where I am just now but I can get messages on the mobile, at least for now.' Maggie was so glad she had not succumbed to Adrian's overtures and immediately texted back. 'And I adore you darling, stay safe, all my love.' And she meant it. How could she have thought even for one moment she and Adrian could even flirt, never mind start a relationship? For all that he seemed to be sincere and Maggie knew she could learn a lot about film acting from him.

Early next morning she got up, had a shower, drank some black coffee and carefully backed Charles's car out of the garage to begin her journey to High Wynch Park. Not expecting a reply, she texted Charles again to say where she was going. The roads were quiet and she made good time to what was now becoming a place where she wanted to be. She had a good feeling about this film and although he was going to a dangerous place, in an odd way Maggie was perversely glad she would be able to concentrate on work and doing well without the distraction of the man she truly loved.

When she crunched up the gravel drive and round to the back door of the big house there were plenty of signs of life. As the imposing frontage was already being prepared for workmen, this was not surprising. What did bring her to realise this was all happening were the portacabins, loos and even a couple of residential caravans. Admittedly they were not close to the door but they were certainly there. She knew Hughie had gone through his trust money and needed to use the house to support his family but for a fleeting moment she was saddened by this. Nevertheless, few families with large houses now were able simply to live in them without either opening to the public or, which was much more profitable, engaging in commercial projects like film-making.

Despite the bustle going on all around the back door of the house there didn't seem to be any family about. Odd, because they knew she was coming. Then, suddenly, the door opened and a slightly dishevelled Virginia appeared carrying Fleur in a sling.

'So sorry, Maggie, Fleur has been acting up all morning and this seems to be the only way to keep her quiet. Don't rush into having a baby when you and Charles get married, they're damned hard work.' This was more like the old Virginia, then she added 'But I love her to bits and so, surprisingly, does the rest of the family. But come in and we'll have some coffee and you can tell me all you know about your film. It sounds really exciting!'

The kitchen was still tidy and warm, thanks to Virginia's long-suffering cleaning lady, Mary, who worked longer hours than she was paid without ever complaining. Mary was a widow of uncertain age and had a propensity to gossip. Virginia had taken to allowing Mary ten minutes or so to talk about her dysfunctional family whilst being careful not to reveal very much about the Bruce and Douglas clans. After that, Mary happily got on with her work whilst fantasising this was her own home.

The arrangement worked tolerably well and at least the basics were done. Virginia had even given up on insisting the silver was cleaned every week! Nappies and baby laundry had taken its place in the priorities she set.

Virginia and Maggie were sitting at the kitchen table drinking mugs of coffee and indulging in chocolate biscuits when the door opened. Piers Romayne, who was directing the film in which Maggie was appearing, came in. He had become a family friend after using High Wynch Park for art films as well as bigger enterprises so there was nothing odd about his coming in unannounced. But behind him came Anthony Goodman, with whom Virginia had enjoyed one night of passion at the very time Fleur had been conceived. They had not met since a stormy lunch at the Lygon Arms in Broadway in the Cotswolds when Virginia had stalked out in a fury. As far as Hughie was concerned, he was Fleur's father and Virginia had never owned up to the very brief liaison with Anthony. She felt herself colouring, up and hoped everyone would think it was the warmth of the kitchen and the coffee.

Piers went straight over to Maggie and gave her a warm kiss. 'Maggie, darling, so lovely to see you again. I have a very good feeling about this film. The subject's very topical and you're perfect for the part.' 'Thanks, Piers. I met Adrian in London and so we are getting to know each other.' 'Oh, watch him darling. He has quite a way with the ladies, which is one reason we've cast him as 'the minister who lied.' This was said with a sweet smile. Anthony had said nothing so far until: 'So this is Maggie, I'm delighted to meet you. Piers has been raving on about his casting you for the part and, as usual, his instincts seem spot on.' He followed this with a casual hug with one arm around her shoulders. 'I'm very happy to meet you, too, Anthony. Without people like you British films would hardly ever be made any more.' He liked the compliment.

Then he turned to Virginia and said: 'What a lovely domestic scene, mother and baby. Perhaps Piers could introduce a little vignette into the film.' The words were spoken with apparent, though silky sincerity as he looked directly at Virginia. She was ready for him. 'Oh, I don't think so Anthony. I'm having such a blissful time with Fleur and her grow-up brother and sister dote on her too, as well as dear Hughie.' Right on cue Hughie joined them, beaming with pride at the sight of his wife and baby daughter, unaware of any tension at all.

'Let's all go in to the sitting room. It's getting very crowded in here. Just about time for a drink,' Hughie said. 'Let me carry Fleur, please' so the baby was handed over to Maggie and they trooped out of the room. Anthony, despite his coolness, felt a stirring of a feeling he couldn't place. He was so close to Virginia they almost touched. Although he tried not to do so, his hand brushed her shoulder and back so it looked, if anyone took any notice, as if he were simply escorting her out of the crowded kitchen into the more serene sitting room. She stiffened but otherwise did not acknowledge his unexpected touch.

Afterwards, Virginia was not sure how it happened but Maggie sat in a low armchair with the now sleeping baby in her arms and Anthony skilfully placed himself on one of the big squashy sofas next to her. Whilst both Anthony and Virginia maintained a cool façade, there was most definitely a frisson which they both felt.

Quite oblivious to any underlying tensions, Hughie was busying himself pouring drinks for them all. As Virginia was still feeding Fleur herself, she stuck to orange juice but the rest of them accepted his usual large gin and tonics and Mary's lovely canapés which was one of the reasons Virginia kept her on!

The conversation moved on to the film and Maggie was able to report she and Adrian were going together to the Houses of Parliament to get a 'feel' for the place and make sure they were 'in character'. While Maggie had absolutely no intention of getting into any kind of relationship, other than professional, with Adrian, even discussing the background and some of the planned scenes raised a feeling which she quickly suppressed.

Virginia announced there was a buffet lunch set out in the dining room but she wouldn't be joining them immediately because she had to feed then settle Fleur for her afternoon nap. It was a plausible explanation and although there was a very knowing, swift look from Anthony, she took Fleur from Maggie's arms and made her escape. When she returned to the others, Roberta and Alexander were there too so, for the moment, the awkwardness with Anthony had passed. She did, though find the presence of the two men one of whom was Fleur's natural father, disturbing. As soon as she could Virginia went away to the nursery.

Virginia had just settled Fleur in her crib when the door opened. It was Anthony. Startled, she jumped. He smiled at her in a way she had not seen before and without saying a word came over and gently kissed her on the lips. 'You look so desirable, I almost wish I were the father.' But there was no malice in his tone. 'See you again soon, even alone perhaps?' Before she could respond, he had gone.

'Darling, Virginia, you're a marvel, what would I do without you?' Hughie and she were sharing the same bed again most nights and on this one he felt amorous. So Virginia closed her eyes and moved obediently, but the face she saw was not that of her husband but of Anthony. Beside her Hughie later slept soundly and snored which did not help Virginia to sleep, and eventually she got up and went into the nursery, pulled over a duvet and curled up on the chaise longue beside the peaceful Fleur.

The next morning Maggie realised she had a few days in hand before rehearsals began for the film and she was filled with a longing to see her grandmother Florette and step-grandfather Nigel at their farm and small estate in Yorkshire. Could she drive there without causing any offence to Virginia and Hughie?

'Of course, darling. You're going to be very busy once rehearsals and then filming starts.' This was Virginia's response to Maggie's tentative bringing up of the subject at breakfast the next day. 'We'll see plenty of each other when you come back and you can, I think, contact Charles on his mobile. Anyway, if he phones here and you haven't been able to reach him, well, we'll just tell him where you are!' So after a brief call to Florette, who was delighted

Maggie was coming for a brief stay, fond goodbyes and hugs and kisses from Hughie and family, Maggie was soon packed and on her way.

Manor House Farm

Maggie had a peaceful drive to Yorkshire from the Cotswolds. Much as she had become closer to Charles's uncle and family, especially Virginia whom she had never really expected to like, it was an enticing prospect to go and see her grandmother and step-grandfather before she got stuck into rehearsals and filming. She knew it would be demanding but hopefully would occupy her completely until her darling Charles' return.

The car radio was tuned to Classic FM, which she found soothing and comforting as she negotiated first the motorway, then the A1. Apart from two carefully worded text messages she had not recently heard from Charles and, for the first time, he was not dominating her entire thoughts.

So Maggie was feeling reasonably relaxed as she drove up the familiar drive and was met, as usual, by a crowd of dogs, her glamorous grandmother and Nigel, quiet and steady as ever, dressed in his usual cords, checked woollen shirt and cashmere cardigan.

'Welcome, darling,' cried Florette effusively. 'Lovely to see you. Down, dogs, down!' was Nigel's greeting. Maggie ran up the steps into the house which had been her natural refuge for so long. 'Just us this evening, but Gillian and Peter would love you to go round in the morning, if you'd like to do. 'Yes, yes, I'd like that, but right now a hot bath and a cold drink would be marvellous.'

After this, Maggie felt refreshed and relaxed. By unspoken common consent, they did not enter into the difficult conversation about Charles, Afghanistan and what might happening there. Both Florette and Nigel were genuinely interested in the film. 'Won't there be a lot of hanging around?' Nigel asked, 'Well, yes, I expect there will be but at least I have a major part this time so it should all be worth it. And I think Adrian and I will get on. He's rather a smooth character but, luckily, I don't feel in the least attracted to him.' 'My darling, Maggie, I am quite sure you would not be attracted to anyone except your darling Charles.' This was Florette's immediate response.

Altogether it was a very relaxing evening and, whilst Nigel had refused Florette's earlier demand to tell Maggie that Charles would be in no danger, because this simply wasn't true, his presence was, as always reassuring and calming. Florette was launching a new line in cashmere pashminas, and colours and sizes were also the subject of discussion. Around ten o'clock, Maggie started to yawn and excused herself and said she was tired and did they mind if she went to bed.

'Of course not, my darling. You must be exhausted after all the excitement and the drive too.' Florette hugged Maggie and so did the usually undemonstrative Nigel. Maggie soon snuggled down in the bed she had shared with Charles. Florette was right. She was exhausted and went into a deep and dreamless sleep. The next morning she woke up to the sound of birds singing outside the window and the sun was shining. Maggie yawned, stretched and looked at her watch. It was eight o'clock. She decided it was time to get up.

When Maggie got down into the kitchen it was deserted. The kettle was simmering gently on the Aga hob so she made herself a cup of Earl Grey tea and found some orange juice, toast, butter and honey and sat at the well-used table for a relaxing breakfast. She had just finished when both Florette and Nigel came into the kitchen.

'Did you sleep well?' asked Florette. 'Like the proverbial log. You were right, I was exhausted.' Maggie replied. 'I think, though, I would still like to go and see Gillian and Peter and catch up with them again.' 'I'll come over with you, if you like.' This was Nigel. He not only wanted to see his young neighbours but also to observe for himself how Maggie would fit in with their way of life. He was very hopeful, if all went well Charles would seriously consider doing a short course in agriculture and then join him as a partner in the business.

Soon Nigel and Maggie were in another kitchen, with another Aga. This time Gillian, who had greeted them very warmly insisted they had some hot chocolate with her home-made pancakes. Although both of them had eaten breakfast already, to be polite they accepted.

'Have you heard from Charles? 'Gillian asked softly. 'Just a couple of text messages but he can't really tell me very much at the moment.' Her eyes began to fill with unexpected tears. 'Oh, I am so sorry, that was tactless of me.' Gillian spontaneously hugged Maggie and the friendship which was to last a long time began. Nigel left soon after that and Gillian showed Maggie her latest painting and they wandered round the garden.

'When do you start filming?' Maggie replied: 'In about ten days time, but rehearsals begin next week. I haven't got time to go to Scotland before then, so tomorrow I'm going back to High Wynch Park to get really stuck in and start to learn my lines. I've met my leading man, Adrian. Actually he is rather dishy, but strictly off-limits.' They both laughed and Maggie said her goodbyes. 'I'm sorry I missed Peter and the children. Please tell them from me and you and I can keep in touch with text, email and mobiles.'

Chapter 11

Scotland

At Whitewalls, Rosie was in an unusually jumpy frame of mind, mostly because of her affair with Michael. They had both tried to end it and return to a friendly but platonic relationship. But one August afternoon Michael called at Whitewalls unannounced and found Rosie in the walled garden dead-heading some of the later flowering roses. He thought she looked so lovely, with no makeup, wearing her gardening clothes and an old polo shirt, Michael could not resist coming quietly behind her and kissing the nape of her neck. She started, dropped her secateurs, turned and fell into his arms. Very quickly, they slipped into the glasshouse and made love hastily, more passionately than ever before. It felt both right and wrong at the same time.

'Michael, what on earth are we thinking of?' 'That was wonderful, Rosie. I love you. Heaven knows I've tried to fight my feelings but I want you and need you so much. I don't want to hurt you or Jamie though and right now I can't see how we can be together in any other way than this.' Michael was holding her tightly when she said this. 'Look, my darling, give me a few minutes and then come to the house and we can talk properly. Nobody will think anything odd about that. In fact, you're considered to be family now.' Her words were spoken without the irony of their meaning but she was shaken, badly.

For once Michael couldn't speak and just nodded his agreement. A little later they sat at the kitchen table, opposite each other. 'I suppose I could go away, ask the church for a new post but I've been here such a short time and with the congregation growing, slowly I know, but in the right direction there would be certain to be questions asked. And I don't want to be away from you, even if we have to be more discreet and not let anyone see how we really feel.' Rosie was quiet for a moment then answered

'Do you think we could do that, be more casual I mean, at least in public? I don't want to stop either but you know Jamie's had cancer, Charles is in Afghanistan, my mother has re-married and is happy for the first time in years, really happy with her colonel. Then there's Polly and her marriage. You know she's had an affair and I'm not certain that's over.' He came round and hugged her gently and affectionately, without passion but with immense feeling.

The conversation was interrupted by, of all people, Betty who came whirling into the kitchen in her usual energetic manner, which belied her eighty years. After the elegant, restrained wedding outfit she had reverted to bright colours and let her curly hair have its own way. One of her qualities which had attracted the rather serious colonel in the first place was this zest for life and colour.

Both Rosie and Michael were quite relieved at the visit because they both knew no conclusion could be reached that day. Quite unselfconsciously, Betty planted a kiss on Michael's cheek, saying with a smile: 'Lovely to see you, Michael. You've become part of the family and it's such fun having another attractive man about the place. Anyway, I'm glad I've caught you. Friends of John are coming to stay at the weekend and I want to bring them to morning service, so this will increase the congregation and you can come back to us for Sunday lunch afterwards. I'm going to leave everything ready and Molly is going to cook. God knows what it will be like, but John's got some lovely red wine and even Molly can't ruin roast beef if she follows my instructions!' Meanwhile Rosie had turned her back and made a china mug of Earl Grey tea for her mother who said: 'Thank you. Let's go outside and get the afternoon sun now the wind's gone down.' You didn't argue with Betty - Not even Michael when it was made clear he was to join them, though after a short time he left, giving both women a hug and light kiss. 'I'd better get started on the sermon for Sunday if the military are coming.' He managed to say this with a tone of amusement, which was far from how he felt.

'I'll just walk Michael round to the front to his car, I won't be long,' Rosie said 'Oh I'm in no hurry darling, John's gone into Edinburgh to collect the guests.' In fact, neither Rosie nor Michael wanted a prolonged goodbye, especially whilst Betty was there so with a rather more passionate kiss, Michael jumped into his car and sped away, not to write his sermon but to try to work out what to do.

True to her word Betty did not go away in a hurry. Indeed, when Rosie came back into the kitchen it was to find her mother had poured two stiff gin and tonics. 'What on earth are these for?' Rosie cried. 'Let's take them outside and sit in the sun.' There was no denying her mother, small though she was, and her strong personality could come to the fore when she chose. So Rosie did as she was told and they went outside to the small paved area outside the kitchen door.

Betty got straight to the point. 'You and Michael. I saw the way you looked at each other. I know that look and what it means. Darling, I'm not going to tell you what to do, we're both beyond that stage of our lives, but Jamie is a lovely man and a marvellous son-in-law. I wouldn't want him to get hurt. Besides, he works so hard running the farm and doing his painting and, in case you have forgotten, has recovered from a particularly nasty cancer.' Ouch! This was direct, even for Betty.

Rosie said nothing at first and took a hefty pull at the strong gin and tonic, then she said 'Oh, Ma, I love Jamie absolutely and he is the only man I've loved. He's given me two great children and is so strong and reliable but, well we were very young when we married and, yes, I do find Michael attractive and he feels this about me. But we both know it won't come to anything.' She crossed her fingers as she said this, a gesture noticed by Betty who did not, however, make any further comment apart from saying: 'Well please, darling, be careful what you wish for! Now, I feel like a little stroll round the walled garden and we can take our drinks with us. Also I would like to stay for lunch if you don't mind.' Rosie didn't dare demur and hoped neither Michael nor Jamie would return before her mother went home.

A chilly breeze meant Rosie and her mother didn't spend a long time in the garden, just enough for Rosie to compose herself and her mother to change the subject. Lunch proved to be calm too. Mother and daughter didn't talk very much and Betty didn't stay for very long before she drove back to her and John's bungalow in Stitcholme. She still had her old Morris Minor Traveller, which was regularly spruced up, with the woodwork being re-varnished every spring. Now she was married to John, she drove rather fewer miles but would not be persuaded to part with her car, declaring: 'It was relatively easy to part with Alistair, but I will not get a divorce from my car!'

As Betty drove along Stitcholme's only road she slowed down outside the manse. Michael's car wasn't there, which was just as well for she would have been very tempted to go to see him and warn him off as far as Rosie went. She reflected you never stop being a mother, even when you are eighty and your children are in their fifties.

When she got back to her new home, Betty still felt restless, so took herself into the studio John had provided for her in the garden in the form of a timber-framed building which was just the right size for her and blended in with the garden. She squeezed bright paints on to her board and moved in front of the easel which was just the right height for her to stand for half an hour at a time. After some very determined application with a thick brush to canvas using reds, blues and yellows, she felt better. Betty had just finished cleaning her brushes when she heard the welcome sound of John's car drawing up outside. The dilemma was, should she tell him about her suspicions regarding Michael and Rosie, or not?

She decided to say nothing in the meantime and certainly nothing to Jamie, her son-in-law, who was such a lovely man. Betty wasn't often angry with Rosie, and had even understood her granddaughter Polly's affair with

David, but this, this would be just too much. Watch and wait! So it was with difficulty Betty kept her counsel John was so pleased she had started to paint again, in her familiar bold style and, also, that she had seen Rosie and invited them all to lunch on Sunday after Michael's family service at the church. 'I think it will really give him a boost to have a bigger congregation. He's a nice chap and he and Jamie get on well together. Rosie, too, I guess but then your lovely daughter gets on with everyone.' Betty thought *but too well in this case.*

Rosie was still in the garden, trying to quieten her thoughts and emotions, when her mobile rang. She fished it out of the pocket of her jeans. It was Jamie. 'Hello, darling. Look I've finished all I need to do in Edinburgh. We've decided on the format for the exhibition. Polly's doing some after-school activity with the twins. I miss you especially for some reason this afternoon, so I'm coming home.' 'That's wonderful, Jamie. Mum was here this morning and stayed for lunch so it will be great to have the place to ourselves for once.' 'Do you want to invite Michael to come round?' She most emphatically did not. 'No, love just you and me and a quiet evening.' 'Bye then, see you very soon.' 'Drive carefully.' He always did, dear, dependable Jamie, she thought. Soon he was home and Rosie tried to put all thoughts of Michael out of her head and to recreate their relaxed, gentle atmosphere. It worked, although that night, in bed she hesitated for a moment as he reached for her. 'Darling, I am thoughtless, are you too tired?' She was but, also feeling guilty replied, 'No, darling. I love you.' She did.

Sunday morning started clear and bright and Rosie was busy marshalling all the brood together to go to the family service at Michael's church. She rang Polly. 'Hello, Lodge House, Polly speaking.' 'It's just me checking to see if you all want to be collected or if you'd rather meet at the church.' She could hear the children in the background and Polly consulting Richard. Well, at least they were speaking.

Then Richard came on. 'Thanks, Rosie, but we'll meet you there and hope the children behave well.' 'Of course they will and Michael is making a great family service with a very short sermon, then we've got lunch with Granny Betty and John.' *Oh God, how was she going to get through all this?* She pulled herself together. This thing with Michael had to stop before it got out of hand. *Be firm*, she told herself. But could she stick to her resolve? She would try.

True to his word Michael had carefully prepared a short sermon about the connection between all living things and God. He spoke well and even John stopped fidgeting and playing with his mobile phone, which he had put on to 'silent' and listened. Yes, he thought, it made sense. The dogs and ponies were living creatures just as much as humans, often easier to deal with too. Although Richard and Polly had been careful to try to keep everything as normal as possible for the twins' sake, both John and Minty had picked up on some of the tensions. Only this morning John had said to Richard: 'Why is David McLean always coming round to see Mum?' Richard's lips tightened but he only said, lightly: 'Because they do business together. Mum cooks for David's clients who live usually in very posh houses.

There were more people in the little church than usual and the hymns were cheerful and uplifting - 'All Things Bright and Beautiful' and 'Praise My Soul The King of Heaven'. The children sang the first with gusto and the grown-ups really loved 'Praise My Soul The King of Heaven'. Such a nice change, they said to each other as they came out of the church into the sunshine, to have good hymns everyone knew.

Both Polly and Richard were very proud of their children not only for their good behaviour in church but also at the lunch afterwards. They realised it could be very boring for the twins, but they ate lunch politely and joined in the conversation. 'What is it like being a minister?' John asked Michael. "I mean, it's not like a real job in an office is it?' Michael smiled at John's serious little face. Rosie looked across and felt her heart pounding. 'It is a job, John, though the Church names it a calling. The idea behind it is God needs people to tell people about the Bible - we call it the Good News - and to run churches, mostly bigger than this one, and help people who want to do good things.' John looked very thoughtful for a moment, then said: 'It sounds really interesting but I'm not sure I could do that'. Rosie, who had been following this conversation, smiled. 'Well, John, you don't have to make up your mind what you want to do when you grow up just yet'. She saw Michael's gaze towards her, which was bordering on the affectionate.

Oblivious of these undertones, except perhaps for Lady Betty, the lunch party broke up. The McDowells, friends of Colonel John, had to go to Edinburgh to catch a train to London. Jamie offered to drive them and so did Richard, but they were very well organised and Percy, who had been driving John for years was booked to take care of that.

Fond farewells were said, and Jamie asked as they left: 'What's everyone going to do now? Tom has looked at the sheep and they're fine, so I think I would like to go to the studio and finish off a landscape I've been working on'. "Grandpapa, could I come with you and do some sketching? This was Minty who was already showing some talent for drawing and painting. 'You'll have to ask your Mum and Dad', he replied, giving her a gentle hug. Polly and Richard had no objections to this idea. They had, anyway, to prepare for the return to Edinburgh in the early evening to get ready for the week ahead and all it held. 'John, what do you want to do? asked Richard. 'I want to go and catch Snowball, tack him up and take him for a ride.' This was agreed, as long as he kept to the fields and promised not to go far. Snowball was a very reliable pony and unlikely to do anything silly. 'Janey might be at the stables anyway and she could help you, even come out with you on Border Prince.' Richard was fond of Janey who was helping with the horses and he knew they could rely on her. 'Great idea, Dad, will you drop me off there?'

Michael stepped in quickly. 'I could give Rosie a lift back to Whitewalls. It's not too far out of my way.' 'That's really kind of you, Michael,' Jamie replied before Rosie could get in with a refusal (which she didn't want to do anyway). She did, however, catch a warning glance from her mother, which she did her best to ignore.

As they all dispersed Rosie felt excited. She knew what she wanted to happen. 'Will you come in for some tea?' 'Well, darling Rosie, I'll come in. As for the tea....' He didn't finish the sentence. Careless of who saw them, they got out of the car and quickly into the house. She made a feeble attempt to draw back. 'Are you sure you don't want tea?' 'Quite sure'. Wordlessly they went upstairs, not to the spare room, which had been Rosie's intention, but to the large, comfortable bedroom she had shared with Jamie for so long.

He undressed her gently as she unbuttoned his shirt and pressed herself closely to him. She threw back the covers and they slipped quite unselfconsciously on to the bed. 'Michael, are you sure?' 'Shush, you already asked me that. I love you, Rosie .'I love you too.' The lovemaking was both passionate and gentle. It felt very loving to both of them. Afterwards Rosie looked at her little bedside clock. It was almost four. They would have to move quickly. Michael had fallen asleep, breathing quietly next to her. Gently she woke him up.

'You are beautiful, Rosie.' She smiled: 'And you are a great lover, but it's time we went back to the real world. Jamie will be back soon with Minty and maybe John too.' So after a quick shower, both together, they made their way downstairs. They were just in time. Automatically almost, Rosie had put the kettle on the Aga to fast boil when they heard Jamie's car crunching on the driveway. 'Granny, look what I've painted. Grandpapa thinks it's really good and it's going to be framed.' It was, indeed, a very pretty painting of an apple on a blue plate, with the

114

red of the apple contrasting with the blue of the plate. 'I think it looks like a heart, so does Grandpapa.'

Her enthusiasm broke any tension there might have been and Jamie gave Rosie a kiss. 'I think she has some real talent. Maybe extra art lessons at school to develop her technique would be a good idea. I'll mention it to Polly.'

Now Minty was showing Michael the picture. It did look like a heart and his own heart he now wanted to give to Rosie - for ever. But how? It was time for him to leave but Jamie insisted he stayed and have a beer as the afternoon was warm and neither man wanted to drink tea. Soon, as expected, an excited John, accompanied by his father joined them and he too had spent a great afternoon. 'Janey was there and she helped me catch the ponies and tack them up. I rode both of them, though not at the same time of course, and she thinks I am very good!' Richard joined in. 'She said that to me as well so I think we will have to spend some more time in the horse world.'

'Right. Time to get everyone organised. John and Minty - we're going back to the Lodge with Mum, okay?' The children didn't really have any choice and neither did Polly, but recognising the stern tenor of Richard's voice they gathered their things together and got into the Rav to go the short distance to the Lodge. This left Jamie, Rosie and Michael making what had now become an inevitable invitation, Jamie, who remained in blissful ignorance about the burgeoning affair between his wife and the minister insisted Michael stayed on.

Rosie was torn between wanting to continue her relationship with Michael and the needs of her family, as well as her enduring love for her husband. This was an entirely new situation for her. There wasn't anyone she could share her dilemma with, though she now knew Betty suspected something this was hardly a situation to discuss with your mother, who was herself newly married and truly happy for the first time in many years.

So whilst she pondered the two men insisted she should

come outside to enjoy a gin and tonic with them, and later they had omelettes for supper before Michael managed to tear himself away.

The Pele Tower

Sir Alistair was very annoyed he and Madeleine had not been included in the lunch after the church service. Especially as he had gone to the trouble to attend with a most reluctant Madeleine. The minister, Michael Martin, had been cordial enough shaking hands as they left, but Rosie, Jamie and the rest of the family had just exchanged 'hellos' with them before going off to lunch with his former wife, Lady Betty and her new husband Colonel Prendergast.

He managed to hide his extreme anger from Madeleine as they drove back to the tower. 'I simply cannot live here much longer, Alistair,' said Madeleine crossly as they finished their healthy lunch in the kitchen. They had given up any pretence of elegant living. The telephone rang and Alistair answered, 'The Pele Tower, Sir Alistair Douglas speaking.' The voice at the other end was that of a youngish-sounding man. 'I apologise for troubling you on a Sunday, but I believe you are interested in letting out the tower house. Sorry, my name is Geoffrey West and my wife and I are coming to Scotland for six months. We would rent in Edinburgh, where I will be working, but we have two horses and want, if possible to bring them as well! *Result* Alistair thought. Geoffrey continued 'I believe one of your family has stabling and paddocks and I am wondering if they would consider some kind of arrangement with us? 'Give me your number Geoffrey. Leave it with me and I will get back to you before the end of the day. I will need to ask my son-in-law about the horses, but his son-in-law is in charge there now. I think it is very probable we can work this out.' Cordial goodbyes were exchanged and Alistair turned back to Madeleine who was sulkily washing the dishes.

'Well, my dear,' he said smoothly, 'I think you can start to relax. That was a man called Geoffrey West who was answering my advertisement in Country Life and he and his wife plus two horses are interested in renting this place for six months. So if it all works out, we can look for somewhere to rent in Edinburgh.' For the first time in a long time, Madeleine smiled at her husband and even hugged him! 'Cheri, this must work or I simply can't stay. Now I am going to read my book and relax. Perhaps you could tidy the garden a little?' With that, not caring whether or not he went into the garden she climbed the first flight of stairs to the little sitting room, which with throws and cushions she had made as comfortable as possible.

Alistair was delighted with this news and set off immediately to find Jamie, or Richard or preferably both of them. He didn't tell Madeleine he was going out. He was annoyed with her. Let her stew. But if this sublet worked, with the remainder of the money from the Leseures buying back the lease on the château, he would be able to buy more time. Also, if Madeleine got a job she could jolly well contribute too.

He got out the small hire car and was whistling as he drove the few miles to Whitewalls. Luckily both Richard and Jamie were at the stables with the rather irritating, even sanctimonious minister, Michael, who seemed to spend a hell of a lot of time with Jamie and Rosie. If he only knew!

'Well, we'd have to meet them and get references,' said Jamie cautiously though he hadn't seen his father-in-law as natural as this for a long time. Then he added 'And I imagine you've asked Betty's permission?' 'She has agreed in principle but I will, of course, consult her once we decide to go ahead. *What a cheek that man has* Jamie thought, but let it go. However hard he tried Alistair, would never, ever get Whitewalls back. Richard said, cautiously: 'I'd also need to check out the horses. Where are they right now?' 'Oh, at a livery yard on the outskirts of

Edinburgh,' he lied but it was plausible. Really he didn't know.

It was arranged Alistair would telephone Geoffrey West and arrange for him and his wife to come down the following Saturday when Richard would be there. *If this works* Richard thought *it would be a great help all round and justify his employing Janey..* Realising he was not even being invited to the house for a drink, Alistair decided he would invite himself. 'I haven't seen dear Rosie for so long. May I pop in to say hello, and maybe have a g and t?' This was put so suavely Jamie, whose politeness and good nature were legendary, couldn't politely refuse.

All the same, it was a somewhat awkward little gathering, and Rosie was glad both Jamie and Michael were there. Richard had excused himself as he, Polly and the children were just about ready to return to Edinburgh before the start of the working week and school.

When he wanted to be, Alistair was quite entertaining and regaled the others with stories, some of them even true, about Whitewalls in the past and the time he had spent in France, making it sound as if he had owned the château, but they were all relieved when he sensed he was about to outstay his welcome and said: 'Must go, darling, Madeleine will wonder where I've got to and the mobile signal isn't any good up in the wilds.' So he kissed Rosie, clapped Jamie on the shoulder, shook hands with a reluctant Michael and departed to give Madeleine his version of events.

Jamie, as was becoming a habit encouraged Michael to stay for supper. 'Rosie always cooks plenty of food, so unless you've got other plans do stay on. You know, we ought to give you a spare room here to save you having to go back after supper. In fact, if you don't mind borrowed pyjamas and dressing gown as well as a disposable razor, why not stay over tonight? You've worked damned hard today. It's time for you to relax!' Michael was tempted, very tempted indeed. So was Rosie, though the idea of

Michael actually sleeping at Whitewalls was disturbing. She did not want to sound too enthusiastic, but when asked by Jamie, replied: 'Oh, do stay, Michael. As Jamie said there's plenty of food, if a chicken and asparagus risotto would tempt you. I made it earlier and there's plenty. I thought we wouldn't want a big meal after the huge lunch.' He hesitated but only for a moment. 'If you're both sure, I'd love to stay. The manse is perfectly decent but rather lonely.'

The decision was made and the two men went off to the stables just to check everything was in order and the ponies, which were out in the field next to the stables, had water and were fine. It was very quiet in Rosie's kitchen and only the regular ticking of the clock disturbed the quietness as she set the table for three and then made a salad. Her heart, though, was racing. Dear darling Jamie didn't suspect anything. She was sure of it, though she had never felt like this about a man before, not even Jamie when they were first married. What was she to do? 'Wait,' she decided and behave as casually as she could. It was not as if Michael hadn't eaten with them before but somehow he had become part of her family circle and she was facing the biggest dilemma of her, so far, comfortable and calm life.

There had, of course, been the worry over Jamie's prostate cancer but the treatment with radon seeds had worked and, thankfully, had not made him impotent. Thankfully, until now that is. There wasn't even this excuse for what she and Michael had started. And she was worried about the state of Polly and Richard's marriage, although Richard inheriting the Lodge and stables after Roddy's death could be the start of a new phase in all their lives. Then too, her mother seemed blissfully happy to have married dear Colonel Prendergast who, it seemed, could not do enough to love and cherish her. On the other hand Charles being sent to Afghanistan was an ever-present worry, lurking beneath the surface. She told herself every day he would come back unharmed. Every day she prayed for it.

The arrival of her sister-in-law's late baby, at the end of Lady Betty and the Colonel's wedding reception had been dramatic but Fleur had been safely born at the general hospital and was thriving. Both her brother Hughie and Virginia had been begging her to go down and stay. Jamie, who hated being away from Whitewalls and his farm and studio, was holding out. 'Why don't you go, darling?' he had said, just the other day. 'You work so hard for all of us and I am sure you could do with a break. Maggie's grandparents would love to see you as well and you could do that either on the way to the Cotswolds or on the way back.' Normally, Rosie would have given the idea serious consideration, but now there was Michael. *Oh stop it,* she told herself firmly. *Go into the garden and do some dead-heading. Think about it later.*

After Michael, Rosie and Jamie had enjoyed the chicken and asparagus risotto, with some perfectly ripe brie afterwards, the men took Tweed Heather, the black Labradors, off for a last walk, then returned the sitting room. The evening had grown chilly, so Rosie had lit the fire and was sitting on one of the sofas flicking through the Sunday Times but not actually reading the words in front of her. Perhaps the answer to the close proximity of Michael throughout the night would be less upsetting if they all had a large glass of Jamie's excellent brandy! In the event, the three of them became tired around the same time. Jamie went to check the locks and put on the burglar alarm. Rosie teased Michael: 'That's so you can't escape'. 'If only I were sharing your bed with you, I would never want to do, he replied, giving her a deep though hasty kiss. 'Jamie's coming back,' she whispered, and they got over the difficult moment when Rosie announced she was going off to have a bath. It had been a long day.

Jamie was very tired indeed. He felt he could sleep for a week. Normally, he had high levels of energy. Even after his prostate gland treatment he had bounced back very quickly. By the time Rosie had finished her perfumed bath and gone back into the bedroom Jamie was already fast asleep and snoring gently. *Could I risk it? I really just want to see Michael has everything he needs,* she lied to herself.

The guest bedroom was at the end of the corridor. Closing her and Jamie's door quietly, she slipped along to where Michael was staying the night. He wasn't asleep. In fact he was reading a rather serious book by James Robertson, 'And the Land Lay Still'. It was a work of fiction but also charted the development of Scotland. His soft grey, curly hair was tousled. Michael was not wearing the pyjamas Jamie had supplied but had left them at the foot of the bed. He looked at Rosie over his rimless reading glasses and smiled.

Neither of them spoke as she took the book from his hands, turned off the bedside light, leaving only the moonlight coming through the window. Rosie slipped into bed next to her lover and quietly, but with deep passion and mutual enjoyment, they came together again. Afterwards Rosie didn't linger but with a final kiss crept quietly back to her own bed. She slipped at once into her deepest sleep for a long time.

Next morning, for once Jamie was not up at six o'clock but was just stirring as Rosie got out of bed and Empress, her little Peke, sensing some movement at last jumped onto the bed. This woke Jamie. 'Hello darling. We must have overdone the brandy yesterday evening, but it was a great day and a lovely end to it.' *If only you knew* Rosie thought, She ought to have felt guilty but did not, not in the least. *I'll think about what to do later. we can't just carry on as if nothing has happened.*

Once fully awake, Jamie was quick to get out of bed, go to the bathroom and get dressed in his customary cord trousers, checked woollen shirt and a pullover. 'I'll take the dogs out and Empress into the garden, I think. See you for breakfast. I assume Michael will be up and about by then.' She smiled at her husband. And with those words he went downstairs, whistling, without a care in the world. She heard Michael getting up but didn't risk going into the guest bathroom, so next time she saw him was in the kitchen. Right on cue, as she was cooking sausages and bacon on the Aga, Jamie came back with the dogs and what could and indeed should rightly have been an awkward moment for Rosie and Michael was over.

She made especially strong coffee to go with the food and had her usual boiled egg and wholemeal toast whilst the men got stuck into the sausages, eggs and bacon. 'Well, boys, you'll have to excuse me, I've got my list of things to be done, starting outside. Molly will be here in about twenty minutes so she'll want to get on too.' This was said in a firm, steady voice and she kept her composure as she went out into the garden, picking up her trug and secateurs on the way.

Michael was not quite finished yet, however, and made sure he went into the garden to say goodbye. 'Rosie, thank you for everything. We're going to have a serious talk at some point soon but I wanted to tell you how amazing last night was, unexpected but magic.' He kissed her lightly on the check and was gone.

Why not, after all, go to visit her brother Hughie and sister-in-law. Virginia, who was now calling herself Ginny because she thought it sounded more youthful and suitable now she was a mother again? It had been a long time since she had visited them. She pushed to the back of her mind the fact Michael had played a major part in getting the expectant mother to hospital and staying to help. So here perhaps was a credible reason to get away, with the bonus of Maggie being there too for the filming of 'The Minister Who Lied'.

The visit had been arranged hurriedly. Rosie knew she had to get away to think. Her affair with Michael had started so suddenly and now, for both of them she needed some breathing space. Jamie, who suspected absolutely nothing about his wife's relationship with Michael, was, perhaps surprisingly considering how much he relied on Rosie, in favour of the plan.

Chapter 12

High Wynch Park

Usually, if she was expecting guests, Virginia made a big fuss about everything in the private area of her home being absolutely impeccable. But since Fleur arrived, she had dropped her quest for constant perfection and as a result was much more relaxed. She found she was really looking forward to the visit from her sister-in-law Rosie, whom she had not really got to know properly.

Virginia thought she just might confide in Rosie, who was so sensible, about her doubts as to who was Fleur's father, Hughie or Anthony Goodman. Then she resolved to wait and see how the visit went. In fact, Virginia was surprised at Rosie visiting at all and without Jamie.

Rosie planned to go by train from Scotland to Bristol and on from there to Bath, where Hughie would meet her and drive to High Wynch Park. She had not fancied driving the whole way, partly because it had been a while since she had taken such a long journey by car on her own and partly because it meant she would have time to think on the journey and get her head round all that was happening, so unexpectedly in her normally ordered life As well, it meant she had the perfect reason not to visit Nigel and Florette in Yorkshire. Fond as she had become of Maggie's grandmother and step-grandfather, she needed to concentrate.

What had happened with Michael was so unexpected, so unlike her and however hard she tried and, yes, fantasised, she could not see a happily ever after ending. Yes, over the years there had been many ups and downs in her life. The worst was probably Jamie's prostate cancer, but, caught early, it seemed to have been cured. Indeed he was as loving towards her in bed as well as in every other way as he had always been. What on earth could she do? The sensible thing, and Rosie was eminently sensible, as a rule, was to end the affair. She didn't feel sensible though. It was not obvious that she would find answers by going to stay with her brother and his wife, with whom she had never been close. But Rosie had never been alone in her whole life, and, whilst others might have gone to a spa or retreat of some kind, she knew in her heart this was not the way for her.

Rosie had been given a comfortable room and en-suite bathroom. After her long train journey, when she had been met by Hughie with great hugs and kisses, she was pleased when Virginia suggested she might want to have a bath and relax before dinner. 'I'll be giving Fleur her bottle as it's the au pair's night off. Just kitchen supper if that's all right with you?' Rosie gave Virginia a warm hug, which rather startled both women in view of their previous quite cool relationship, though this had thawed a great deal after the drama surrounding Fleur's birth.

'Of course, it's all right! I will, though, go and have that bath and unpack,' Rosie replied.

'Hughie will be back from his wanderings round the garden soon, so we'll have drinks in the drawing room about seven o'clock, then supper in here.'

Right on cue Fleur started to grizzle and needed to be fed, so, whilst Virginia prepared her bottle, Rosie went upstairs, already beginning to relax. As soon as she got into the bedroom, she checked her mobile. She had a message. It was from Michael. She opened it. 'Missing you already, darling girl, please reply and let me know you arrived safely and you are missing me too!' She smiled, happy to have heard from him. Rosie replied: Yes arrived, yes missing you, about to run a bath, wish you could join me in it. Before she got into the bath she looked at her naked body in the full-length mirror. *Not bad for 56,* she thought before immersing herself in the warm scented water. Her hands trailed in the suds and moved to and fro.

She lazed in the bath for quite a while. Then her mobile phone bleeped. Hoping it was another message from Michael, and excited at the thought, she jumped out of the bath and wrapped herself in one of the huge white bath towels. Virginia had not relaxed all of her high housekeeping standards! The message was from Jamie. 'Please phone love. I've tried the house phone but it's engaged, xx'. Guilt-stricken, she dialled Whitewalls straight away. Jamie picked up immediately and she said: 'Sorry, darling. I meant to call but we got talking Ginny, as she's now calling herself, shoved me off for a bath before dinner. But is everything all right at home? Any problems with Polly and Richard and the twins?' Jamie sounded much more cheerful. 'Yes, darling, no dramas except Maggie has had an email from Charles which she's sent on to us. He's safely, if you can call it that, in Afghanistan, but of course you'll be seeing her, if not this evening then tomorrow. She might be going up to London to check the house this evening. Oh, and I'm going to Michael's. He's promised to make a curry, like he used to do in India. But stop me from rambling on or you'll run out of battery. Love you, 'bye for now!' She managed a loving-sounding 'lots of love, speak again tomorrow.'

She sank down on to the bed. *What on earth was she doing?* Rosie had always held very strong views about faithfulness. This was not surprising, considering her father, Sir Alistair's shocking sexual behaviour over the years. Then there was Polly, now she was going in the same direction.

Rosie pulled herself together and quickly dressed in soft cream trousers and a lovely cashmere sweater bought from Florette. The top was a lighter shade of cream, which suited her silvery blonde hair. A quick application of make-up and she was ready.

When Rosie went downstairs to the drawing room, she found Hughie about to pour himself a large gin and tonic. 'Just in time, old girl. Come and join me. Ginny will be down in a minute. She's just seeing to Fleur. Oh and Maggie has gone up to London to check on the house there, but will be here tomorrow to start rehearsals for the film.'

For no good reason, her spirits lifted and she gave her brother a hug before accepting her very generous drink. He looked a little startled and then grinned. She asked: 'When did Virginia decide to be called Ginny?' 'I suppose it was after Fleur was born. I think it suits her and, I'll tell you what, this late baby has given her, and me a whole new lease of life. It's hard work but somehow all for the better.' For Hughie, this was a long speech. 'Anyway, drink up!'

The door opened and Ginny came into the room. 'She's gone to sleep, thank God.' But she was smiling, 'Come on, husband, large g and t. I've earned it.' After a couple of stiff drinks, which made Rosie feel giggly, they went down to the kitchen. 'I've done a beef and red wine casserole,' said Ginny. 'It's in the Aga and the veg can be done in the microwave.' The table had been set in the conventional style with crystal wine glasses and stiff white napkins. There were flowers in the centre of the table.

Rosie laughed and said: 'Well Ginny, glad to see some things haven't changed.' 'What do you mean?' asked Ginny. 'I mean the food smells fantastic and the table looks up to your usual high standards.'

In the past Rosie would never have spoken to her sister-in-law in such a teasing way. But things were different now. Hughie produced a very good claret to go with the casserole and though Rosie thought she couldn't eat another thing, the late raspberries with thick cream rounded off the meal. She really enjoyed eating them.

'Right, announced Ginny, with a touch of her old bossy tone, 'Let's leave this lot, Sally can clear it up in the morning. Do either of you want coffee?' They didn't. Then Hugh said: 'Well let's go back up for a nightcap. I've got some really good brandy.' By now Rosie was so relaxed she thought: *Oh, what the hell, why not? Should she tell her brother and sister-in-law about Charles' impending return from Afghanistan? No, it wasn't her story to tell and it hadn't actually happened yet.*

Over the brandy, conversation turned to family and Charles and Maggie, Polly and Richard as well as Ginny and Hughie's grown-up children, Roberta and Alex who were both now settled in good jobs and sharing a flat in Camden. Rosie told them about Minty and her leg maybe needing more surgery. Ginny said sympathetically: 'Oh, poor little mite. She looked so lovely at Betty and John's wedding. Let's hope she doesn't need another operation!'

Hughie yawned, drained his brandy glass and announced: 'Well girls, I'm knackered, so I'm going to turn in. We've got Piers and Anthony coming in the morning. I think you'll like both of them, Rosie. See you soon,' he said to Ginny. 'Goodnight, Rosie, sleep well.' Because they had been talking so much Rosie and Ginny had not finished their drinks.

'Rosie, can I tell you something in absolute confidence? 'Of course you can.'

'Let's have a drop of brandy first.' Now Rosie was definitely feeling squiffy. But it was, she decided, a warm, slightly surreal feeling and not unpleasant.

Ginny refilled their glasses with another generous measure. Rosie couldn't remember when she had last had so much to drink in one evening! 'Well, you know Hughie and I have had our ups and downs over the years, mostly over money and his hare-brained schemes. Then things started to get better, mostly when he met Piers and Anthony. There's a lot of money to be made using here as a film set and so on. I even get commission from the bed and breakfast people who put up the technicians and cast acting in the productions. I'll be honest, we hadn't been having sex for ages, even more or less stopped sleeping together. Anyway,' she stopped, 'am I boring you?' 'Absolutely not,' Rosie replied, fascinated. 'Well, Piers' financial backer is Anthony Goodman, he's a bachelor, very good-looking and, well, sexy. I couldn't resist when he came on to me and Hughie was away. So I had a very brief affair with him. I didn't think about contraception, well, you don't, do you? Rosie thought: *well, no you don't.*

Ginny went on. 'Then I had sex with Hughie as well. I guess I was back in the mood. Afterwards I found I was pregnant. I honestly didn't, and still don't know who is Fleurs' father. Anthony turned very nasty when I told him I was pregnant. It didn't seem to be the same loving, sexy man. So I was in quite a state.' 'Did you say anything to Hughie? No, how could you?' Rosie interjected.

'Hughie was so pleased, and I said nothing. It seemed easier that way, at first. But I still really want to know. You'll meet Anthony tomorrow and I wanted to confide in you before that. As well, I'd like to know what you think of him. I've never told anyone this before. I know I can trust you and you won't say anything.'

Rosie decided, of course I won't say anything Ginny, actually, can I share something with you?'

'Absolutely, though I can't imagine it's anything like my situation.'

'Much closer than you think.' Ginny was now really intrigued. Rosie began by saying 'I'm not sure where to begin.' It was Ginny's turn to be was silent, and expectant.

'Well, you know Jamie and I married when I was twenty one and he was twenty four. It's a cliché, I know, but it was love at first sight. We met at a Borders Hunt Ball. He asked me to dance, and that was it! Ginny had a pretty shrewd idea of where this was leading. *Rosie, she thought is still quite naïve.*

'Anyway, you know our new minister, Michael (she loved being able to say his name) at Sticholme. He's a lovely man, and he's a bachelor. I found out he had spent most of his ministry in Africa, then India. He was engaged, but she died with some awful tropical disease. He never found anyone else. Ginny, you've met him. He's lovely. Not very tall, but he has a wonderful smile and thick curly hair, lovely silvery-grey, and the most beautiful hands' Ginny had by now guessed and could keep quiet no longer. 'So you've been to bed with him, had wonderful sex!'

'How did you guess?' Rosie exclaimed. 'Was it so obvious?' Ginny was both amused and intrigued. 'Well, no, but I could tell you liked each other, got on well together and I remember how sweet and kind he was coming into the hospital with me when Fleur decided to arrive which, of course, she wasn't supposed to do for another three weeks.' How did it all happen? You and Michael, I mean?'

Rosie realised she had a sympathetic listener and went on: 'Michael started spending more time at Whitewalls instead of the rather bleak manse which is his official home. As well, Jamie really liked him and started inviting him for meals. Then one night Jamie was staying over in Edinburgh with Polly and Richard and he suggested Michael stayed with me! It was wonderful, different and it's all gone on from there. It probably seems odd but neither of us feels guilty.' 'And Jamie has no idea?' Ginny asked. She, of course had been in a similar situation, although with a more tangible outcome.

Rosie paused, pulled herself together. 'No, he is as kind as always and even invited Michael to stay the night! So, quite apart from wanting to see everyone here, I decided I needed to get away for a while. I've hardly ever been away on my own, always with Jamie and children and grandchildren. So this is ideal and it's so kind of you to have me to stay.'

'Don't be silly, It is great having you here.' It was now almost midnight so they drained their glasses, hugged each other and went off, rather unsteadily, Ginny to check on Fleur and Rosie to sink into her bed and a deep and dreamless sleep.

Although Ginny too was tired and had a lot to drink when she had finally settled her baby and slipped into bed beside Hughie she felt sexy, probably because of talking about sex so much with Rosie. She woke him up and they had a very satisfactory, though fairly brief coming together before going to sleep.

Maggie, meanwhile had gone to London to check on the mews house and have dinner again with Adrian, her leading man in the film. They by now enjoyed flirting with each other, but Maggie had made it very clear this was as far as it was going to go, especially with Charles away in

Afghanistan. In fact, this was a good arrangement as in acting it was always good for the leading actors to have at least a frisson of feeling between them.

They were due to come to High Wynch Park the next day to see Piers, meet Anthony Goodman and plan rehearsal schedules. Most of the cast would be billeted in local bed and breakfasts with just Ginny's chosen few at the house itself.

Rosie woke early the next morning, roused by her mobile phone bleeping. She had a message and grabbed her glasses from the bedside table, hoping it was Michael. It was Jamie. 'Good morning darling. Hope I haven't sent this too early. I didn't phone because I thought you'd be asleep and this seemed better. I'm in the top field with the dogs, though your Empress preferred to stay with Michael! Give me a call when you are properly awake.'

Her mobile bleeped again. It was Michael. 'I think it shows how much I care for you because I have your little dog with me. We've been for a walk and I am now sitting, along with Empress outside your kitchen with a cup of coffee! Lots of love. Michael xxx' She instantly replied 'You are so lovely, I'm almost tempted to come straight back before Empress falls in love with you too! Seriously it is quite good to be away, get some perspective. I love you too. R xxx' She pressed 'send' before she could change her mind. She would telephone Jamie after breakfast.

Rosie went to the en-suite bathroom and then was soon dressed in chinos and a smart checked blue and white shirt. It suited her and had been bought especially for the trip.

She went downstairs to the kitchen to find Ginny sitting at the table, which had been so elegantly set the previous evening. Ginny was feeding Fleur. 'Did you sleep well?' she asked 'I was going to leave you to have a lie-in.' 'Yes to the first and this is actually me having a lie in. Have you had breakfast, or can I make something?' Ginny replied: 'If you could just forage for yourself that would be great! And perhaps make me a cup of Earl Grey for when I have finished with this one. We've given up on formal breakfast since she arrived.' She smiled lovingly at Fleur and soon the baby had finished.

So Rosie duly made herself some wholemeal toast, found the butter and ginger marmalade as well as some freshly squeezed orange juice. She made Earl Grey tea also for Ginny and popped the baby in her Moses basket.

The kitchen door opened. It was Maggie. 'Hello, darlings, late breakfast? Just teasing, I don't know how on earth you cope, Ginny, especially without a full-time nanny! But you look well on it. You look good, too, Rosie, my mother-in-law elect.' All this came out in a rush, then Maggie hugged and kissed both women. 'Now, let me see this beautiful baby, and what a lovely name! My grandma thinks it is after her. Well, I suppose Fleur and Florette are just about the same. May I pick her up?" Before Ginny could say the baby had just been put in her basket, she was in Maggie's arms. As Maggie's green eyes met the baby stare of Fleur's blue ones, Maggie felt a rush of, she supposed, love and in that moment decided, whatever happened, she and Charles would have a baby as soon as they could.

Whilst all this was going on, the front door bell rang. 'Hughie will get that,' Ginny said, 'Piers Romayne is coming for a meeting about your film, Maggie, so I'm glad you're here. I believe he's bringing Adrian with him.' Maggie knew this but thought it better not to comment. Ginny got up from her seat at the kitchen table, gently took Fleur from Maggie and shepherded them out of the kitchen. 'Do go into the drawing room, I'll take Fleur to her room.

As Ginny went upstairs her heart was pounding. She didn't know whether or not Anthony would be with the others. Well, she would soon find out as she went to make coffee for them, after settling Fleur down. The little one fell asleep almost immediately. Before going downstairs again, Ginny checked her make-up and hair - fine though not as immaculate as she would have wanted. The morning had just whizzed by. Now she just might, have to face Anthony.

She took a deep breath before going into the drawing room. The men stood up as she entered. Yes, as well as Piers, her husband Hughie and Maggie's leading man, Adrian, was Anthony. Ginny still didn't know if Hughie was Fleur's father or the result of her very brief affair with Anthony. Maggie stayed in her chair with her enviably long legs crossed. She, too, was remembering she might have succumbed to Adrian if her deep love for Charles had not stopped her. Piers kissed Ginny's cheek but Anthony, before she could turn her head away kissed her on the lips.

Ginny gave them all the benefit of her brilliant smile and offered coffee. However, Hughie intervened and said: 'Darling, the sun's nearly over the yardarm why don't we have a gin and tonic and toast the success of the film? I really like the title, "The Minister Who Lied" Who thought of that? 'As a matter of fact, I think it was me.' This was Anthony in his deep rich voice. So they acceded to Hughie's suggestion. He did make good gin and tonics and Ginny opened some nibbles, which Maggie handed round. Piers proposed a toast to 'The Minister who Lied' which they all repeated in varying tones. After the drinks had been finished and top-ups declined the men all disappeared to the office to finalise the plans, after which Adrian went to the cottage he had rented. This left Maggie to go back to her room to try and to send a text to Charles telling him all was going according to plan.

Right, that's a relief. It's kitchen lunch and the men, apart from Hughie, are not staying, but we'll see plenty enough of them soon. Ginny thought At this point, Sylvia arrived. 'Good morning, Mrs Bruce. And this will be Maggie whom we've heard so much about!' Sylvia, a widow in her early fifties, was one of the old school and didn't hold with too much familiarity, rather like her own Molly, Rosie thought, and feeling nostalgia and a desire to go home soon. She shook hands with Sylvia before going to her room to phone Jamie. He answered almost at once. 'Whitewalls, Jamie Douglas speaking.' 'Hello, darling, it's me. How are you?'

The sound of his voice made up her mind. She would go home. 'Darling, I'm missing you all, so I've decided to come home a couple of days early. I'm going to fly from Bristol and get you to meet me in Edinburgh, if that's alright. I've haven't booked anything yet, but Hughie can do it for me.' 'That will be great, Rosie. Whitewalls is just not the same without you! We're all fine and Michael is being a great help as well. Polly and Richard seem to be getting on better, thank God, so no new dramas. Must go, my love, and check on the sheep. Michael's coming round later and has offered to cook dinner again so I can get some time in the studio.' Rosie inwardly groaned. How on earth was she going to sort out this situation? Her husband and her lover seemed to be getting closer all the time. The sensible thing to do would be to talk things through with Michael and try to end their affair amicably so nobody was badly hurt. Having made a sort of plan, she would then, with Hughie, set about making arrangements for her flight back to Edinburgh.

'Darling, I'll call you again the minute I know what flight I am on tomorrow. Love you,' and closed her phone before Jamie could say anything else. After this events moved quickly. Whilst Hughie and Maggie tried to persuade Rosie to stay, Ginny, who knew what was uppermost in Rosie's mind, was conciliatory and supportive. There was no further opportunity for a private conversation, though Ginny did manage to say: 'If you want to talk, give me a call on my mobile. I don't want to pry, just to help if I can. And you know you are welcome here at any time.' Rosie felt comforted and replied in a similar vein 'Please bring Fleur to see us at Whitewalls whenever you are ready. After all, she is a Scot! 'Of course, I hadn't really thought of it that way,' was Rosie's reply. Whatever the issues might bring up the two women, who had been distant with each other in the past, parted with hugs and kisses, before Hughie drove off with Rosie to the airport, to return to Scotland and face her future.

When he dropped her at the airport, Hughie gave his sister a big hug, then said, uncharacteristically for him: 'Take care, old girl. You've got a good life and it all seems to be sorted but, oh, it's probably nothing, you seem to have changed! Whatever it is, remember what you already have is probably better than what you think you want.' 'I'll remember, Hughie, and thank you for my lovely visit. Ginny has changed too, you know and Fleur seems to have really brought the two of you closer together'. After another hug, Hughie saw Rosie safely into the departure hall and left. The flight to Edinburgh left on time and was not busy, so Rosie had a window seat with nobody sitting beside her. She tried to marshal her thoughts to make some sense first of the dangers of disrupting her relatively calm family life, and then how wise or not it had been to confide in Ginny about Michael. In fact, she didn't regret doing so, after all, she told herself, Ginny's dilemma about who was Fleur's father was a much greater issue than a brief affair with Michael.

Before the flight was called Rosie, had tried to phone Jamie. 'This is Whitewalls, I am afraid we can't take your call at present, please leave a message after the tone.' So she did, briefly, 'Hello darling, the plane is on time and I am so looking forward to seeing you,' She had followed the answerphone message with a text to Jamie's mobile, which he was also not answering. She managed to relax to a greater extent than she had expected and even dozed off during the smooth flight.

After swiftly getting through to the arrivals hall, Rosie looked around for Jamie. But Jamie wasn't there. Michael was. He gave her a huge smile and hug before she could even ask why Jamie had not come to meet her. When she did ask he just said, 'I'll tell you in the car. Don't worry, there's nothing wrong. *Oh wasn't there?* she thought as her heart started to pound and desire flooded through her. Quite unselfconsciously, Michael took hold of her small suitcase and tucked her arm through his as he led her to the car park nearby.

'Tell me what's happening,' Rosie demanded as they set off from the airport to drive back to the Borders. 'I think it's very exciting for Jamie. One of the London galleries, quite out of the blue, wants to exhibit his paintings but he had to fly down early this morning to see the owner. He should be back this evening though. Apparently one of Polly's clients recommended him to the gallery so it was too good a chance to miss. I know he tried to phone you at High Wynch Park, but you had already left so he asked me to pick you up and explain.' Rosie had a premonition. She knew the answer before asking the question. 'Did he say who was the client? 'David McLean, I think that's the name.' David was, of course, Polly's lover who had caused so much trouble in her marriage and Rosie thought this was another trick of his to try and get Polly to choose him and ask Richard for a divorce.

'Anyway, my dear Rosie, it is so lovely to see you. Shall we have lunch on the way back? 'That would be lovely,' she replied 'What about the Horseshoe at Eddleston? That's on the way.' 'Then that's what we'll do and you can tell me all about your visit south. It sounds to have been quite an experience.' *Also* she thought *having lunch out would give her a chance to compose herself* again before they arrived back at Whitewalls.

The journey to Eddleston near Peebles wasn't difficult. Michael had Classic FM playing softly in the background and Rosie related some, though not all of the events of her stay with Hughie and Ginny.

Whilst neither of them was very hungry, they sat closely together at a window table and both ordered salmon. As he was driving, Michael stuck to sparkling water but Rosie felt she needed calming down and had a large glass of Pinot Grigio. 'How's the congregation campaign going?' Rosie asked, more for something to say than because she really wanted to know. Michael answered in the same, light tone: 'Pretty well, I think. The family service and the bonus of lunch afterwards has raised the profile and the numbers.'

They finished their meal, declined coffee and went outside to get back into the car for the rest of the journey to Whitewalls. To Rosie there was an feeling of unreality but Michael seemed very relaxed and the wine had helped to relax her too. All she had to decide, for the moment, as they sped through the Border countryside alongside the River Tweed, was whether or not to ask him to come into the house. It wasn't a difficult decision.

'Coffee, darling?' she asked. This was the first time she had called him darling but it didn't seem wrong or out of place. He smiled and pulled her close to him. 'I think the coffee can wait.' Neither of them saw the red twinkling light of the telephone answering machine as they made their way upstairs to the bedroom. Rosie felt a fleeting surge of disloyalty as they entered the room which she had shared with Jamie for so long. Then they undressed each other and were lost in magical love-making. Sometime later, Michael stirred, still wrapped around Rosie. 'Darling, have you any idea what time it is?' Gradually she opened her eyes and looked at the bedside clock. 'Oh, heavens, it's five o'clock. I think we'd better get up, just in case. Richard, Polly and the children are coming down later and they're sure to come round.'

'We'd better get up then. I ought to go back to the manse and do some work anyway. But please phone me if it's going to be possible for me to come back later this evening.' She kissed him lovingly and they both dressed as quickly as they could. This was fortunate. After a last kiss Michael jumped into his car and drove off down the drive. Minutes later Rosie heard the crunch of tyres at the back of the house and went to greet Richard, Polly and the excited twins who were full of their own news. She took a deep breath and tried hard to compose herself

'Hi, Granny, guess what? I came top in my maths test this week, Mr Brown was really pleased and nice about it.' This was young John's greeting accompanied by a big hug.

'And I've started swimming again. Dr Cluny says it should help my leg to get strong, so I'm really happy. As well he says I can start riding again, as long as I don't go fast and someone is with me.' Rosie hugged her lovely granddaughter and her eyes met those of her daughter Polly who came into the sitting room after the children. Polly did notice two wine glasses but at the time didn't think anything of it.

Richard was the last to come in. 'You know Jamie's in London, I hope. We thought we'd better come and keep you company for a bit. He's really excited about the chance to exhibit there. We were going to meet you at the airport but, as you know, he fixed up for Michael to do that so I hoped it worked alright?' Richard was so thoughtful. He might be quiet, even gentle but was truly considerate and very clever. Rosie often thought he and Polly were a great contrast to each other which, in her experience seemed to work well, although she had been very upset at Polly's affair with David McLean. She hoped this was now over, Richard gave her the choice of a divorce with his having custody of the children or trying to make a go of their marriage and staying together. Richard wasn't a lawyer, a recent partner in his prestigious Edinburgh practice, for nothing!

'Yes thanks, Richard. Michael met me at the airport and came in for lunch. He's gone back to the manse to do some work. He might pop back later. Do you all want to stay for a meal? The freezer is pretty full of goodies.' Feeling a little uneasy about it, Polly replied: 'No thanks, Ma, we've a lot to do at the Lodge and I've brought food with us. Do you want to come over?' Rosie pretended to pause for thought, then replied 'Darling, no thanks. I've had a hectic time. Why don't you come round for lunch tomorrow and I'll tell you about everybody. You wouldn't believe how maternal Ginny has become!'

'Daddy, mummy, can we go and get the ponies?' John asked. 'Well let's go and look at them and you can take them out tomorrow,' said Richard. With that they left

Rosie with her thoughts and, yes, her expectation. She was torn between ringing Michael and putting him off coming back and inviting him to return. She could hardly drive up to the manse, going past the Lodge when she had just declined going there with her family! Still, it was worth the risk and she picked up her mobile phone.

Michael answered at once. 'Darling, are you able to get away for even a little while, or shall I come back? I think it's easier if I come to you. If any of the family see me, well I've had to go in to the village to collect something!' 'If you're sure, this will be a bonus and maybe we can talk a little about what we're going to do, apart from the obvious,that is.'

Rosie's heart was beating faster than usual as she drove carefully down the long drive and past the Lodge. She was in luck. Polly was busy inside whilst Richard and the children were down at the stables. The short journey was accomplished in ten minutes and soon she was inside the manse. Michael was waiting for her, a bottle of her favourite white wine already chilled in the fridge.

She went quickly into the manse and was at once enfolded in Michael's arms. He kissed her warmly and led her to the sitting room. He poured the wine but it was not long before they went upstairs to Michael's bedroom, taking the wine with them.

Rosie had left her mobile phone in her handbag downstairs. So she didn't hear its persistent ringing. It was Richard, calling from the Lodge. He had been walking Pixie and Pod, the twins' Norfolk terriers, and saw Whitewalls in darkness. Walking further towards the house, he noticed Rosie's car was missing. It could, of course, be that she had gone to Stitcholme to see her mother, Lady Betty, and husband John, but why would she do that in the early evening, especially after saying she was fine and wouldn't eat with Richard, Polly and the children at the Lodge.

He made up his mind and drove to Sticholme. All seemed quiet at the Prendergasts, and Richard hesitated to disturb them and seem as if he were worried about Rosie's whereabouts. A little further down the road he came to the manse. There was his answer! Rosie's car was parked rather untidily outside. The lights were on both upstairs and downstairs. He hesitated. What was she doing there? He hazarded a guess, surely the saintly Rosie was not following her daughter down the same path?

Inside the manse, Rosie had hastily dressed, and both she and Michael, he still in his dressing gown, his curly hair even more rumpled than usual, were downstairs in the sitting room. 'Darling, I really must go,' she said and opened her handbag for a comb. She saw the message light on her mobile. It was the message from Richard, carefully worded, hoping she was all right.

'Darling, I really must go. That was Richard and he must have been up to the house for some reason and wondering where I am. I think I might just call there on my way back with some plausible excuse.' 'Oh, can't you stay?' asked Michael. She gave him a very passionate kiss, which aroused him again so she pulled herself away and said: 'No, no I have to go. Come round tomorrow. Jamie might be away for another night and back early on Monday, but I don't know until I have spoken to him'. With that Michael had to be satisfied. As she got into the car to drive away she vaguely noticed a familiar Rav up the road but it didn't register until she was nearly home. What to do?

Rosie thought quickly then decided the truth was better than a made-up story about going to see her mother. So she stopped at the Lodge just as Richard pulled up beside her. He spoke first. 'Ma, you had us worried! I was walking the dogs and saw there was nobody at Whitewalls and with you being on your own, well, I just drove up to your mother's in case you were there.'

'No, actually I went to the manse to return a book Michael had left when he was here earlier!' Even to Rosie it sounded very feeble. So she pulled herself together and said lightly: 'If the offer is still open I will come in and have supper with you all. Then maybe you could help me walk Heather and Tweed'. So the awkwardness passed, for the moment.

They had just finished supper when the phone rang. 'Yes, yes, Jamie, she's here.' Richard handed the phone to Rosie, saying: 'It's Jamie. He was getting worried about you and your mobile doesn't seem to be working.' Well, it wasn't working because when she went to bed with Michael, she had turned it off. She took a deep breath. 'Hello, darling, sorry you couldn't get me on the mobile. I think I've run out of battery.' *If only he knew.* 'Anyway, darling, how are you? Did you get on well with Oscar at the gallery?' Jamie sounded really excited. 'Yes, darling, I did! Your husband is going to have his first London exhibition in two months' time.' 'Oh, that's marvellous. I am so proud of you.' This was true. Jamie was a talented artist but to be offered an exhibition in a small, but highly prestigious London gallery was a real accolade. 'Anyway, what have you been up to?' 'Oh, just the usual, she said lightly. Michael has been a great help. And he's looking forward to hearing all your news'.

Thankfully for Rosie, who was getting even more flustered, he added, 'Anyway, I'm staying at the Chelsea Arts Club this evening and flying back to Edinburgh tomorrow afternoon. There's a few loose ends still to tie up with Oscar in the morning. I'll call you when I know what plane I'm getting, Maybe you could meet me? Love you, darling. 'Bye.' With that, and after Rosie had agreed she would meet her husband at the airport in Edinburgh, the conversation was at an end.

'Are you sure you don't want me to stay with you at the house tonight, Mum?' Polly asked. 'Quite sure but thanks for offering, darling. I still have some tidying up to do and I'm going to Edinburgh tomorrow to collect your father from the airport.' 'Does that mean you won't be at church tomorrow? Michael will be disappointed.' This last remark was delivered with just a hint of a barb. Polly didn't want to believe her sainted mother was having a relationship with Michael Martin, but they did seem to enjoy each other's company.

Then Polly told herself she was being stupid. Her parents' marriage was the strongest she had ever known. Whereas she and David had almost destroyed the relationship between herself and Richard. Almost, but not quite. Not yet! Rosie was still wondering what to do to deflect any suspicions her family might be harbouring about her visit to the Manse.

'Michael has been such a support to your dad and really encouraging him to go for a London exhibition. He's also, at Dad's request been keeping a bit of an eye on me to make sure I am all right. We've hardly ever been apart before, your dad and me, that is' Her inner voice was saying *stop before you say anything incriminating or unbelievable!* So she pulled herself together and said: 'I'll be fine at the house. I've got the dogs for company and I'll keep my mobile on all night! Maybe you could do the same?' With that, and loving goodbyes, she got away.

As Rosie let herself into the almost eerily quiet house with the Labradors snoozing in their baskets in front of the Aga and Empress curled up with her favourite, Tweed, Rosie burst into tears, *What on earth had she been thinking about? Taking risks with Michael, sleeping with him for God's sake...* She stopped and laughed shakily, although there was nobody there to hear.

She poured herself a glass of brandy, threw some more logs on the sitting room fire and, with Empress transferred to her knee and Tweed and Heather lying comfortably at her feet Rosie began to calm down. Her mobile rang.

For a moment she thought she would ignore it but picked it up. It was Jamie. 'Hello, darling' he said 'Are you still okay for picking me up at the airport tomorrow morning? The plane gets in at eleven. If that means too early a start for you I could give Michael a call, I know he's an early riser.' This made her feel mildly hysterical, with a double entendre thrown in for good measure. 'Darling, of course I'll be there. We mustn't impose on

Michael. Besides, I am dying to see you and hear all the news.' 'That will be wonderful, Rosie. Are you all right on your own tonight?' He was so caring. 'Yes, yes, I'm fine. The dogs are snuggled up with me and I had supper with Polly and Richard and the twins. So all's well. Love you. See you in the morning. Goodnight and God bless'. With this the called ended. She took another swallow of the brandy and realised how close, how very close she had become to wrecking everything. *But what to do?* Like the famous line from Scarlett in 'Gone with the Wind', she decided *I'll think about that tomorrow.* Rather to her surprise, Rosie slept very well.

She woke early as her phone was ringing. She looked at the name and number. It was Michael. With a great effort of will, she didn't reply. He left a message. 'Rosie, darling, if you're there, please pick up. I just want to know you are all right.' A few minutes later, after she had let out the dogs, Rosie's phone went again. This time it was Jamie. After a moment's hesitation, she answered. She half-hoped he was ringing to say he was staying on in London. But no! 'Hello, my darling, I've really missed you but I'm at the airport and we should be on our way very soon. Are you quite sure you are fine with collecting me? If not I can always ring Michael.' No, love, don't do that. I'm sure he'll be busy. I'll be there to meet you.' This sounded rather hollow but it was the best she could think of. 'I'll say goodbye for now and see you at the airport I'll be waiting.'

As soon as she came off the mobile, the house phone rang. It was Polly. 'Mum, just checking you're fine. Are you still going to meet Dad at the airport and do you want me to come with you?' Rosie inwardly sighed. *Why this sudden interest in my welfare? Could my family be checking up on me?* Polly hadn't quite finished 'I know, Mum,' she said with an air of studied casual enquiry 'you could always ask Michael to go.' Rosie was rarely irritated, but she was now. 'Polly, I'm going to collect Dad and I've things to do. Besides aren't you forgetting it's Sunday? Michael will have church services. Darling I really must go. 'Bye.' She hung up before Polly could say any more.

Rosie's thoughts were in turmoil as she drove to Edinburgh airport to collect Jamie. She knew she ought to feel guilty about her affair with Michael. Although, so far, it had been brief, the feelings of both of them were not simply physical. There seemed to be a synergy between them. Of course the relationship was new and still had all the excitement of first meeting and getting to know each other. On the other hand she had loved Jamie for so long there seemed to be nothing about each other they did not know.

It was a pleasant morning and the roads were very quiet. She had Classic FM on the car radio which soothed her jittery feelings as she drove through Peebles and on to the west side of Edinburgh where the airport was situated. Almost inexplicably her mood changed. Yes, she was still tremendously attracted to Michael, but in her heart she knew the relationship could never be long-term.

When Rosie reached the airport she managed to park without difficulty and made her way to the arrivals lounge, still feeling nervous but wanting to see Jamie. For once, the airport wasn't crowded and she got a seat close to the arrivals door. Looking at the arrivals board she saw the flight was on time. This was a relief as it would give her less time to think and less time to worry about Michael.

Then the doors opened. Jamie was one of the first passengers to come through. He saw her first and smiled happily to see his darling wife waiting for him. Rosie waved to him and, for the time being, her relationship with Michael was put quite firmly to the back of her mind!

He was carrying not only his hand luggage, which was all he had taken with him to London, but also a pale blue small carrier bag with the word 'Tiffany' printed on the side. Her heart leapt. It must be jewellery. But in all their long relationship, Jamie had never bought her jewellery, except for her engagement ring, a sapphire and diamond, her platinum wedding ring and a gold watch, which she kept for special occasions!

'Where's the car?' he asked after giving her a warm kiss on the lips. 'What's in the bag?' she asked. 'You'll have to wait and see!' was his response. As they walked to the car, she said: 'You haven't told me yet how it all went with the London gallery.' 'Tell you over lunch. Let's stop on the way home and go to Peebles Hydro. Save you cooking for once!' 'Thank you, darling, but do you know everything is ready at home and I've even put a bottle of champagne in the fridge.' Jamie smiled again. 'Well I had sort of hoped you would say that, I am actually quite tired. It's all been very exciting, but I really don't sleep well away from you. If the exhibition goes well, perhaps you can come with me next time. We could leave Michael to keep an eye on the house and if it's at the weekend, Richard can do the farm. As well, the horses are all turned out and Rachel can look after them.

Oh, no, not Michael again. What am I going to do? Naturally, Rosie didn't voice this but realised she would need to do something soon about the situation with Michael. As she drove up to the house Rosie had a brief feeling of remorse, but beneath this she knew her feelings for Michael were still strong.

'Great to be home darling. Let's open that bottle and I have a present to give you as well as all the news. Do you want to ask Michael to join us?' It was the last thing she wanted! 'No, just you and me!' she replied hastily. 'Let's go into the sitting room whilst the fish pie finishes off in the oven. Then you can tell me all about London and we can drink some champagne. 'Fine, Rosie, we'll ask Michael round later. I want to ask his opinion about my next step with the gallery.'

'First, though, here's a small present I bought for you in London.' He smiled proudly as Rosie went into the distinctive blue bag and pulled out a tissue-wrapped small parcel. 'Oh, Jamie, it's lovely!' The silver chain with its pearl drop and silver web around it was beautiful and, in fact, really suited her understated style. 'Put it on for me, please'. He did and she felt a warmth bordering on the sexual, which she had not experienced with Jamie since the start of her affair with Michael. He kissed the nape of her neck then poured the champagne. Rosie took a deep sip and, using the excuse of checking on lunch went briefly into the kitchen really to compose herself.

'Well, the London gallery want to stage my first exhibition with them in November when they unexpectedly have a vacant slot. As you know, galleries plan their exhibitions a year ahead of time, but the artist whose work was going up then has been taken ill and is going to have major surgery so I've taken the chance and said yes! The downside is I am going to need more help with the farm and it might be we have to cut back on the horse side of things, unless Richard can take more of that on and we can get a really good assistant permit holder. Anyway, I'm sure it can all be sorted out later. Right now I want to enjoy our lunch and then we might have to have a rest!'

Rosie didn't want to say 'no' but neither was she sure she could cope with going from Michael to Jamie to have a sexual encounter in the space of less than twenty-four hours. She took a gulp of her champagne, placed her hand in Jamie's hand and went upstairs.

In contrast to the feverish couplings with Michael, she found the gentle lovemaking, resulting from their many years of compatibility, easier than it might have been. But the face she saw when she closed her eyes at the moment of climax was not Jamie's but Michael's.

Almost immediately, the bedside telephone rang. It was Michael. Jamie answered the call.' Thanks, Michael. I got on really well. In fact, I'm thrilled. It will be hard work getting everything ready in time. Luckily I've got quite a number of paintings Oscar wants to exhibit but I reckon three or four more will round off "Border Scenes". Supper this evening? But what about the sermon? Already finished? You must have been working very hard. I'm sure Rosie would like to come. I'll just ask her. Darling, Michael wants us both to go for supper this evening, is that alright with you?' What could she do but agree? 'Well, that's very kind of Michael. We'll take some wine, shall we? Did he say what time? 'There's no evening service so he suggested six o'clock which sounds about right.'

'Darling' she said, trying to sound very natural, 'I think whilst you unpack and either put your feet up or go and see the sheep I'll go round to the Lodge and see Richard and Polly, though I expect the children may be out with the ponies. I know Richard wants to sort out the other horses, but he can talk to you himself about that.'

'I'll go and check on things outside, though I'm sure everything will be okay. Then I'll join you for a cup of tea with Richard and Polly, before we go off to Michael for supper'. 'Sounds like a plan' she replied trying to sound nonchalant, but I don't think we want to have a particularly late night!' Jamie grinned: 'Not if this afternoon is anything to go by!' She just smiled.

When Rosie reached the Lodge, she found only Polly there. 'Come in, Ma, you must be psychic I was just about to call you. Where's Dad? 'Gone to look at the sheep.' 'Now, why am I not surprised? Anyway, come into the kitchen and we can have some tea and a catch-up.' *If only you knew*, Rosie thought. 'I'm sorry everyone's out. Richard is talking to the couple who are interested in renting the Pele Tower if they can rent a field for their horses and use a couple of loose boxes down here. John and Minty are out on the ponies. Rachel's with them so they'll be quite safe, before you ask!'

Rosie felt uncomfortable. What if Polly, and indeed her own mother, Betty suspected something about Michael? Well, she would simply emphasise the friendship between Jamie and Michael and laugh off any suggestion of involvement with Michael on her part except for being pleased Jamie had found a new friend. Everyone seemed to have forgotten the close friendship between Roddy, Jamie's father, and Jamie. After all it was only three months since Roddy's untimely death from heart failure. Why shouldn't Jamie enjoy the company of an intelligent, educated and at times humorous man? What she and Michael did, was, of course, quite different. As Polly poured the tea, Rosie took a very deep breath.

Polly didn't waste any time. 'Mum, do you think you and Michael Martin are seeing, well, a bit too much of each other?' Rosie felt herself blushing a little. 'What do you mean? Yes, I like him and he is a good friend for Dad, so it's a very nice relationship we all have.' Even to her ears it sounded rather lame, but she persevered. 'And what about you and Richard? Is everything working out for you both?' *Tables neatly turned,* Rosie thought.

Polly made a face, trying to appear inscrutable, but really looked quite cross. She sighed. 'Well, Mum, we are trying, but honestly, if it weren't for the children, I don't think we would still be together. I really did fall in love with David. I mean it wasn't just physical. But Richard has made it pretty clear if it came to it he would divorce me, name David and try for custody of John and Minty!' Glad to have moved away from her own situation with Michael, Rosie gave her daughter a sympathetic hug. 'Darling, I think you have made a wise decision. Though I must admit I never thought Richard would be so tough!'

At that moment, Richard arrived, closely followed by the twins. John, as usual was jumping up and down with excitement. 'Hello, Gran. We had a race on the ponies and Snowball and I won!' As ever, Minty's greeting was more sedate. 'Oh, Gran he's exaggerating as usual, but it was fun and my leg didn't hurt at all.' Rosie hugged both her lovely grandchildren and gave Richard both a beaming smile and a cuddle. 'Hello, mother-in-law, what's all this? A love-in?' But Rosie could tell he was pleased.

'Well I've just met Geoffrey and Pauline West. They seem a very nice, sensible couple. Geoffrey works in IT and has a six-month assignment in Edinburgh. So wily old Alistair has wangled it with Betty and they are going to rent the Tower and Geoffrey is going to commute. Pauline will be here pretty well full-time and will look after the horses and help too, with ours!

'What does Betty think about all this?' Jamie asked. 'I honestly don't know,' replied Richard, but he must have sorted it out with her, and Madeleine was never going to settle there, so I think it's best to assume everything has been agreed. Plus we won't have them hanging round here much with Madeleine playing the Lady of the Manor.'

John came into the kitchen which was still in the process of being modernised, 'Minty and I are hungry. Mummy, Any chance of tea?' With this the party broke up and Rosie and Jamie went off together to have supper at the manse with Michael – without mentioning this to the family. They had left the dogs at home and would walk them later.

'Are you sure you're not too tired?' Rosie asked. 'No, I'm getting my second wind, I think and anyway Michael's making a special Indian curry for us and we don't want to let him down.' She couldn't think of another excuse and, anyway, she wanted to see Michael too though it would be hard to remain casual with him in front of Jamie. 'Right,' said her husband, 'don't want to keep Michael waiting'.

As they drew up outside the manse Rosie could smell curry. During his time in India Michael had perfected how to make curry. For no logical reason, she felt a chill running through her.

They enjoyed an excellent authentic curry with warm poppadums, nan bread and yoghurt and cucumber salad. Rosie chose to drink white wine whilst Jamie stuck to low alcohol beer as he would be driving back to Whitewalls. 'That was delicious Michael,' Rosie said and thinking it safe in front of her husband, kissed him lightly on the cheek.

'I've something to tell you both. I had a telephone call earlier asking me if I would consider going to Mumbai for two or three months to sort out a problem. The John Wilson college there was started after independence and has a good number of students. Robin Seaton is a senior lecturer and he's got one of these stomach bugs. I'm pretty immune, so that's why they've asked me to help out for a couple of months. George Taylor from Peebles, helped by Robin Seaton, who is studying divinity in Edinburgh, will look after the church and as many events as possible. I wonder if either or both of you would be willing to help?'

Jamie was quick to answer 'I'm sure we can. I've nearly finished painting for the London exhibition and the new farm manager, Giles, is shaping up really well .'What about you, Rosie?' 'Are you coming back?' she asked. Michael smiled warmly at her. 'Of course, home for Christmas, if not before.' 'Then I'll be happy to do what I can. Maybe Polly can help too.' Her heart was beating fast but she hoped she looked calm.

'When do you leave?' asked Jamie, practical as ever. There was a brief pause then Michael replied: 'In ten days' time so there's a lot to do before then.' 'Well, we'll all muck in and help. I can't say I'm thrilled at your going, but we'll make the best of it and I'm sure you'll sort things out and soon be back with us, where you belong, Now, Rosie, I think it's time we went home, and we'll see you tomorrow.' So the departure was fairly easy and Rosie had no time to dwell on the consequences of what was happening. When she and Jamie got home, he parked the car in the drive and said: 'I'll just get the dogs for a quick walk, then I think a brandy, a bath and bed. We'll start making plans tomorrow for whilst Michael is away and I'll tell you all about London.' Rosie managed to smile her assent and replied: 'Well at least I don't need to cook this evening.'

Rosie's head was spinning. Possibly this surprise move for Michael would help her to work out what her feelings for him really were and whether or not they were simply physical, or something more! By the time Jamie had returned and the dogs were settled, she was more composed.

Jamie poured two large glasses of brandy and threw some more logs on the fire. 'I was thinking whilst I was out there, we should throw a party for Michael next Saturday before he goes away. We'll have it here with all the family and open it to church members. We can ask Polly to do the catering and give him a good send-off. I really do like him and he's such a straightforward guy and there aren't too many about like him. What do you think, darling?' Rosie thought it was the last thing she wanted but couldn't think of a reason to say no. 'Why don't I phone Michael in the morning and see if this would appeal to him? Maybe he won't want any fuss and it's too late to call him now, she said.'

'Good idea, Rosie. Right, drink up and we'll go and have that bath and say hello to each other properly. I've really missed you, especially when you went to stay with Hughie and Ginny!' Again her heart turned over. Perhaps Jamie would be too tired to make love, but he wasn't. At the moment her husband climaxed, she closed her eyes and thought, not of England or any other country, as the saying goes, but of her lover.

Rosie was up and about early the next morning and, after taking Empress out round the garden, sat outside with a cup of coffee and her mobile phone. Jamie was out with the Labradors, Tweed and Heather, and would soon be back for breakfast. She picked up the phone and dialled Michael. 'I am going to miss you so much, but the reason, or one of them, I am calling you now is to see if you like the idea of a big party here next Saturday with all the family and people from the church too.' There was a brief pause. 'That's a lovely idea, Rosie, and kind of you to think of asking church members. One condition though.' 'What's that?' 'You and I have an afternoon together when Jamie goes into Edinburgh tomorrow to see his agent.' 'Lovely, could be tricky but we'll manage. I'll have to go, Jamie is coming back for breakfast. 'Bye darling.' The conversation ended just as her husband returned with the two bouncing dogs to head to the kitchen where Rosie went to prepare his usual bacon and eggs.

'Did you phone Michael?' he asked. 'Yes and he's very pleased at the idea. In fact he's coming here to talk right away so I'll get onto Polly and do a ring round everyone. We'll put a notice up on the board outside the church so people will know to come. I thought three o'clock until six would be about right.' Jamie always enjoyed his cooked breakfast whilst Rosie just had her usual wholemeal toast. Michael accepted the offer of a bacon sandwich, then they began to discuss plans. 'As it's a week on Saturday, why don't the three of us have a planning meeting at the manse tomorrow afternoon?' Michael asked with every appearance of innocence, knowing Jamie would be away. 'Good idea, but I can't come. Rosie you can though. I have to go into Edinburgh to see my agent and I want to go and see Polly and the children so I don't know when I'll be back.' 'Well, I had better get back to the manse. 'And I'll start phoning round and make some lists' said Rosie, reverting to the ways she had always run her busy life so efficiently, until now. So the three went off to continue their days. Michael gave Rosie a light kiss on the cheek and left. Jamie spoke to her. 'I'll just go and check the top field, back at lunchtime. There's a lot to do!' He kissed his wife gently, put on his Barbour waistcoat and left.

The following ten days passed in a whirl of activity for everyone. Polly was in a good mood, especially when her father said he would pay for the food she was going to prepare for the party to wish Michael well with his trip to Mumbai. When the word got round people offered to supply wine. They all agreed the best time would be on Sunday after morning service with everyone in the congregation invited and family friends too. Putting up a couple of gazebos in case the weather was poor was accomplished by Richard, with, naturally, help from John who loved being with his father in the country.

It did not take Michael long to pack and put together bibles and prayer books for his trip. Rosie and he managed to see each other on a number of occasions, always at the manse. One afternoon, as they lay coiled in each other's arms in a bed now as familiar to Rosie as her own, she said. 'Michael: I am going to miss you so much. I want to come with you'. He kissed her deeply with great passion and love, but said: 'My darling, that is simply not possible now. I'm coming back just before Christmas and if we both feel the same then, maybe we can find a way of being together. But you would have to be very, very sure as it wouldn't be easy.'

The Sunday of the party was warm with September sunshine. Whilst Polly, Richard and young friends from Edinburgh as well as the new occupants of the Pele Tower got the food and drink organised, Jamie and Rosie went to church. It was very difficult for her and she hoped she wouldn't cry. She came very close to doing so as Michael based his sermon on the text ' Now abide faith, hope and love, and the greatest of these is love.' Then she realised he had chosen it deliberately to reassure her of his own deep and genuine feelings.

The marquee outside Whitewalls was crowded, not only with friends of the Douglases, but also members of the congregation who, in the relatively brief time Michael had been there, had become very fond of him. They were not happy about his going away for almost three months, but in his short, sincere speech Jamie reassured everyone that Michael had given his word he would return after filling in for a time for a sick lecturer at the John Wilson College in Mumbai. 'Michael in the fairly short time we have had the pleasure of your reviving the church here and your being so kind and helpful in the community, we absolutely insist you return, even if I have to come and fetch you myself.' Rosie felt tears pricking behind her eyes and at this she and Michael looked briefly at each other, then looked away. Briefly, Rosie was overcome by guilt as, indeed was Michael, then the moment passed.

Polly had excelled herself with the buffet and Mrs Morrison who did the flowers in the church had made a huge cake for the occasion with the words 'Haste ye back' on the top. People had brought wine and canapés so there was no shortage of food and drink.

Then Jamie tapped his glass with a spoon and called for

silence. 'Michael is going to say a few words now.' Michael who, in truth, was never short of words, as befitted a minister paused before he spoke. Everyone became quiet. Rosie looked straight at Michael who returned her look with a smile. She hoped nobody had noticed.

'I simply want to thank the whole family, especially Polly, Rosie and Jamie for making this lovely party so memorable and enjoyable. Also to say to the congregation even though I will be a long way away, I will know you are keeping the faith and recruiting new members to our church. In order to keep in touch with you I propose to see if I can send news to you over the Internet. Before you even notice I have gone, I shall be back. I'm very grateful to Robin Seaton here for taking time out from university where he has almost finished his degree in divinity, for helping to hold the fort, which I know he will do extremely well.' Everyone clapped and Robin briefly stepped forward and thanked Michael for his encouraging words.

After this the party gradually ended and people left feeling replete and even inspired.

Jamie invited Michael, Polly and Richard as well as Minty and John to go back to Whitewalls. Polly and Rosie did some clearing away, but Polly said to her mother: 'Let's leave the rest, Molly is bringing her sister along tomorrow to help finish off. Richard is in charge of taking down the marquee but the weather forecast is good so it's safe enough to leave it. Rosie agreed. She was feeling tired and beginning to feel depressed at the thought of losing Michael. 'Mum, I think you like Michael very much, don't you?' 'Well, yes, he's very likeable and he and Dad get on so well. Also he's encouraged Dad to be more ambitious with the painting and get this London exhibition off the ground.

Polly refrained from asking any more questions and, understanding what her mother was feeling, linked arms with her as they strolled back to the house. 'I'm dying to sit down and take my shoes off and you must be tired out, Polly. You've worked so hard' 'Mum, when everyone's gone, could we have a talk? I'm really in a quandary about Richard. He's becoming more and more insistent and I think he wants us all to move down here from Edinburgh and he would commute as well as driving the children in to school every day.' Rosie thought quickly. She was really hoping to have even a small amount of time with Michael, somehow, and they had still to decide who was driving Michael to the airport in Edinburgh to begin his long journey to Mumbai the next day.

'Darling, why don't you go and relax with Richard and have a good talk after the children have gone to bed? I mean it might be, if he is serious about this commuting business, you stay in Edinburgh during the week and all get together either there or down here at the weekends?'

Polly wasn't sure how much or how little her mother knew but sensed then was not the right time for the talk she so badly needed. Then Rosie had an idea. 'Why don't you go back to Edinburgh as you've planned tomorrow and I'll get in touch? We can have a nice girls' lunch together and see what we can come up with?' 'Ma that's a good idea. I am tired after all this, and I know you and Dad will want to say goodbye to Michael on your own.'

Rosie was relieved. She too was tired at the thought of Michael going away the next morning and knew already how much she was going to miss him. When she caught up with the men Jamie piped up: 'Well, I don't know about either of you, but I think we all deserve a nice brandy. Come on, let's go inside I'll take the dogs out for a bit and Rosie can keep you entertained!'

Once Jamie had taken the dogs out for a run Rosie and Michael went into the sitting room. As if he had been doing it for years Michael put some logs on the fire which immediately sprang into life. So did they! Then Jamie came back with the dogs and a suggestion. 'Michael, I'm assuming you've packed and are ready to go tomorrow. So why don't you just stay the night, and Rosie and I will drive you to the airport in the morning after we've collected your things?' Rosie and Michael hardly dared to look at each other. It was not an ideal situation but Jamie seemed set on the idea, so they agreed.

Michael was flying to London then on to Mumbai with Virgin airlines and it was not a particularly early start. Neither Michael nor Rosie could think of any convincing reason why this plan would not work. Well, they had a reason, but not one they could mention - sleeping under the same roof but not in the same bed! So, after another large brandy each Rosie went into the kitchen and popped the shepherd's pie she had made earlier into the Aga and told the men she was going upstairs to get the best spare room ready for Michael. 'Get Michael to go up with you and you can remind him where everything is, said Jamie' They both agreed to Jamie's suggestion with great alacrity, knowing this was the last time they could be alone together for the next three months. 'Don't be too long, though. I'm getting hungry for the shepherd's pie,' Jamie added.

Rosie and Michael went quickly upstairs and into the spare room. No explanations were needed but they kissed passionately and he said: 'It won't be easy, but we can keep in touch with texts and email, and when I come back we will need to talk seriously about the future.' This rather scared Rosie, and instead of agreeing or disagreeing, she kissed Michael again. 'We'd better go downstairs. There's no point in spoiling everything now.' she said' So they did and managed a kitchen supper, helped by a bottle of Merlot and casual conversation. They were all tired and Rosie announced she was going up to bed. Both men kissed her goodnight and she left the kitchen as quickly as she could.

Much to her surprise, she went to sleep quickly and slept soundly until the small hours of the morning when she started to think again. Jamie was beside her, snoring gently and Michael through the wall was also lying awake and thinking of the future. Eventually they both slept again and soon the autumn sunlight was shining through the windows.

The morning passed in a swift blur. The men went off to the manse after breakfast to load up Michael's luggage for Mumbai. Rosie, who despite her whirling feelings was not capable of leaving it in the kitchen sink, did the washing up. It gave her something to do. The phone rang. It was Polly. 'Hi, Mum. How are you after yesterday? What a party! We're all about to leave for Edinburgh. When am I going to see you for our talk?' Rosie thought quickly. 'Well, we're taking Michael to the airport. I'll find out what Dad is doing next. He and Michael have gone to get things organised at the manse.' Polly thought her mother sounded over-bright but didn't comment except to say: Well, give me a call later and we'll fix on a date for our girlie lunch!' So there was another issue postponed.

They drove in to Edinburgh airport on the west side of the city with Classic FM playing quietly in the background on the car radio, but little conversation. To her surprise, instead of a brief stop at the dropping-off point, Jamie drove into the short stay-car park. He said to Michael 'We can't just dump you like a parcel. Both of us want to see you safely on your way.' So the departure was prolonged until Michael had checked in for his flight. He then hugged Rosie and kissed her warmly on both cheeks before shaking Jamie by the hand then, oddly, hugging him. 'Try and keep in touch, we'll miss you!' said Jamie. And Michael was gone - for now.

'Do you want to go into the city centre, Rosie?' 'Not really' She felt sad, drained even. Perhaps Jamie was more perceptive than she thought. 'Tell you what, you're always looking after other people, cooking, organising and being a lovely wife. Why don't we go home but have lunch at Peebles Hydro on the way?' She smiled at her husband. He returned her smile in the boyish way she had always found attractive. 'I'd like that.' The only other reference to Michael was over lunch when Jamie said: 'You'll miss Michael, we both will but I think he'll come back before we know it.' Maybe Jamie knew, after all. No, he couldn't, surely?

Rosie and Jamie enjoyed lunch in the traditional surroundings of the hotel dining room which they both knew so well and they quickly relaxed. It was almost as if the last few months had not happened.

London - The Mews Flat

Maggie was at her London mews flat having some time off from the hectic filming schedule for the film 'the Minister Who Lied' being largely made at High Wynch Park in the Cotswolds.

She saw her mobile phone was blinking and quickly opened the message. It was from Charles. 'Back safely, with you in half an hour.' Maggie burst into tears but they were of happiness! How did he know where she was? Of course he must have contacted Ginny and Hughie at High Wynch Park and been told she had gone to London.

Soon she heard the door key turn downstairs and then the sound of the love of her life running up them towards her. Charles was out of uniform, clearly unhurt, well-dressed and looking, for all the world, as if he was ready to go out for dinner, which he was.

'Darling, when did you get back? Where have you been? You were still away last week!' These questions and many more kept spilling out from Maggie until Charles stopped her from talking with another deep kiss, holding her tightly at the same time. 'Come on. We're going to Luigi's for dinner, then back here. I want to make love to you all night long!'

They quickly found a taxi just outside and were on their way to begin talking, celebrating and making plans. Luigi greeted them like old friends and, taking only one look, realised this was going to be a major celebration so ushered them to a discreet table, already lit with candles. Next he produced a bottle of champagne announcing: 'This is on the house.' Before they could protest he had started to pour the champagne so they toasted him with thanks.

After a lovely meal and the rest of the champagne, they could wait no longer to be together, alone again. Again, as if intended, a taxi was outside the restaurant door and they sped back to the mews. Over dinner Charles had relayed as much information as he could do - apart from the messages he had managed to send – while away- about his last, mercifully brief tour in Afghanistan. He would have to rejoin his Regiment for another six months before he could leave and begin a new civilian life. These plans, however, could wait. Maggie went into the bedroom, leaving Charles sipping a brandy. She drew the curtains, put on the soft-glow bedside lamps and had a quick shower, pulled on her silk dressing gown and went back into the sitting room. Charles leaped to his feet, put down the glass and drew her with a mixture of gentleness and passion into the bedroom and the soft, downy bed. This was not, of course, the first time they had shared such deep love and passion but it was very special and eventually they both slept, satiated and in love, their bodies wound round each other in perfect harmony.

The next morning Charles and Maggie woke up feeling languid but also wanting to plan what they would do next. She had four days off from filming and they decided on a long but potentially very happy trip around the country.

They had decided to phone round the family immediately after a breakfast of fresh orange juice, croissants and some pretty strong coffee. 'Could we do the long drive to Scotland first, to Whitewalls, so we can let Ma and Pa be the first to know?' Charles asked. Maggie thought this was a great idea and agreed. 'Then,' she said, 'we can make our way back stopping at the grandparents at Manor House Farm and then back to High Wynch Park. I'll then need to go on filming and you will probably be going back to the regiment for a while anyway.' And so it was agreed.

Although it would be a long drive they had been thrilled at the warm response from Charles' family, especially his parents and Nigel and Florette had been equally delighted to hear the good news. Nigel had enough sense, as well as tact, to say nothing to Charles about his future plans although he would be delighted if Charles accepted his offer to go into partnership at Manor House Farm. Already Nigel had offered to pay for an accelerated farm management course to bring Charles up to date on farming methods and management.

It was a long drive but the miles seemed to fly by so quickly they hardly noticed and apart from pulling in to a motorway café for coffee and a sandwich they didn't stop. Neither did they talk very much. Maggie drove for part of the way but stopped a few miles before they reached the Scottish border. There Charles got out his mobile phone and rang his mother. 'Hello Ma, we won't be long now. Yes, I'm fine and so is Maggie. We're really looking forward to seeing you all.'

Rosie had hurriedly organised the family to come to Whitewalls for an early supper. She knew both Charles and Maggie would be tired, but Richard, Polly and the children were at the Lodge for the weekend and it was easy for the Prendergasts to come round. Then Jamie said something which unwittingly jolted Rosie out of her mildly euphoric state. 'What a pity Michael's already left, I know he would have loved to meet them.'

More sharply than she intended, Rosie replied 'Well, he has gone so that can't happen- not right now anyway.' Puzzled by this answer but in a way rightly thinking his wife was worked up about the flying visit of her darling son and Maggie, he thought nothing more about it.

By the time the crunch of gravel heralded the arrival, everyone was ready to dash out and give the warmest welcome they could, which was not difficult. So the couple got out of the car to a melee of family, including dogs. After hugs and kisses all round, Jamie took charge again. 'Right now, come on in. You must be exhausted!' In a way they were, but also buoyed up by the sheer warmth of the welcome.

Rosie said: 'Spare bedroom all made up and there's time for showers before we have drinks and early supper.' Charles kissed his mother warmly and they went into the comfortable room which Rosie had prepared, with stacks of white towels and matching white dressing gowns, for all the world like being in a luxury spa, but better.

Soon they were back downstairs into the sitting room where everyone apart from John and Minty, who had gone to feed their ponies, was gathered. Jamie expertly opened the first bottle of well-chilled champagne. They drank a toast to the very happy couple and John Prendergast collared Charles with a few, but not obtrusive questions about Afghanistan and the campaign there. John and Minty came dashing in and Rosie ushered everyone into the kitchen, announcing supper was ready.

It was a happy meal and a sense of contentment prevailed. Then Jamie started talking again about Michael and how much he valued their friendship. Rosie said nothing but Polly and her grandmother, Lady Betty, exchanged meaningful glances. Richard and Polly at the same moment looked at each other and she wondered whether it would be worth giving in to David's ever-growing pressure to get a divorce when she already had so much and Richard appeared to have forgiven her past infidelity.

Sunday morning meant an early start for the next leg of Charles and Maggie's journey round the country needed. With lots of hugs and kisses and 'see you again soon', the happy couple left with a picnic hamper in the boot thoughtfully prepared for them by Rosie. Although Molly's full-time housekeeping duties were over because of semi-retirement, she still came at weekends and was there to take part in the 'launch' party. She had always been very fond of Charles and whilst not too sure about his choice of an actress to be his wife, she too had been won over by the way in which they clearly adored each other and gave her important seal of approval to the match!

Yorkshire – Manor House Farm

Charles and Maggie took turns to drive to Yorkshire. Although the route was longer they avoided the A1 and took the rural A697 stopping near Alnwick to have their picnic. As well as sandwiches and one of her famous quiches, Rosie had included a flask of creamy soup and one of coffee, with fruit to follow. 'I can't understand why you're all not as fat as pigs the way your lovely mother feeds everyone up, Charles' 'I think it's one of the ways she shows her love, but we've always been a very active family and walking dogs, riding horses, gardening and playing tennis have all helped.'

Not wanting to arrive at Manor House Farm too late they finished lunch, repacked the basket, shook the grass off the tartan rug and set off for Nigel and Florette's Manor House Farm. It was a working farm on the outskirts of a small Yorkshire village and also the hub of Florette's mail order company. She sold luxury cashmere clothes and scarves. She had done this even before she met and married Nigel. Her first husband, Francois with whom she had lived in France, died suddenly, leaving her with not quite enough money to survive in comfort. Once her business had become successful, Florette was able to buy the mews house in London for Maggie, whose parents had sadly both been killed in a car crash.

They arrived at the farm around four o'clock to a very warm welcome both from Nigel and Florette as well as assorted dogs which milled down the steps, but being well-trained, did not jump up.

'Darlings how lovely to see you,' cried Florette. 'Did you have a bad journey?' Without waiting for an answer, she swept the pair inside after hugging them both. As ever, Nigel was more restrained but just as welcoming. 'So pleased with your good news and, Charles, just as much for your safe return – brave but unhurt I believe. Charles almost winced at this. So many of his comrades had been hurt, some of them fatally, and he really didn't want to talk about his time in Afghanistan. Nigel understood perfectly and did not return to the topic. Following afternoon tea, Charles and Maggie went upstairs to their comfortable room to have a rest and bath before 6 p.m. drinks in the library.

When they arrived downstairs, Charles was not altogether surprised to see Peter and Gillian there for drinks. He had a shrewd idea this was part of Nigel's plan to get him to take up a career in farming once he left the army, though during a very convivial hour or so the subject was not mentioned. They brought their lovely, well-behaved children with them and, as Nigel had hoped, the idea of his going into partnership with him at Manor House Farm was beginning to appeal to Charles. Florette, who knew her husband better than anyone wisely did not comment on this but left it to Nigel to choose the best moment. The visitors did not stay for very long and over dinner it was Charles, not Nigel, who raised the subject of the proposed partnership.

'I'll need to make some enquiries about agricultural college but I think they do an accelerated course at Cirencester or even somewhere nearer,' Charles said. Nigel had already rehearsed his answer. 'Do you know, Charles, I don't really think you will need to do that. I reckon with all your army experience plus everything you've learned from your father and growing up at Whitewalls, if you decide to do this, that should be enough. Anyway, think about it.' Maggie had been quiet during this conversation but simply said: 'Thanks so much for this. What Charles and I will need to discuss is our future once he leaves the army, which is still a few months away. Right now I am so glad to have my darling safe home from Afghanistan.' Stifling a yawn, she then said: 'Would you mind awfully if we went up to bed now? It's been a long day and we'll be here tomorrow before we go to High Wynch Park.' With hugs and kisses all round, the evening came to a very happy conclusion and the couple who were by now very tired went up to bed and soon slept in each others' arms.

'I'll just take the dogs out if you want to go up, darling.' Nigel said to his wife. I think we've sown enough seeds at least to get Charles and Maggie to think about the plan. I'll see you upstairs! Florette laughed. 'Is that meant to be a pun about the seeds?' Nigel laughed too, gave his wife quick hug and kiss and went out with the dogs which, by now, were becoming impatient for their ritual evening walk.

Charles and Maggie would not did not have so far to drive next morning to reach High Wynch Park where they would have a couple more days before she began filming again and he rejoined his regiment for a final three months. so breakfast was a relaxed affair. 'How about staying another night, then leaving early tomorrow morning'? Nigel enquired. Whilst Maggie suspected this might be part of a plan already discussed between Florette and Nigel, she and Charles were happy with the idea.

'I'll go and phone Ginny and tell them about the change of plan. She won't mind a bit'. Maggie said. Charles dressed casually in full expectation of Nigel wanting to take him round the estate. He was right. 'If you're not too busy, Nigel, could we take the dogs and go out round the estate again.' This was exactly what Nigel had hoped would happen. So, collecting the assorted dogs, the two men pulled on wellington boots and set off

'Let's have some fresh coffee'. This was Florette who wanted to quiz her step-grand-daughter about both the engagement and future plans. So, over freshly brewed coffee they sat at the kitchen table and talked. Florette said: 'Darling you must be so very happy to have Charles back unscathed and now you can make plans. Has he given you the ring yet?' Maggie laughed 'We're going to choose it together in London and if all goes well I know Charles would absolutely love us to get married around Christmas time or early in the New Year at Whitewalls – as long as you don't mind coming up to Scotland for the wedding.'

She looked anxious for a moment but her naturally sunny character re-surfaced especially after a loving hug from Florette who then wisely said: 'Of course we don't mind. Last time Nigel really liked Charles' parents, in fact both of us did. Now come and pick something from the latest collection'. Which is just what they did. Maggie found a lovely, soft, pale green sweater which really suited her colouring and soon it was lunchtime and the men and dogs reappeared.

Whilst they had been out, Charles had not said very much to Nigel but he began to feel the possibility of making a future from farming in partnership with the older man and had already started to see things he would like to do, including getting sheep to use some of the free pasture land.

In the early evening the 'boys' as Florette called them visited the village pub where Nigel was not only well-known but also very popular with the locals. After a couple of pints of Yorkshire beer, Nigel and Charles strolled back to the farm with the dogs. Wisely, Nigel didn't mention again future plans for the partnership and neither did Charles. Instead they spoke of Maggie's career and the positive way in which it was developing. Charles volunteered some information about his time in Afghanistan but did not dwell on his experiences.

After very convivial drinks again in the library while talking about a range of subjects from politics to films and the theatre, the four of them – without the neighbours this time – enjoyed another dinner of salmon, spinach and new potatoes, Béarnaise sauce, followed by late strawberries, then cheese. Because they intended to have an early start on the next leg of their journey south, Charles and Maggie decided to miss coffee and have a relatively early night. With all the passion of a young couple who had been separated for some time, they made very satisfying love and drifted to sleep in each other's arms.

All too soon it was seven o'clock in the morning and they

packed, had quick showers and went downstairs for breakfast. Light-hearted and fond farewells were the hallmark of Charles and Maggie's departure to drive to the final destination of the long journey round the country for them to share in person the good news of Charles' safe return from Afghanistan and his official engagement to Maggie. She felt so happy to be an 'official' member of this fascinating family with all its up and downs, people and places from Scotland to France and back again.

Nigel hugged them both and kissed Maggie. He said quietly and briefly to Charles: 'You're part of us now whatever you decide to do after the army.' Charles smiled warmly. Florette kissed them and said: 'Drive carefully, and call us when you arrive at Hugh and Ginny's.'

Maggie and Charles were quiet on the journey south. The roads were not busy and they arrived at High Wynch Park in good time and they received the same warmth of welcome as already shown by the other members of the extended family.

With all the activity at Hughie and Ginny's house including film-making occupying large areas of the grounds as well as part of the public rooms, and little Fleur growing rapidly, some of the glamour of the lovely Elizabethan mansion had become diminished. But there was an improvement in the ambience and Hughie, whose lack of financial acumen had led to serious losses in the past, was a happy man, especially since Ginny's 'late baby had softened her previous imperious manner. Hughie and Ginny were happier than they had ever been and even their grown-up children had taken to the late addition to the family.

So after they arrived Charles and Maggie fended for themselves with their usual room and en-suite. By the time pre-dinner drinks in the library came round order, had been restored and Ginny announced in honour of their guests and dinner would be in the dining room with a cook brought in for the evening. Hughie had splashed out on Dom Perignon so they could drink a toast to Charles and

Maggie.

'What's it like being a mum again, Ginny?' Maggie was genuinely curious as both she and Charles had discussed the subject of starting a family although they had decided to wait a while after their wedding. Ginny was about to answer when Brigitte, the Norwegian nanny, brought Fleur into the room before putting her to bed. After the baby had been duly admired, Maggie looked at Hughie and said: 'she really does look like you, I mean, lovely blue eyes, rosy cheeks and curly hair and the sweetest smile.' Hughie was delighted with Maggie's words and Ginny smiled very brightly with an inner sense of great relief. Her brief affair with Anthony had not, after all have resulted in his fathering Fleur, which he had always denied in any case!

Maggie and Charles were ready to go to London again as Maggie had a few more days off before filming continued – at least the scenes in which she was needed the doorbell rang. It was Anthony Goodman and Piers Romayne. Maggie noticed Ginny went pale and then began flapping around. Fortunately a delightfully unsuspicious Hughie went forward, shook both men warmly by the hand and said: 'This is an unexpected pleasure. Come into the library and we can have a chat.' Anthony strode across the kitchen and gave Ginny a kiss on either cheek, which flustered her even more. 'You look absolutely blooming, my dear. Clearly, motherhood suits you!' Piers simply gave her a hug and the men left the hallway with Hughie offering the visitors coffee which Brigitte was then asked to make.

It transpired they were very pleased with the way the film was progressing and one of the larger film distributors in the United States had shown interest to Piers in distributing the finished film. He explained: The Americans love anything to do with British political scandal and with this development on top of the interest already shown here at home we stand to make a lot of money.' Then it was Anthony's turn. 'So I've decided I can increase my investment as and when it becomes necessary'. Hughie's faced was wreathed with smiles and just at that moment Brigitte came in with the beautifully laid coffee tray as well as chocolate biscuits. After this Anthony and Piers left, closely followed by Charles and Maggie.

The two visitors shook Charles warmly by the hand 'Jolly glad you're back in one piece Charles. I'm so proud of what you had to do in Afghanistan.. I hope you and this beautiful girl get properly hitched as soon as you can'. Anthony said Charles answered briefly, but politely 'Thank you sir, and yes, we will.' So they went their separate ways. After they had gone, Ginny's relief was enormous and she started humming as she went about her daily routine.

Chapter 12

Whitewalls

Rosie was restless. Jamie, once again, was away in London making the final arrangements for the London exhibition taking place in November. These days he left much of the work on the farm to Tommy, the farm manager. She missed her husband but also yearned for Michael whose three month secondment to college in Mumbai felt as if it would last for ever, even though he had not long departed! She hadn't heard from him, which made it worse.

Richard, whilst commuting daily to Edinburgh with Geoffrey West, was staying at the Lodge. Polly had based herself in Edinburgh with the children and both she and Richard came with Minty and John to the estate each Friday for the weekend. The children certainly really enjoyed this arrangement, particularly John who spent a good deal of energy as well as time with the ponies, Snowball and Butterball. Rosie really hoped the David Mclean affair between her daughter and the charming, but ruthless self-made man was over. However, since her own entirely unexpected entanglement with Michael understood much more than before how it had happened.

During this reverie, so rare in her busy life, Rosie had been sitting at the kitchen table nursing her second cup of strong coffee, again unusual for her, when the telephone rang. This took her out of her introspection. It was Lady Betty. Certainly after divorcing her rascally former husband, Sir Alistair, she had acquired many friends but no special man in her life and Beatrice, John's late wife, had been a special friend. Betty had spent much of her life painting and had greatly encouraged her son-in-law with his art. She had told him: 'You can't just spend all your time farming. Let's see if you have any talent with art. He had and loved it, as well as being successful with his beautiful landscapes of the Borders countryside.

'Hi Rosie,' Betty said 'are you very busy?'

'No, Ma, for once I don't have anything I absolutely have to do!'

'Why not come to me for lunch? John has gone to have lunch and catch up with one of his old army friends at the Royal Scots Club in Edinburgh. I want to see you very much and, for once, make a fuss of you!'

'I'd love to come. What time?'

'Oh whenever you like. Around twelve? See you then. 'Bye darling.'

Rosie wasn't really sure she could be bothered, which was so unlike her but she gave herself a mental shake and went upstairs to change into something more respectable than her old comfortable cords and realised she hadn't seen her mother without other people around for a long time.

As she drove the short distance to Sticholme and her mother's home, where John had built a studio for her in the garden, she began to look forward to a gentle lunch with her mother. Little did she realise there might be an unexpected price to pay.

Betty, from whom Rosie had inherited her own highly developed sense of punctuality, was waiting at the front door of the bungalow she and John had transformed into a very attractive and comfortable home.

'Darling, you look a little peaky – and no wonder with all the running around after other people, including the minister as well as darling Jamie.'

'Oh, Ma, I'm fine but, yes, a little tired I guess and life has been very complicated recently.'

'I know darling Let's go and sit in the garden. It's sunny and quite warm still. I've made some lemonade and lunch is ready. It won't spoil whilst we have a chat.'

Rosie wondered if there had been a specific reason why her mother had mentioned Michael. Later, she discovered there was!

It was very pleasant for both women sitting in comfy

loungers in the well-tended garden with its studio in one corner. For once, Rosie had absolutely nothing she immediately needed to do. Then apparently from nowhere she realised how much she missed Michael. Was it because she heard her mother speak his name?

Betty gently raised the topic. 'Darling, forgive me if you think I am interfering in your personal life – because, yes, it's true!'

'What do you mean?' she had a defensive note in her voice.

'Well my love, it seems there is some strong attachment between you and Reverend Michael which, heaven forbid, I think could develop into something more and harm your marriage. You and Jamie from the very beginning have always seemed perfect for each other and so happy together. I think this would be very difficult now, especially since Richard and Polly's marriage seems to be on firmer ground after her relationship with that awful man Mclean. I never trusted him, smarming round Jamie, buying pictures and bribing the children. Anyway, let's finish talking about you. I am only saying all this because I love you dearly and think you are a wonderful daughter, wife and mother.'

Rosie knew she was blushing – something she never normally had cause to do. But she managed to produce a sturdy, if not an entirely truthful response. 'Jamie and Michael get on really well together and Michael has no family of his own so we've sort of adopted him.'

'Darling, please be careful. I could tell from the way you look at each other there is an attraction between you. If this hasn't already gone too far, don't let your feelings develop any further. There's too much to lose!'

Rosie then realised far from being judgemental her mother was being protective of her daughter, which, of course is how good mothers act.

'Thanks Ma, I'll be very careful, and when, or for that matter, if Michael comes back from Mumbai, I will leave the relationship between him and Jamie to return to what it was'. Rosie knew this was a somewhat ambiguous and not entirely truthful answer but it satisfied both women, for now.

'Come on. Let's go inside and have lunch in the kitchen. It's just a quiche and salad but at least I made the quiche myself and it will be a change for you from the constant cooking you do for everyone else.'

After the earlier tense conversation the two women relaxed, chatting about family and friends as well as children, particularly Minty's leg which was still causing her problems and the possible need for further surgery. Also Rosie asked to see her mother's studio and her latest pictures. They went back into the garden and the studio which John had provided for his new wife. Betty's style had always been bright and colourful, though perhaps the latest pictures were more restrained than her earlier work had been. Then Betty came up with a completely new and to each of them surprising idea.

'Darling, why don't you try some creative work yourself? I don't necessarily mean painting or drawing but what about writing – articles, short stories for magazines or even a novel?'

'Ma, I've never even considered anything like that. For one thing, I always seem to be busy, but thanks for the idea. I'll think about it. But now I'll leave you in peace and do some work in my garden, which is always soothing.'

The two women hugged and parted on warm, loving terms. As Rosie drove back to Whitewalls in a thoughtful mood she couldn't help picturing Michael. She really believed they loved each other but was it deep and real enough to be worth the inevitable destruction of her family and not least her long and happy, though sometimes eventful marriage? Then there was Michael's career to consider. Adultery was not included in the job description of a Church of Scotland minister.

As she drove up the gravel drive and parked at the door, a deep feeling of exhaustion hit her and far from

172

gardening she simply went inside, made a large china mug of Earl Grey tea and sat with it in the absolute peace of her own garden. It was Friday and Richard, Polly and the twins would be arriving soon so she could then stop being so tense and enjoy their company, make a meal for them and have an early night.

Rosie came out of her reverie in time to hear a car coming up the drive to the house. For a glorious minute she thought *Michael's come home*.

'Hi, Mum.' it was Polly! Rosie was pleased to see her daughter, who jumped out of the car and hugged her warmly. Already Rosie was standing outside the open car door and after the affectionate welcome they shared she began to feel better.

'Sorry, I've not organised anything yet for our meal this evening.'

'No need! We all want you to come to us at the Lodge and the twins are in great form and really looking forward to seeing you, without you dashing around looking after everyone else.' 'Rosie was delighted. 'Thanks, darling. I'll just lock up and I'll walk down with the dogs.' 'No, let's pop them in the back of the car and we'll take them with us! Richard can bring you back with you later and walk them too.'

A few minutes later they arrived at the Lodge to a tumultuous welcome from the twins. Richard was quieter but he was very fond of his mother-in-law who had been so supportive to him, especially over Polly's affair with David Maclean. That had been such a difficult time and there were still issues to be resolved. He gave Rosie a hug and kiss. 'Good to see you. You must be missing Jamie. When is he due back from London?'

'Tomorrow I'm going to meet him at the airport. His plane gets in mid-afternoon.' Immediately Richard suggested 'Why don't you both come to Murrayfield? I'll drive you back here with Geoffrey West. This commuting arrangement's working well so far though I know it's early days.'

'I'll speak to Jamie about it when I phone him this evening.' Rosie's mobile rang. She answered quickly, hoping irrationally it was Michael. It was Jamie and his familiar loving voice.

'Darling, are you alright? I rang the house phone but it went straight to the answerphone.' 'I'm fine at the Lodge with Polly, Richard and the twins as well as dogs and even Buttons! Richard has just suggested a plan for tomorrow. Here, have a word with him and he can explain it.' She passed her mobile to Richard. Jamie told him: 'That's very kind of you but I'm keen to get home and away from cities, even Edinburgh, as well as missing my darling wife. See you all at the weekend.' Richard handed the phone back to Rosie. 'Can you get Polly to stay overnight with you? It's a pity Michael's away or I'd have got him to take care of you'. Rosie felt her face colouring up and hoped nobody noticed. Polly did but made no comment.

'Come and stay with us in our house soon'. This was Minty, John joined in: 'Yes, please, please do, Gran I've some new model planes I've made and I want to show you.' 'Of course I will, darlings, once Grandpapa isn't away so much, but we'll all go to London for the start of his big art exhibition in November'

Mother and daughter managed to relax together in the sitting room – a change from the kitchen. Rosie lit the fire as the evening was becoming cool and they happily consumed fresh coffee and a large brandy each.

It was Polly who first raised the subject which had been on both of their minds 'Ma, you've been so supportive of Richard and me and not condemned me for having what I now see was a stupid and dangerous affair with David. He's still trying to get me to commit to him and to ask Richard for a divorce. But I am steeling myself to tell David I won't do that. Richard has, he says, forgiven me though things will never be the same again I know that. But I can't bear the thought of what all this would do to the twins. As it is, they are growing up and need both of us together. This commuting idea is only temporary as is

Geoffrey and Pauline staying at The Pele Tower and the horses being with Pauline, who helps too with the ponies during the week. I've always thought you and Dad had a practically perfect marriage and when he was diagnosed with the prostate cancer I'm sure it was your love and care helped him get through the treatment and make sure you were and still are so well looked after! You've been a wonderful example. Please don't do anything to change.' Rosie took a very quick decision to change the subject as she knew the subject of Michael would be coming up next. So she yawned and smiled after this. 'Darling, I'm tired, and you've got an early start tomorrow. Let's have a quick walk outside with the dogs, then turn in.' Polly was wise enough to agree and the difficult topic was closed, at least for the time being.

Edinburgh Murrayfield

Rosie decided she wanted to spend a couple of days in Edinburgh staying with Polly and the twins. Travelling arrangements were complicated, with Richard spending more time at the Lodge and commuting daily to Edinburgh with Geoffrey West and the family coming to the Lodge every Friday. There was, she felt, little time before the end of term at Minty and John's schools to see how Polly felt about the ending of her affair with David and the decision agreed with apparent harmony between Richard and Polly to give their marriage another chance.

What had not entirely been resolved was whether or not David had accepted Polly's commitment to continuing her marriage. David was still unwilling to give up and had refused to leave her alone. Even though, on the surface, he had accepted she would not, in fact, leave Richard, this was one battle in his life he was determined to win.

The ideal opportunity arose for Rosie to put her plan into action when Jamie felt he needed, and indeed wanted to spend a solid week at Whitewalls checking on the various farming issues requiring decisions. As well, after the mental and physical exertions of the past few weeks, the appeal of returning to the countryside and his roots was very appealing. Jamie asked his wife: 'Why don't you spend some time in Edinburgh with Polly and the twins and have a change from organising and problem-solving? It's a pity Michael is away in Mumbai or he could have kept me company as well as learning more about the Borders' culture and doing some physical exercise!' So with Jamie's approval and a surprisingly free conscience about Michael, Rosie gave Jamie a hug and announced: 'I'm going to ring Polly right now and get organised. You'll manage. The freezer is full of food and you and Richard can spend more time together in the evenings.'

'My darling wife, will you please stop trying to make sure everyone is happy and put yourself first, for once?' Yes, she reflected, until the arrival of Michael with all its ups and downs her marriage to Jamie had been loving and caring from the start. They were regarded by everyone as the perfect couple!

Luckily Polly was at home when Rosie rang. 'Hello, darling, I'm coming to Edinburgh on Tuesday to do some shopping and it seems Dad will be busy with farming and I'd love maybe to come and stay over with you and the twins. I don't have to hurry back but we can talk about that when I see you.'

'Mum, I would love to see you here in Murrayfield and so would the twins. Please stay for more than one night.' Polly's immediate warm welcome of the idea was in a way a relief for Rosie. Polly continued: 'Can you arrive here at lunchtime? We can have a good natter then collect the children together later.'

Both mother and daughter felt relaxed and happy about the plan and, whilst Jamie pretended to grumble he too had been very aware of tensions in the family, though he had no idea about the relationship between Rosie and Michael, nor how far things had gone. Would he ever find out? Michael's temporary absence in Mumbai at had removed the issue – for the time being.

As she replaced the landline phone, Rosie heard her mobile buzz with an incoming message. It was brief, but she smiled as she read 'How are you, hot and tough here, students fine so that's good, but I miss you so much. Love you, M xxxx'

Before she could press 'reply,' Jamie came into the back lobby outside, kicked off his wellington boots and whistled happily as he entered the kitchen, then gave Rosie a kiss on the nape of her neck, followed by: 'I'm hungry, not just for lunch. May need a rest later? Somehow she managed to give her husband a convincing hug and said: 'Lunch won't be long, it's good to see you in your working kit again!' Feeble but it was the best she could manage.

The following day, Geoffrey West was driving Richard back to the Lodge at Whitewalls and although both men were tired after a full day's work in Edinburgh they chatted as usual on the journey. 'Richard, you know we really do appreciate this arrangement with the Pele Tower we're renting from Sir Alistair and Pauline loves helping with your horses and ponies as well as her own. Frankly, I think we would have had to give all this up without your help.'

'So far, so good,' Richard replied, 'but what makes you think Alistair owns the Tower? It's Lady Betty's, but for reasons best known to her, she's keeping quiet about it now she is very happily married again to the dear old colonel.

'Oh hell, I was going to sound you out to see if we could stay on until the end of the year. The consultancy I'm working on has been extended for three months and we were hoping to keep the arrangement going until then.' Richard thought for a moment or two then said 'I'm sure there won't be a problem if we all just carry on pretending it's simply going to be an extension of the existing arrangements. And quite honestly once I've sorted things out here with Jamie and issues with Polly and the children, this could be a very positive outcome for all of us. No, tell you what, I'll have a word with Betty and I'm sure there won't be any more complications. We can deal with our side of the family when we're all sorted out – if families are ever in that situation!'

Both men felt more relaxed as Geoffrey stopped outside the Lodge, before going on to help Pauline with the horses and ponies. Luckily, all the livestock were still out at grass and there wasn't a great deal to do before he went back to the Pele Tower and his loving wife Pauline. Geoffrey reflected, for the present, life for them was much simpler without children!

Feeling some trepidation as well as concern, Rosie drove to Edinburgh with the soothing music of her favourite classical music programme playing on her car radio.

Giving herself a mental shake towards a more relaxed and positive frame of mind. Rosie looked forward to time shopping for herself in Edinburgh as well as seeing Polly and the twins with no 'agenda' to pursue. She wanted to get away from Whitewalls for a little while and not feel responsible for everyone and everything there – whether or not her help was needed or even wanted.

The traffic was not heavy, and street parking on a meter in the centre of the principal elegant shopping area in Edinburgh's George Street proved surprisingly easy for once.

So after a restoring coffee and croissant on the top floor of Harvey Nichol's department store overlooking St Andrew Square, Rosie went to buy new shoes, a pair of smart fine corduroy trousers and an elegant jacket for herself as well as a lovely silk scarf for Polly, a pretty shoulder bag for Minty and DVDs for John. She had not intended to buy a present for her son-in-law Richard. This wasn't because of any feeling of enmity towards him – indeed she hoped very much he and Polly would repair their marriage and renew their love of each other. However, on the way to her car she saw and bought smart leather driving gloves to complete, at least to her own

178

satisfaction, impromptu family presents!

Polly was waiting in the kitchen, feeling quite tense, for her mother to arrive though as soon as the door opened mother and daughter hugged each other with warmth and smiles, genuinely happy to see each other.

'I've had a lovely morning shopping for a change. As you know, usually I can't stand it, but I parked easily and the place wasn't too busy, so I bought a few things for you and Richard and the twins.' Polly's eyes filled with tears. She hadn't expected her mother to be so cheerful, nor had she thought her mother would be so comforting after all the unhappiness her affair with David had caused and some of the issues around it that had still not been resolved as it seemed David was not prepared to give up without a fight.

Polly had organised the school run so Minty and John would be dropped off at home from their respective schools. 'I thought we could all four of us go out for an early supper at Giuliani's so the twins can make their own pizzas – they haven't grown out of the fun of doing that – at least not yet! We can always have pasta! Whilst this plan did not immediately fill Rosie with enthusiasm, quickly she realised it could be fun for the twins and relaxing as far as she and Polly were concerned. So Rosie's response was light-hearted. 'That's a lovely idea, Polly. You and I can be together for a couple of hours until the children come home. Do you want to go out for some lunch or shall we put our feet up here?' This was an easy decision and mother and daughter made themselves comfortable in the sitting room.

At least it gave both of them some quiet breathing space.

Rosie and Polly looked at each other and mopped up the tears and both instinctively knew this line of conversation should end until – if ever – a more appropriate time came along. 'Shall we have tea or coffee?' Polly asked. 'Oh, let's have some Earl Grey and some of your lovely ginger cake.' Polly went off to the kitchen, leaving her mother to sit quietly for once in her life. When Polly returned with the tray, the conversation turned to much safer topics, school choices, renovating the Lodge and ponies now almost outgrown by their young riders. Both Snowball and Butterball could be given to the riding for disabled children organisation and, if things worked out well, larger ponies would be possible, provided John and Minty wanted to continue with this part of their lives.

The front doorbell rang and Polly looked at her watch. 'That's odd. The twins aren't due home for another twenty minutes or so.' 'I'll go and see who it is,' Rosie interjected, and before Polly could stop her she went to the door and opened it. It was hard to know who was more surprised! Carrying a large bunch of red roses, David McLean began to say 'Darling Polly, you're not getting rid of me so quickly ....' When he realised Rosie had opened the door and not Polly probably for the first time in a long time, David didn't know what to say to save himself from making matters worse.

'Please go away and leave my daughter and her children alone. You've caused enough trouble, in fact more than enough trouble already!' So rarely did Rosie raise her voice in anger, she surprised herself.

'Aren't you going to let me come in, Mrs Douglas?' David asked, trying to charm Rosie and gain the upper hand again. 'After all, it really isn't any of your business, is it?' Rosie took a deep breath but didn't move, praying Polly wouldn't come out to see what was going on. Fortunately, recognising David's voice, even though the sitting room door was closed, Polly stayed where she was.

'That is not true. It is my business when my family is being torn apart,' Rosie replied in a strong, calm voice.' So please go away now and I will tell my daughter you were here, then without doubt she and her husband, who loves her so much in spite of all you have done to wrench them apart, will talk about things again and I hope repair their marriage. Goodbye, for good.' Before David could have one more try at getting inside the house, Rosie gently but firmly closed the door.

David retreated in great haste but as he did so he hissed: 'Tell your darling daughter I will be back and soon, whatever you think about it.' Rosie felt shaken but at least David had gone away. This had to end and soon. Fleetingly, she wondered about Michael and whether or not her own behaviour was even worse! No time for regrets now!

When Rosie went back to the sitting room, all she said to a white-faced Polly was 'That was David McLean and I said this wasn't a good time for him to come in, with a bunch of red roses! I hope you don't mind. He's gone away.' Before there was time for Polly to say anything at all in reply, John and Minty arrived home from the school run. Laughter, cuddles and hugs with 'Hi Gran, cool to see you' from John and a more gentle but equally loving 'Gran it's ages since you've been here on your own. Big hugs and lots of love, and how long can you stay with us? from Minty.

The arrival of the twins stopped the negative feelings which might have developed into a nasty situation and ruined Rosie's plans for Polly, Minty and John to have fun without any tensions to spoil things.

They had decided to have an early evening supper at the local Italian restaurant not far away which had recently adopted the strategy of similar eateries where children under twelve years could construct pizzas with toppings of their own choice. This was all carried out under the careful but jolly supervision of the chefs who then baked the children's creations!

Because she wasn't driving, Rosie decided to order for herself a large glass of Prosecco. Polly and the children were happy with their cool fruit drinks, served with brightly coloured straws and paper umbrellas in the glasses.

Once the linguine and spaghetti Carbonara respectively had been ordered for the adults, the last vestiges of any tension simply melted away After the party had enjoyed ice cream and lots of 'bella, bella' compliments, an hour-and-a-half later they were all back home in Murrayfield. Luckily, with no homework needing to be done for school by the twins, who were then indeed tired but happy, baths and early to bed was in fact welcomed!

Although mother and daughter had tacitly agreed to discuss the issues of marriage and family in general, including trying to work out the best strategy to enable Polly and Richard to save their marriage and family after the near-disaster with David McLean, it did not now seem to be necessary.

Rosie felt sleepy and yawned. Polly felt more relaxed than she had done for ages. Life seemed possible again! They drank soothing camomile tea from pretty china mugs and the evening came to a gentle conclusion

After a deep and dreamless sleep, Rosie woke early next morning, feeling refreshed and feeling relaxed and more in tune with life in general than she had done for many months. Rosie left to drive to Whitewalls feeling better but still anxious about Polly, Richard and the children. Big hugs and kisses from the twins accompanied by 'see you on Friday, Grannie, love you lots' from Minty and 'Cool, Gran, be good' This was the mildly daring parting remark from John! Rosie laughed and simply said: 'Cool all round, darlings'

Neither mother nor daughter had wanted to prolong the discussion on the issues which at least been had aired between them. Indeed, Polly was grateful, although she had not said so, and was secretly relieved Rosie had been there when David arrived and had politely but firmly dispatched him without his seeing her.

As Rosie drove out of the city to the relative tranquillity of the Borders and Whitewalls, she found herself looking forward to spending some time with Jamie. She felt more hopeful. Somehow, because Michael was so far away in Mumbai for three months at least, she was able to calm her mind over the need to make a potentially heart-breaking choice between two men who she believed were the great loves of her life.

The mood of optimism persisted until she drove past the Lodge to Whitewalls which, for once, was clearly empty. Where were Jamie and the Labradors, Heather and Tweed? A feeling of foreboding briefly came to her, quickly dispelled by the unmistakeable welcoming barking of the dogs as Jamie came round the side of the house to meet her! Jamie was a man of great kindness but did not easily express his inner feelings. However, he smiled at Rosie and hugged her, saying 'Darling wife, do you realise we're going to have some time together at last? Just the two of us and it seems months since we could simply be ourselves without other people around.'

Chapter 15

London – The Mews Flat

Maggie and Charles were enjoying a relaxing few days together before the next phase of their lives. Happily they were looking forward to being married in Scotland at the little church where Charles's parents and Lady Betty and Colonel Prendergast in turn had enjoyed a simple marriage ceremony followed by a happy reception in the Whitewalls garden.

As far as the practical side was concerned they were in complete agreement. Charles would finish his present army duties and Maggie would continue to further her career as a stage and screen actor and pursue her dream with the full support of her family and now his. However, if Maggie looked deeply into her own heart, this ambition burned less fiercely than it had done before she and Charles had fallen so deeply in love and committed themselves to a life together, with children, and the apparently idyllic unions of Rosie and Jamie and also of Florette and Nigel, virtually Maggie's only close family. Life is never all it seems looking in from outside, this had not, of course, entered their thoughts, nor would it do so for many years to come.

Increasingly, Charles was interested and attracted to the change of direction offered by the opportunity to join Nigel in the Yorkshire farming enterprise and to become a partner with Nigel and Florette in further developing both the thriving arable farm and their way of life. They had been so welcoming and delighted about the young couple's impending marriage following Charles's safe return from the hell of the Afghanistan conflict.

The physical passion between Charles and Maggie continued to be as important to their relationship as ever. Now the wedding plans were going ahead quickly, they knew they would need to make decisions about the future very soon.

It was not often they had the opportunity to lie in bed with the lovely afterglow of a night of love-making combining intimacy and absence of inhibition or any feeling of a need to hurry. All this made this particular morning all the more precious. Maggie's head nestled with ease into Charles' neck and their naked limbs were wound around each other with total ease.

'I've had a thought!' Charles announced. 'Really, how hard was that?' answered Maggie teasingly.' In return Charles kissed his fiancée again deeply and for a long time. While this was going on, the conversation stopped.

Eventually though, they sat up on the soft downy pillows and made a plan, suggested by Charles ,to get away for a few days together – no family, no need for anyone else, just each other. 'Where shall we go for our practice honeymoon?' Maggie asked. 'Let's go and eat whilst we decide I'm very hungry, 'No wonder.' Replied Charles.

After enjoying a meal together at their favourite Italian, restaurant Charles proposed a city break in Vienna for four days, flying direct and staying in a luxury hotel. They could see the amazing sights and wander wherever they wished or simply be together, go out to restaurants, afterwards strolling around the landmarks of the Museum of Applied Arts, the State Opera House and all the other architectural gems for which Vienna is famous.

'On the other hand, darling,' Charles said, 'why don't we have a long weekend at a luxury health spa, not too far away and no airports, planes, queues and hassles – just lots of pampering, luxury, massages and hot tubs and you and me?' Inwardly Maggie was relieved. Charles had only recently returned from a gruelling time and deserved some pampering and luxury even for a few days as they moved towards their next adventure with marriage, a new job and a home, new life and, hopefully, though not for a while, children of their own.

By day two of their visit, Charles and Maggie were, in

his words 'so relaxed I feel horizontal.' Maggie hugged him tightly again. 'You, my darling man, seem to have a wonderful way of doing and saying just the right thing at the right time!' As well, you are a great lover and so brave. You have had to be, even before you marry me and even more afterwards!'

At ease and in love, any tensions seemed far away and, whatever the future held, this moment was captured forever in their hearts and minds! Maggie recalled what seemed to her appropriate words from 'The Little Prince' a slim volume penned by Antoine Saint-Exupery a World War Two pilot, concerning an individual whose plane crashed in a desert: 'It is only with the heart one can see rightly, what is essential is invisible to the eye.'

By the third day, before they needed to think about parking, moving or arrangements for the future of any kind, both Maggie and Charles were more convinced than ever, not only of their love and passion but also of the foundations already in place for the rest of their lives together. They would survive and thrive!

Edinburgh Murrayfield

'Richard, I want us to try again, get the past where it belongs. It's a huge ask, I know but it has all been my fault. I see that more clearly now! Can you possibly forgive me?'

Silence followed. Polly and Richard were alone in the kitchen. The simple meal, one of Richard's favourites – homemade cottage pie with fresh vegetables and then fruit and cream as well as a bottle of red wine - was eaten in what seemed to be a companionable and relatively quiet atmosphere, with the subject still hanging in the air between them. Polly hadn't wanted to look as if she were desperate, but she was in emotional turmoil. This, she felt, would be the final chance to try to save not only her marriage to Richard, whom she truly did love but also to move forward to a better future.

Richard tried to look at his wife, the mother of his children, as if for the first time, although he knew the road back to what had been so stable and happy for so long would not be an easy one. Later, Polly realised her mother's firm intervention, indeed altercation, with David had been the crucial turning point. At this stage, of course, Rosie's own fall from 'perfection' had not been discovered, although suspected, by Lady Betty!

Richard remembered a song from his own youth 'Walking Back to Happiness', sung by Helen Shapiro. Could this be achieved for them? Eventually, he spoke. 'I don't think we can do this without some professional help. Do you, darling?' There was a word she had not heard from her husband for a long time. Darling! He continued. 'Polly I won't pretend I have not been deeply hurt but I need to share the blame, if this is the right word and I am willing to try again as long as you are sure McLean is out of the picture for good.' Polly gave him her most brilliant and loving smile, took a very deep breath and replied. 'Thank you darling husband and, I hope, in time you can forgive me and we can be happy again.' The words sounded very formal, even awkward. After that, words did not seem to matter.

They stood up, embraced and went upstairs together. Their long journey to renewal began in the most loving and very passionate way! Later, when Richard and Polly continued to discuss the issues surrounding the past, present and more importantly the future they decided to make a plan. Partly owing to his feelings of residual anger and bitterness but also reflecting his resolve to retrieve from near-breakdown what had been such a good and happy marriage, Richard felt some mediation from a professional outside individual would be helpful.

Polly seized on this as a very positive move and agreed Richard would arrange for them to receive counselling privately and away from Edinburgh and, for that matter, away from the Scottish Borders, where gossip had destroyed more than one private family relationship. Also,

Richard was conscious his fairly new partnership with McLures meant he didn't want any further obstacles in his professional life. This may have been selfish on the surface but, in fact, it was a good idea. After making discreet enquiries they arranged an appointment with a highly recommended individual, a woman with an excellent reputation in the field of human relationship counselling, whose practice was in Dunfermline, just over the Firth of Forth in Fife.

Because of the build-up to this new development of trying again to salvage their marriage, Richard and Polly managed to keep entirely to themselves the fact that they were arranging counselling, a venture on which they pinned hopes of success without felling certainty as to its outcome.

Musselburgh Races

As life at Whitewalls and the farm and stables became less frenetic, Geoffrey came up with the idea of a visit to the racecourse in Musselburgh – on the east side of the city of Edinburgh - as a foursome with Richard and Polly, to see whether or not this was an area of interest, at least between the two men, and also Pauline. The idea was that they might have fun days out and think about the possibility of applying for a training permit for continuing the racing tradition established by Roddy Douglas. Rosie's late father had devoted his later years to building up a small string of National Hint horses, both breeding and racing them, mainly around the Scottish and North of England race meets. The flat racing season had finished as racing was now under National Hunt rules involving horses hurdling over fairly low obstacles and more challenging higher ones known as jumps. At first, when the idea was put to Polly by Richard, she almost rejected it out of hand. However, Pauline intervened: 'Oh come on, Polly. Let's at least have a day out, the four of us, and see whether or not we all enjoy ourselves, and we don't have to make any commitments immediately!'

Richard didn't allow his feelings to show, but he felt close to happiness at the prospect of something good about to become real. Arrangements were easily made. The children were 'parked' happily with friends in Edinburgh and Richard made the booking for the next Saturday meeting at the racecourse and reserved lunch in the bistro there at the same time. Rather to her own surprise, Polly looked forward with relaxed anticipation to this expedition. She was used to the racing world but not in the sense of being involved with the ownership of horses and the breeding and training which had been so much an integral part of her late and much-loved grandfather Roddy's life and achievements.

A new enthusiasm for owning and training horses to race and jump seemed to be growing not only for Richard but also Geoffrey and Pauline, as well as the next generation, John and Minty, now her leg was strong enough to ride her pony once more. They agreed to find out the essential requirements and procedures after the visit to Musselburgh races. On the face of it, this seemed a fairly straightforward task and by looking through Roddy's meticulously-kept records, they would be able to find out exactly what was involved.

Although Polly had never been as interested and involved as the rest of the family either in horses or racing, apart from the social side, it did seem another way forward to repair some of the harm done during her affair with David. Together with the counselling which they had started, it was another way forward for her to show how serious she had become about saving her marriage to Richard.

It was both interesting and potentially exciting, not simply as a way of continuing the excellent reputation of Roddy Douglas as a breeder and trainer of winning horses, but also in turning round the disaster which had nearly ended the marriage of Richard and Polly. This might be a tradition to be carried on in a new and 21st century way to involve future generations of the family. In this manner the legacy would continue and become a fitting memorial to Roddy.

For Richard, in particular, continuing this family tradition was a very important part of the jigsaw and he knew the man who had almost ruined his happiness, David McLean had no interest in or knowledge of horse racing, or indeed horses in general.

Jamie thought it would be an excellent idea to ask the Hon Jane Gillies, who had served for many years as a steward with the Jockey Club and was herself an owner and trainer of racehorses, to come to Whitewalls and stay overnight. She would then see what she thought about the facilities at the Lodge, the paddocks and the possibility of Richard being able to obtain a permit to continue the training there as well as to include Geoffrey and Pauline. They were increasingly likely to stay in Scotland as Geoffrey's bank intended to open a branch in Edinburgh and, as well, they hoped to start a family and put down roots in the Borders within easy commuting distance of the Capital.

Once Richard, with Polly's support, Geoffrey and Pauline had agreed a plan to look first of all through how Roddy had started his horse breeding and subsequent training career, they didn't hang about but set to work with enthusiasm and commitment. It was, therefore with more optimism and enthusiasm than anyone in the Scottish members of the Douglas family had felt for many months, during which events had been at best fraught and at worst almost catastrophic, the plans began to take shape.

The next stage of positive family activities proved much simpler and happier than either the Douglas or Bruce branches of the extended family could have expected.

Yorkshire – Manor House Farm

Once the engagement between Charles and Maggie had

officially been announced in the Daily Telegraph, The Scotsman and The Times newspapers, events moved swiftly

Initially, Maggie had thought the marriage should take place in the Yorkshire village where her grandmother and step-grandfather had nurtured her since the untimely death of her parents. Then the thought came unbidden to her that Whitewalls was the family home to which she would in future belong. Whilst Nigel was, at first, somewhat disgruntled at a choice he saw as unfair to Florette, the wife whom he adored, he kept his own counsel and there were certainly no arguments between them.

Whitewalls

Before further arrangements could be made, there was the matter of Charles serving the remainder of his army career, but, thankfully, not in Afghanistan. Events moved on again, even more quickly and in the organised manner so familiar to the trained soldier, leaving Rosie feeling a little left out but also relieved. For once, not everything was left for her to organise! As well, she and Jamie were becoming closer again - that was, until an unexpected telephone call to Jamie from Michael in Mumbai.

'Hello Jamie. How are you and Rosie? Just a quick call to say I'll be coming back earlier than I had expected. The lecturer whose job I've been doing has made a great recovery so I am surplus to requirements. I'll be back by the end of this month at the latest!' 'That's great news Michael. We've all missed you, even Rosie here! Have you time for a quick word? 'Rosie, have you missed me as much as I hope?' She was very conscious of blushing and with her husband sitting right next to her. Trying to sound casual yet welcoming, she briefly replied with what she hoped was enough, but not too much warmth in her voice without paying attention to her heart while trying to ignore her heart pounding. 'I was listening in to what you told Jamie and, yes, we're all glad you'll be back soon, 'Bye for now.' And without giving him a chance to say any more, Rosie gave the phone back to Jamie, smiled brightly and escaped to the kitchen. Michael had hoped to have a longer conversation with Rosie, but prudently didn't try to do so and simply said: 'Hope you are all in good heart and Rosie isn't working too hard. I am going to try and get back in time for your grand exhibition in London. Remind me when it begins.' Jamie simply said as they ended the conversation: 'It's early in November but don't worry about rushing home for that. We've had a few issues at the start of the month but getting on with things. Let us know the date you expect to arrive and either Rosie or one of the family can meet you at the airport in Edinburgh.' With those brief but cordial parting words Jamie ended the conversation.

Chapter 16

Yorkshire - Manor House Farm

'Of course I'm happy and proud to give Maggie away when she and Charles get married, but why the hell do we have to traipse up to Scotland again?' Nigel Hardcastle was generally a mild-mannered man and loved his step-granddaughter Maggie as much as if she were from his own family and not from his wife. Florette gave her husband a hug which managed at the same time to be both conciliatory and firm.

'Oh, darling, after all Charles has been through with the army, Afghanistan and he is so in love with Maggie. Besides, I am almost certain he will take up your offer of coming here as a partner in the farm, so you will probably see more of him than the Scottish family!'

Nigel had never been able either to be cross for very long nor to ignore the logic in any situation. As well he still adored Florette so conceded she was right, especially as it was looking more and more certain Charles would be joining the Manor House Farm business.

So, when he answered the telephone a little later and found Jamie Douglas on the line he was able to answer Charles's father truthfully and without rancour. 'Hello Nigel, Jamie Douglas here. Look, I do hope you won't mind another trek up here for the next family wedding. By the looks of things it won't be until early January after all the loose ends are tied up with both of the young lovers!' 'I must admit, Jamie, I had thought, with our being Maggie's only family, we might hold the wedding down here in Yorkshire. But no, you're right, Charles is your only son and if you can bear the thought of my poaching him finally to come down here and help me out, then that's fair!' Without anything more needing to be discussed and to avoid any further misunderstanding, the rest of the conversation turned to the safe topics of crops and

European farm subsidies and away from emotional matters.

Rosie had been anxious regarding the idea of Nigel and Florette coming to Scotland for a second time to celebrate a family occasion and had not expected the two men to reach such an amicable conclusion. She did sigh inwardly a little, though, yet again another big family event for her largely to organise. 'Darling, we'll all help including Polly and Richard now they are back on track, as well as your mother and the colonel. Hopefully Michael will be able to conduct the wedding ceremony in Stitcholme church.' Jamie said. Whilst Rosie felt jumpy at Michael's name being spoken by her faithful husband, she simply smiled, hugged Jamie and retreated to one of her safe havens. As it was getting cooler outside, the kitchen provided the escape route instead of the walled garden or greenhouse.

The phone rang at Manor House Farm again. 'It's Maggie. Darling Florette, I've had a brilliant idea!' 'And what might that involve?' replied Florette, a touch drily, although Maggie sounded so excited. 'Well I know you've been persuaded we should have our wedding in January in Scotland and Grand-pere is not very keen but has been persuaded, so I wonder if you could design and make my dress and one bridesmaid's dress for a grown-up bridesmaid and another one for little Minty if you would! Of course I'll pay for them.' As Maggie had hoped and expected, Florette riposted swiftly: 'Oh yes, I will be happy to do that and no, you will pay nothing except your love and I am so very happy for both of you.' Florette continued. 'Who is going to be the grown-up one?' The reply from Maggie came as a surprise. 'Well, I thought as Polly and Richard are back together I would ask Polly if she would be willing to step in. What do you think, I haven't asked her yet?' This seemed a high-risk strategy but also a good one provided Polly's affaire really had ended. 'Why not, if you are sure it is a lovely idea, though don't be too surprised if Polly and, for that matter Rosie are not sure!' 'Thanks Grand-mere, I knew you would be wise.' Nigel came in to the room partly to see who had been on the phone to his wife for such a long time and Florette judged this was the opportunity to end the conversation so she quickly said 'Au revoir, Cherie, be in touch again soon. 'Bye, thanks so much, I will.'

Nigel had given in generously. He loved not only his wife but also her granddaughter, even if he did not entirely approve of, nor understand why she wanted to be an actress and film star. But increasingly, he was becoming more admiring of Charles and as a former military man himself, Nigel knew how military action was at any level always carried danger with it, even in so-called peace time. He concluded, in his own mind, Charles would be an asset to Manor House Farm and in the long run well worth the trek to Scotland for the marriage ceremony in the New Year.

Just as Nigel began to feel relaxed the phone rang again. 'Damn and blast, is there no escape from the bloody phone? he muttered.' Nevertheless, he picked up the receiver. 'Yes he barked. 'I'm sorry sir, Is this a very bad moment to call?' The caller was Charles. 'Sorry, Charles, This thing's been ringing non-stop for the last half hour.' ' Well, I've just heard from my mother you are not only going to give Maggie away when we marry in the New Year but also you've agreed to come to Scotland, which all of us really appreciate. Oh, and there is something else. I've looked into the possibility of a sandwich course at the agricultural college and if you'd still like me to join the Manor House Farm team after I've finished with the army in a few weeks, I'd be really honoured to join you!

At once, Nigel's mood lightened and after a few words of discussion and an arrangement to meet soon at the farm he reiterated his genuine pleasure at the news and ended the conversation by saying: 'I know Florette will be so pleased, as well as the others whom you've met. So I'll go and tell her right now. Oh, and please, Charles, it's not 'Sir. It's Nigel! ' There was a smile in each man's voice as they said goodbye for the moment.

High Wynch Park

Maggie was tired but exhilarated at the same time as she neared the end of the strenuous closing scenes of the filming of her first major screen role in 'The Minister Who Lied '. She realised how much her acting skills had improved since the beginning of the lengthy process. As she walked slowly off the set, Maggie was looking forward to tea and a shower.

She was brought out of her reverie by Adrian, her co-star, coming up to her. 'Nearly there, Maggie. It's looking good! What a pity you turned me down though when your soldier hero safely returned - and I don't mean in the film.' The words might have sounded mocking but were delivered in a pleasant, almost jocular way. Maggie smiled sweetly at Adrian. Eventually, when he realised she was not attracted to him, he had stopped pursuing her and eventually they became a compatible team when acting in their respective roles as minister and mistress. As well Adrian, was an older and accomplished actor as well as experienced and had decided to help Maggie achieve her best possible performance.

'I've really enjoyed working with you, Adrian, but I am looking forward to a break. Charles leaves the army for good in a few weeks' time and we have made some plans. I'd better keep them to myself for now though. Come on, let's go and find some tea. Ginny said we should go into the kitchen and be with the family.'

As they walked toward the mansion, Maggie's mobile phone, concealed in her shoulder bag, bleeped. 'Darling, I'll be quick, I know you're working, but Nigel and I have agreed the deal. There's only the legalities to sort out and I've even found a short course to bring me up to speed on the practical side of farming.' Adrian had waited for her but, realising it would be more tactful and kind, he walked on leaving her to speak to her fiancé without being overheard.

When she went into the kitchen, which now served as a

refreshment area for those actors decreed by Ginny to be family or else suitable and of sufficient importance or family Maggie was smiling broadly. 'Come on, spill the beans. What have you just heard?' demanded Charles's future aunt by marriage. 'Good news by the look on your face,' chimed in Uncle Hughie. 'Sit down in the rocking chair and tell us all about it.'

Maggie knew she could trust Ginny and Hugh not to gossip to the film producers and cast though she was reasonably discreet about Charles and future wedding plans. She did, however, feel it was safe to tell them about the decision they had just reached concerning Charles' future occupation in the New Year after his Army discharge. 'That's splendid news. Ginny, did you hear that?' boomed Hughie. 'Yes, fantastic,' his wife replied although becoming distracted by little Fleur demanding attention. The little girl had come to know Maggie due to her presence while filming at High Wynch Park and in fact provided Maggie with a welcome diversion so she did not need to give away any more information at this point.

'Oh, I'm being so thoughtless', Ginny said. 'Off you go and have a lovely scented bath and take a glass of champagne with you!' 'I was going to have Earl Grey tea, but you've talked me out of it.' 'See you for drinks in the library at six o'clock.' As she hurried up the wide oak staircase which had become even more attractive with the passage of time, Maggie reflected on how well life seemed to be turning out,

The Lodge - Whitewalls

Richard and Geoffrey West had decided between them it was just the right time for Pauline and Polly to meet again as the prospect of the training permit for the horses to run under National Hunt rules was now a distinct possibility and with Geoffrey's permanent transfer to the bank in Scotland, Richard in particular wanted to press ahead with the arrangements to get things underway. Also

Geoffrey and Pauline were keen to continue to rent The Pele Tower, whilst still retaining their house in England, for the time being letting it to friends. So lunch on Saturday seemed a good plan.

After Rosie's altercation with Polly's former lover, David McLean and the counselling undertaken by Richard and Polly their lives were regaining some harmony. The prospect of the developing legacy of Roddy's successes in breeding and training horses and the growing friendship between Richard and Geoffrey both enforced this positive mood. It was the Richard's fervent hope the horse venture would help to bring their two couples and for that matter Minty, John and the various animals closer together.

So, leaving the older generation, including Rosie, out of the plans, a boisterous picnic lunch took place at the Lodge early in September. 'You've already seen our ponies, Geoffrey, haven't you?' asked John, knowing full well the answer. 'Why don't we go and catch them, tack them up and you can come out and watch us riding.' So leaving everything up till later – something which Rosie would never have done - it was a jolly and noisy party that made its way to the stable block.

Then came a surprise. Almost casually, Richard said 'We're all invited to go and visit Lucy Normile who is a successful trainer of National Hunt horses and she has a great yard and facilities at Duncreavie in Perthshire. Lucy has children, too, and so you two horrors - meaning John and Minty - are invited too! She'll perhaps be able to run our horses until we get the training permit sorted out and anyway it should be another fun day out.

There was a closeness and a stirring of sexual desire between Polly and Richard that night. The twins had been tired after their exciting day and happy to go early to bed. 'I'm going for a bath and maybe we could have an early night too?' said Polly. Richard grinned, gave Polly a big hug and kiss and said: 'I'll be upstairs in ten minutes!' 'Make it twenty, darling. It will be worth it, I promise!' Polly could hardly believe she had said this but, oddly, she meant it. Later it was as if the affair with David had never taken place, Or could it be so simple?

A very excited and happy party, including Geoffrey and Pauline West, began the journey to Duncreavie racing stables in Perthshire to talk with the team led by Lucy Normile, They went in two vehicles as the enterprise had been kept somewhat 'under wraps' from Rosie, Jamie and the rest of the Douglas family since there was no decision yet on the possibility of leasing the Lodge horses, or maybe having them trained at Duncreavie in the interim before Richard and Geoffrey could get their permit.

It was a fine September day and the drive to Duncreavie was effortless, once they had sorted out who was going to sit in which car. Minty and John chose to go with Geoffrey and Pauline, whom they did not know very well. The grown-ups were fun for the children as they chatted with them about horses, dogs and riding and didn't ask stupid questions about school.

Lucy was waiting outside the house to meet them as they piled out of the cars. 'Lovely to meet you all. Come into the house and have some coffee and we can talk then go down to the stables. My children will be very happy to show you two around if you like.' This was addressed to John and Minty. Lucy's children didn't stand on ceremony in making the young visitors welcome. Both Minty, who was still a little unsure about her ability to walk easily, and John, who liked the look of the Normile children immediately, soon felt part of the place.

'I'll see what I can do to help and decide, if you agree, the best way forward,' said Lucy. 'Don't worry about the children, they'll be fine and, anyway, Richard, you said your twins have ponies of their own so my three can bring your pair into the house after they've had a good look around.' Polly warmed to Lucy and her welcoming, relaxed manner as well as increasingly warming to Pauline, whom she didn't really know very well.

After a very amicable discussion, Geoffrey came up with a plan. Lucy, would you train Border Prince for us and we will bring on the foal whilst looking to establish our little syndicate as permit holders?' Before very long the plan took clearer shape. 'Why don't I train Border Prince for your syndicate and leave you all to develop at the Lodge whilst Border Princess comes on and you can think about breeding from her?' suggested Lucy. All at once it seemed very simple and whilst Richard, wearing his lawyer's hat wanted to make sure every detail of a deal was recorded, it felt right.

So Richard spoke for them all. 'We'll get the paperwork done and organise transporting Prince to your yard, Lucy, and we can take if from there. That sounds like a plan folks, Geoffrey, Pauline do you agree?' They did and immediately the idea of Pauline taking a greater role in the running of the Lodge horses and ponies made sense.

'That's more or less settled then,' Lucy said 'and don't worry about transporting Border Prince here. I can bring him in one of our boxes after the next run at Newcastle. But come back here very soon and we'll get the horse race-fit and then look for race entries.'

The mood on all sides was happy and warm as the Whitewalls contingent piled back into the two vehicles and, for the time being, said their goodbyes to Lucy and her children. Both Minty and John fell asleep during the journey back to the Borders, so Richard and Geoffrey decided to press on and not stop on the way.

Once over the immediate excitement of the arrangements for Lucy Normile to train Border Prince and Pauline agreeing to take on the greater role of running the yard and possibly opening up for livery clients at the Lodge, a certain normality returned - at least on the surface.

Whitewalls

Knowing nothing of the purpose of the Duncreavie trip, Rosie was feeling aggrieved and left out, despite her lack of real involvement with the horses. So she had retreated to the garden which was where Jamie found her. He came up behind her quietly, put his arms around his wife and, ruffling her hair, kissed the nape of her neck. For a moment it felt wrong, then realising it wasn't Michael, Rosie turned and snuggled into the familiar and comforting warmth of Jamie.

'Darling, I know you love to be involved in absolutely everything this family does, but please let them get on with the horses and getting their own lives back, as well as making new and solid friendships, which is just what they all need.' She replied softly 'I'm just being stupid. Let's go and take the dogs for a walk whilst it's still fine and fairly warm. Then we can go back together, just the two of us.'

With this renewed feeling of closeness, Rosie and Jamie collected the dogs, which were always ready for a walk, and the need to talk any more had gone.

Back at the Lodge, the happy atmosphere continued. Pauline and Geoffrey were very pleased with the outcome of the trip to Duncreavie to make plans with Lucy Normile, and when Jamie and Rosie - at Rosie's insistence - popped in to say a brief hello, they left reassured without a great deal of explanation being necessary. They all seemed happy. As a parting shot, Jamie said: 'Well done, from the sound of things. Now, Rosie and I are going home for some peaceful time together, just the two of us.' There were smiles all round and a very satisfactory feeling concluded that part of the day.

When the couple arrived home the phone was ringing. The answering machine kicked in. The call was from Michael. His voice was warm. 'I'll be brief, Jamie and Rosie but good news. The chap whose work I've been covering here in Mumbai has confirmed he is fully recovered, so I'll be back next week. I hope everything's going well. I miss you and I'll call again when I know the arrangements. Goodbye for now, God bless.'

Apparently not noticing the colour draining from his wife's face Jamie simply remarked: 'That's good news, darling. Michael coming back early, my London exhibition and Rachel and Polly making a go of it again. This calls for a glass or two of bubbly - just the two of us.' Quickly recovering her composure, Rosie linked her arm through Jamie's and they went into the drawing room. 'Sit down, darling, I'll get the champagne and glasses.'

Edinburgh

Finally Sir Alistair had accepted his legal challenge over possible flaws in the original divorce settlement all those years ago when Betty divorced him, had no chance of success. So he decided to 'go to ground'. He telephoned his London friends, who still found him and Madeleine entertaining guests for a short time, and wangled a visit. Madeleine was running out of patience very quickly, and separately making plans of her own to cut her losses, but not to surrender her title as Lady Douglas! For his part, Alistair, whilst plotting to see what, if anything, he could do next to restore his fortune, booked two cheap flights, one way only, to Heathrow. All he said to his wife was: 'Darling, a few days in London staying with my friends will give us a welcome break from all this family stuff. I've booked the airline tickets and we'll leave tomorrow? Madeleine just gave him a quizzical look and said: 'Well, that will be a welcome change. Scotland is so boring with all your family practically ignoring us. I'll go and pack for both of us.'

Whitewalls

Jamie felt more relaxed than he had done for some time. He reflected on his good health, now the prostate cancer had been successfully cured, plus he welcome Sir Alistair's sudden exit south. The fact of the upcoming art exhibition he was doing in a highly regarded London gallery gave him a feeling of great achievement.

Even more important than his own well-being and success were the positive events in his family. Thanks in no small measure to Rosie's intervention, Richard and Polly were reunited as a couple and David McLean seemed to have decided to stop trying to reignite his affair with Polly. Even Jamie's mother-in-law, Lady Betty, had found renewed happiness with her marriage to Colonel John Prendergast.

Jamie felt, as well, highly relieved that Rosie's father, Sir Alistair, seemed to have accepted he had no chance of winning a legal battle over the estate and divorce settlement all those years ago, hence his sudden departure south. The relief felt by the rest of the family was a heartening bonus.

They were quietly enjoying their glasses of champagne in the drawing room when Rosie said: 'You're very quiet, Jamie, even for you.' There was more than a touch of amusement in her voice as they enjoyed the break from routine with no distractions, apart from each other.

'Come on, lovely wife. I've locked the doors and we both deserve our time together and I want you, so now, upstairs.' The time for talking was over and they wordlessly, eagerly proceeded to do as he suggested.

The Lodge

Everyone involved with the horses and training issues was very relaxed and pleased about the progress they had made. Lucy Normile had agreed to take on training of Border Prince for the newly-formed syndicate of Richard, Polly, Geoffrey and Pauline, whilst Pauline was particularly happy to be officially in charge of the operations at the Borders end.

Butterball and Snowball, the twins' ponies were part of the arrangements and John and Minty were thrilled, promising to do their share of work at the stables at weekends and during holidays.

Altogether it had been an exhausting time but the outcome more than promised to repay the effort.

After the upheavals in the lives of everyone in recent

weeks, the even tenor of the Douglases' existence in the fast-approaching autumn months meant the future seemed so much more promising all round.

Rosie felt calmer and her passionate feelings for Michael had become less intense during his absence in Mumbai, although with his imminent early return she knew she would need to stay strong.

It was mid-week. Jamie had made a brief visit to London finalising arrangements for the exhibition in November. He was due to return on Friday. Her mobile rang 'Darling, we'll be home on Friday. The flight gets in to Edinburgh at half-past-two. Could you leave Pauline to look after the dogs, as well as the horses, and meet us from the flight?' 'Of course,' she replied, 'but did you say *we* just now?' 'Yes, love. Michael is coming in overnight from Mumbai so we'll travel home together. I've said he should stay with us overnight. Is that okay with you?' 'Of course,' she replied faintly.

By Friday Rosie had managed to regain some of her usual equilibrium, and by the time she parked the car at Edinburgh Airport and walked across to Arrivals she felt relatively composed.

The flight arrived on time and it didn't take long for Michael to collect his luggage. Rosie looked up and saw the two men who meant so much to her emerge smiling, relaxed and apparently at ease with each other.

'Rosie, this is so kind of you.' This was Michael's greeting. Jamie came in with: 'We're all so pleased you are safely back. We've all missed you, especially Rosie!' She took a deep, and hopefully calming, breath and then, accepting a kiss from Jamie and one from Michael, she said 'Yes, absolutely, Michael. I've missed you in exactly the same way as everyone else.' She went on: 'Jamie has asked you to stay with us tonight then I expect you'll have a lot to do sorting out the handover and settling in again.' They looked steadily into each other's eyes and she could not resist adding 'and, of course I'll be available to help as much as I can.'

For the time being this would be the ongoing situation.

The End

About the author, Christine Richard, OBE

'I have been writing stories since I was a small child. I still write poetry for personal pleasure and commercially for an on-line magazine called Lothian Life. I have interviewed local personalities including Scotland's female political opposition leaders, Kezia Dugdale and Ruth Davidson, these were published in the Edinburgh glossy magazine Edinburgh Life.

The original Whitewalls was published by New Generation and we continue with these helpful publishers for Autumn at Whitewalls. My inspiration comes from observing the lives of families for whom everything seems to be going so well. Then, into this 'Scottish Eden' real life intrudes and all is not what it seems, mirroring real life.

The books are set in the present day with lovely and varied locations, animals – including horses and ponies – and, of course human relationships, which are the centre of the action.

My family are all grown up though we remain close. My late husband, John and I lived and worked in Edinburgh for many years where I was involved in politics, public life and I served as a non-executive director on many Boards, including six years at the Edinburgh International Festival.

I hope all my readers enjoy this sequel Autumn at Whitewalls which I have structured so it can stand alone but the reader may like to read Whitewalls too.

Lightning Source UK Ltd.
Milton Keynes UK
UKOW03f0932151216
289999UK00002B/20/P